man's
best
friend

man's best friend

ALANA B. LYTLE

G. P. Putnam's Sons
NEW YORK

PUTNAM
— EST. 1838 —

G. P. Putnam's Sons
Publishers Since 1838
An imprint of Penguin Random House LLC
penguinrandomhouse.com

Library of Congress Cataloging-in-Publication Data

Names: Lytle, Alana B., author.
Title: Man's best friend / Alana B. Lytle.
Description: New York: G. P. Putnam's Sons, 2024.
Identifiers: LCCN 2023056489 (print) | LCCN 2023056490 (ebook) |
ISBN 9780593715024 (hardcover) | ISBN 9780593715031 (ebook)
Subjects: LCGFT: Novels.
Classification: LCC PS3612.Y787 M36 2024 (print) |
LCC PS3612.Y787 (ebook) | DDC 813/.6—dc23/eng/20231208
LC record available at https://lccn.loc.gov/2023056489
LC ebook record available at https://lccn.loc.gov/2023056490

Printed in the United States of America
1st Printing

Book design by Kristin del Rosario
Title page art: background © simplf/Shutterstock.com

For Mimi
who told a great story

I just want these holes

For when I try to run

For no reason

Or so I'm told

SHARON VAN ETTEN,
"SAVE YOURSELF"

man's
best
friend

chapter one

Come spring they slept with the windows open, and every morning she woke to a tickle in her nose courtesy of the magnolia tree that blossomed outside their bedroom. Still, she restrained the impulse to fidget: she didn't want to wake him. She savored these moments, when his normally restive body was quiet and warm. Her cheek to his chest, she matched her breath to his. She *was* him, she felt, as much as she was herself. Whenever he was sick or angry or miserable she bore it, too, as a prickling on her flesh, a chill in her bones.

She never contemplated Alone if she could help it. Occasionally, though, an aberrant sound in the distance or an unsettling shadow on the wall of the barn, on the brick exterior of the house, awakened the haunting knowledge she tried perpetually to repress: that Alone lurked beneath their routine, beneath his murmurs of reassurance, beneath his wide, steady hands on her back. When this awareness overcame her she trembled, her gaze darting and hunting unsuccessfully for the place where it wouldn't be true. Where Alone would be a lie. Where their bond would not be fragile. In time, her spells of panic grew less frequent. She relaxed into the idea that Alone, while real, was probably *not* her destiny—that her relationship was a lasting one. And then the dreams began.

She couldn't fathom why these particular dreams would visit someone like her. She was content with her life! She was old! Her kneecaps cracked like splitting firewood when she overextended, jumped from too great a height. Dreams like these were meant for the young. But we don't choose our dreams: they choose us.

The dream always began in the same place, by the far edge of the property. Sometimes it was cold dawn and the wooden posts of the fence were wet with dew. Sometimes it was late and lightning bugs winked against a smoky, baleful sky. The pasture grass that usually came to the level of her belly was, in the dream, well above her head, grown wild. Concealed among the stalks, she crept right up to the fence. Between the squares of sturdy wire she could see the forest, where it sloped down and met the creek. Beyond that lay a valley dotted with several other ranches and beyond that—hills, dense with hickory and oak. It was a massive swath of land, and she'd never explored any of it. And this was just *one place*. This was just what she could *see*. She had never questioned the life she'd been given; in fact all her most difficult moments could be boiled down to a fear of losing what had been allotted to her. She had never thought to mourn missed opportunities, untrod paths, unknown faces. She had a home in Ohio, yes, but surely there were other homes. She had love, but was there more love, different love, elsewhere? Was there another place, another situation in which *she* would be different? Whatever pain her leaving might create, she had a right to know.

She began to dig. Invigorated, her paws spit and churned soil so fast that, in mere minutes, she had burrowed a hole under the fence big enough to slip through. As she crawled into the dirt and scrabbled out the other side, her mind raced. *I'm doing this. I'm really doing this.* All her life she had stayed within bounds: never, ever, could she have imagined crossing the line to be so *easy*. The thrill of her own capacity for rebellion, for destruction, filled her with a kind of electric purpose—a transporting heat swept through her body—

And then she woke up. Every time, the dream cut off in this same place. When she opened her eyes and surveyed her real life—the thinning bedspread, the scuffed hardwood, the antique clock with the broken chime, even him, sleeping innocently—none of it stimulated her. Gone was the Midas touch that had been her gratitude.

But abandoning home, in reality, was unthinkable. *Out of the question*, she told herself, as she trailed him, day after day, through the house and the fields, as she rode in the truck with him to the feed store, the package store, the country mart. But even as she banished the idea of leaving, she caught herself regarding him with pity, as if she'd already left. And then she felt guilty for pitying him, which made her feel even more sorry. She wished she could just explain—it wasn't that she *wanted* to fantasize about running away, it was the dreams, infecting her mind! After several weeks of self-loathing, ruing her terrible ambivalence, she began to feel . . . something else. She noticed herself jerking away when he bent to touch her. Fussing with the collar he'd given her that bore her name. Not waiting for him while they made the morning trek to the barn but going ahead on her own. Sleeping farther and farther away from him (his stubble and his snoring grated her now, as they never had before). She had become *angry*. Maybe it wasn't fair, maybe she was holding him to too high a standard, but, really, after years of unwavering devotion she becomes moody and withdrawn and he notices *nothing*? If he paid one ounce as much attention to her as she did him, he would have known something was amiss. He would have made overtures—her favorite dinner, to cheer her up. A special outing to bring them closer. He took her for granted though. His cheerleader. His shadow. *But I bet he would notice*, she brooded, *if I were gone.*

She didn't acknowledge to herself that she had made a decision. It was early May, and every year at this time his brother came to stay for several weeks. The brother was a careless, distracted man, prone to leaving the door ajar when he came in from smoking on the front lawn. One evening after dinner, while relaxing on the couch, she saw the brother making his way back to the house. She rose. She could hear him, her companion of so many years, cleaning in the kitchen. The rushing of water, the clanking of pans. She moved to the front door. When the brother lumbered over the threshold he did not even notice her by his feet. She watched the brother shuffle to the kitchen, heard him mumble something and heard, in reply, her love's gravelly laugh. Her chest constricted; for a moment she felt she would suffocate from sorrow.

And then she slipped outside. A lean wind rippled through her fur. She picked up the scent of something rotting and thought of carcasses by the side of the road. She could end up like that. And there were greater threats than speeding cars— there were coyotes. Snakes. Sadists with cold eyes. She would do her best to avoid all the terrible things she knew about . . . but what about all the things she couldn't conceive of? The most dangerous things probably didn't look dangerous at all. She'd spent her whole life in captivity—she wasn't a predator— how could she possibly keep herself safe?

She worried over this for a long, suspended moment, drawing shallow breaths of chill night air. And then a possibility occurred to her, and she set off resolutely down the driveway, down the road and onto the turnpike. Maybe you didn't know whether you were a predator until the hour arrived, until the world opened its jaws and you were staring down the black throat of terror. *Whoever tries to harm me*, she reasoned, *might discover, at their own peril, that I have teeth.*

chapter two

The city is a dull parade of chill and half-hearted light—then, all at once, it's boiling hot. Things were different when El was young. Back then, winter slush gave way gradually to clement weeks of rain and pollen, and only after people started packing away their serious coats and ordering their coffees iced did true summer emerge with its choking humidity and overfull trash cans, vile and baking on every corner. There used to be time to adjust: not anymore.

El dabbed sweat from her hairline as she hustled up the steps of the West 4th Street station, glancing at her phone: *12:04.* She texted Darcy, her manager: Sorry sorry! 3 min.

From the mouth of the subway she rushed to the corner of Sixth Avenue. Taxis and boxy SUVs raced past, uptown. Little sedans scrambled to skirt wide buses. El eyed her phone anxiously: *12:06.* The light changed and El power walked, as one with the throng around her: the elderly, the uber-fit, the un-happy teenagers of tourists. As a pack they stalked across the avenue, the sun flaming their backs, ridiculing them all for their misfortune to be on foot in such inhospitable heat. El pushed to the front and broke into a jog, which she maintained until she reached the aqua banner of the small high-end bakery where she was a "team member." She worked the register, cleaned the floor, sorted out the cold room. She opened, mostly, but worked the second shift when Darcy asked her to, like today. Occasionally she helped frost cupcakes, the uncom-plicated ones.

Gently she pushed the door open and squeezed into the packed shop. There were eight or so couples in line, a few fam-ilies. Darcy stood at the register, harassed bun atop her head. Whoever had been on shift before El, probably Pia—they must've had to leave at noon on the dot. Not a great day to be late.

"Really sorry," El murmured as she charged past Darcy down the stairs. She shoved her bag in her cubby, pulled her apron on and took the stairs two at a time on the way back up. When she made it to the register she was sweating more than ever, and Darcy moved aside with an exasperated raising of eyebrows.

A woman in head-to-toe athleisure stood waiting to be helped. Her young, serious daughter hugged her leg. "A short-cake cookie and the green olive ciabatta," the woman said. No hi, no good morning, no thank you.

El pulled on a glove and bent to grab the shortcake cookie

from the case to her right. Through the glass the daughter's hazel eyes kept watch, and El, on a whim, puffed out her cheeks and swung her head from side to side, like someone exploring underwater. The daughter didn't smile.

El bagged the cookie and ciabatta carefully. She made sure to keep her expression pleasant as she broke the woman's twenty and returned her change. El saw the woman glance to the open Mason jar, affixed with a blue ribbon, marked TIPS. But the next moment, the woman had slipped her money into the pocket of her fitted sweatshirt and steered her daughter to the exit.

Asshole, El thought. Although really it was stupid to be upset—hardly anyone tipped in cash anymore. Paper money had more value now that you had to pay a fee to get it even from your own bank. True it only cost a couple dollars, but still. El certainly coveted her own cash: there were two creased singles that had been in her wallet for months.

The next customers were a pair of teenage girls, their hair in identically high, glossy ponytails. El wondered if this was some new summer trend. Totally possible: being twenty-nine, El found herself less and less in step with current fashion, more and more reverting to the mid-length layered cut, cap-sleeved tees and boot-cut jeans she'd favored for a decade. Despite their youth, both the girls were taller than El. One of them stood at least six feet in her kitten-heeled sandals, and she was the one who moved toward the counter, her eyes meeting El's with arresting confidence. She ordered two hazelnut milk flat whites and one lemon cupcake, cut in half. Her friend continued to hang back—out of respect, it seemed to El, for the taller girl's preeminence. Their dynamic reminded El a bit of Anna and Julia.

While El fixed the coffees, she thought about how this very week fifteen years ago, she, Anna and Julia had been about to graduate eighth grade. El had been extremely naïve: she had assumed that even though Anna and Julia were matriculating to a prep school in the Bronx and she to a public performing arts school in Midtown that they would still hang out all the time. Not so. El eventually realized that she, Anna and Julia had never lived in the same Manhattan. She had accessed theirs fleetingly, during her single year at the private middle school where, despite the mandatory uniforms, there had been constant, hungry comparison among the girls—which sneakers did you own, which earrings, which hair ties—and El's things had always been inferior, secondhand, drugstore-bought. As a suburban transplant, El had found New York City not only intimidating, but alien. She hadn't even recognized the brands worn by her classmates: Betsey Johnson and Longchamp and Lacoste—that tiny crocodile had seemed to sneer at El's own collared shirts, whose cheap unstarched necks wilted like soggy leaves when she tried to pop them.

The other eighth graders had whispered about El: that she was on *financial aid*, that she and her mother lived with *friends*, they didn't even have their own *apartment*—all of it was true and nothing to be ashamed of, but El had internalized the meaning of these observations: having less made her less. Then, on the Friday before Halloween, Anna and Julia had approached El in the computer lab, and Anna had asked—no, had commanded, that El come hang out with them.

"Why?" El had asked, her tone unintentionally rude. Anna had simply caught her off guard. She was about to apologize when—

"Oh my god. You're so *funny*." Anna's doll-like face shone with incredulous delight.

"You're hilarious," Julia had agreed.

After her public adoption by the grade's most popular girls, no one had trash-talked El anymore. Instead they'd jockeyed to hang out with her on weekends or on the sidelines in gym. The boys had made a "hot list" and El had come in *second*, right behind Anna. El had felt sorry for Julia, whose allure had been obscured by braces with elastic bands between the upper and lower teeth. Julia had seemed to know she was in an unfortunate phase, though, and had borne her mid-tier ranking without complaint. Some of the other girls had decried the hot list as sexist, however, and though El had agreed on principle, privately she'd taken comfort in having an allotted place. Actually, if El really thought about it, eighth grade had probably been the happiest year of her life.

El placed the flat whites on the counter beside the boxed-up cupcake and turned the card reader in the taller girl's direction. The taller girl paid with an absent wave of her phone, picked up her drink and moved aside to let her friend grab the remaining coffee and cupcake box. El grimaced as the friend struggled to situate the box under her purse arm, but the friend either didn't notice El's compassion or didn't need it. She swept after the taller girl, ponytail swinging like a metronome.

Traffic in the store finally began to slow at five o'clock. El's calves had begun to cramp and she needed to sit, but didn't dare do so until Darcy left at a quarter after: Darcy's new boyfriend, a sous chef at a Thai fusion place in Chelsea, had miraculously been granted the night off.

As soon as she found herself alone, El removed her apron, pulled out her phone and allowed herself to begin moping. It was Saturday and she had no plans. She scrolled through her feed, pausing at a post of Julia's: a video of clinking champagne glasses captioned *never too early*. Julia's birthday was the following day. El commented with two purple hearts and two crowns. The last time she'd actually seen Anna and Julia had been at Julia's twenty-sixth, three years earlier. Julia's then-boyfriend, Keegan Handler, owned a deeply exclusive restaurant, the kind of spot where even Ivy Getty's and Leonardo DiCaprio's assistants had to call in favors to land same-day reservations. Keegan had closed the restaurant for a night to host Julia's party, and El remembered how she'd felt being on the VIP list, being led to the main table where Julia had greeted her with a cry of delight, Anna with her trademark beguiling smirk, where cocktails made from top-shelf liquor had been freely supplied, where everyone had looked like they belonged in a *Vogue* spread or on a French car commercial. El had been reminded that night of how special she always felt in Anna and Julia's company, and she had sworn to herself that she would get together with Anna and Julia more often. But once again El had been naïve, because her infrequent meetings with her old friends were a matter not of motivation but of physics—of parallel universes.

Straight out of college Anna and Julia had settled in the East 70s, just blocks from their parents' brownstones. For El's other friends, living in the pale, stodgy prewar monoliths on Madison and Park would have been *nice* for sure but definitely dull. Her other friends lived in Astoria and Greenpoint and Bushwick and Bed-Stuy. They all, like El, lived paycheck to paycheck but still felt queasy about being part of their neighborhood's gentrification; they cringed when an exclusive artistic cooperative moved into the vacant space on the corner where the family-owned lighting store used to be, and, sure, was Jeff Bezos to blame for the lighting store losing its market? Probably, but weren't they all Amazon Prime members? They settled in with their guilt and their plants. They stayed at nearby bars until closing, steering clear of the sad fortysomething separated guys who kept dropping hints about how nice the High Line was that time of year. They hurried home with their sharpest keys between two fingers just in case, drunk texting all the while with that retail-store-manager-cum-glassblower they'd been stringing along. Once home they pillaged the fridge and fell asleep. In the morning they took the train to their destination—work, therapy, improv, Bikram—and later they took the train home.

But not Anna and Julia. El had learned during her year at private school that some people were so removed in their extreme wealth, even their feelings were untouchable. Anna and

Julia certainly knew the Upper East Side wasn't a cool place to live in their twenties, knew the subway was always cheaper and usually quicker than a cab, but it would never have occurred to them to care. Their world was *the* world, with its own capitals, routes and boundaries.

So that was it: El was never on the Upper East Side, never in the Hamptons, never "upstate" at a country house. Home was a cramped walk-up in Williamsburg and work was here, in the West Village. El commuted between the two and that was her life, basically. That was all she had energy for. Her phone buzzed with a notification. *Julia had liked her comment.* Then a text came in—

> babe! having a birthday/memorial day thing on sunday. you've been to the beach house, yeah? come come come. xx

El, Anna and Julia had practically lived at Julia's family's beach house in the Hamptons the summer before high school. It was the first place El had gotten drunk, thanks to Julia's older brother Tom, who had used his fake ID to buy Julia hard lemonade in exchange for her silence about the girls he snuck in at midnight and out at dawn. El remembered the place vividly: a long, renovated farmhouse with green shutters. A giant lawn of fresh, soft grass; a pool, heated and pristine; a gate that led to a secret path to the beach. At night, she, Anna and Julia had imbibed and watched movies in the home theater Julia had begged her father to put in. El had memorized all of Kate

Hudson's lines in *Almost Famous* and had sometimes performed them off the cuff to Julia's applause and Anna's incisive critiques. She had told herself that, when she became a movie star, she would buy her own beach house. This fantasy had allowed her to feel like Anna's and Julia's equal—like they had it all for the moment, but later on, in ten or twenty years, she would be able to host them. Over lunch on the patio Julia would ask, what was it like to work with so-and-so, was he a dick like everybody said? And even Anna would lean forward to hear El's answer.

The fact that Julia didn't even remember taking El to the Hamptons house . . . That was kind of devastating.

Yeah, think I've been but it's been a minute! El texted back. I'd love to come.

chapter three

would bring you if I could," El said.

In her full-length mirror she eyed Crystal, who was picking at her frayed jean shorts on the bed. Three years El and Crystal had been roommates, and until very recently they had enjoyed the easy friendship of two people fundamentally uninvested in one another. They had caught up in passing, over coffee in the kitchen or between episodes of *Love Island*, often griping about flaky reps and bad auditions and about how, even when you did get a decent speaking role, being bottom of the call sheet inspired nauseating existential dread. Now, what was there to say? Crystal was still auditioning, still trying, and El wasn't. El had fired her manager and had quit her bartending gig (the bar having been frequented by her former acting coach). She had taken the job at the bakery five months ago and had been trying, ever since, to become a morning person and to forget all the things she used to want.

To Crystal's credit, she had not tried to convince El to stick with acting, which was not to say that she was giving El space. Quitting must have been in the air when El had given up on her dreams, because Crystal's long-term girlfriend, Nicole, had chosen that same week to break Crystal's heart. Once Crystal had gotten past the initial shock of being dumped, she'd come to the realization that she had no platonic friends: she'd been El's shadow ever since.

"Where is it again, Long Island?" Crystal asked.

"East Hampton." El stripped off a stretchy T-shirt and tossed it over the closet door.

"Fan-caaaay."

El started flipping through hangers. She pulled down a loose, thin blue dress that made her nipples stand out.

"What time do you leave?" Crystal asked.

"Not till tomorrow, but I have a double shift so I won't have time to come back here and change."

"Oh, right."

Crystal's voice was so saturated with self-pity El felt almost embarrassed for her.

"Maybe I can text Julia, feel out the deal with plus-ones."

El hoped that Crystal recognized she was merely being polite—that she would not, under any circumstances, be messaging Julia to see if she could bring her roommate to the party. El just wanted to get drunk with her old friends and gossip about the weird trajectories of the people they'd known in middle school. She wanted to pretend that her own trajectory was blessed. That she was Enough, had Enough. Crystal would only be a reminder of the uncertain present. Plus—and why this even mattered El couldn't say, because did it make her like Crystal any less? No, not at all, but it was a fact that Crystal's personal style lived somewhere in the ballpark of an old Kid Rock music video. Rhinestones and lace, wife beaters, everything skintight. Crystal made her own rules about what to aspire to. She wore what she liked, what suited her. She had no concept of wealth like Anna's and Julia's, their upper upper echelon, and therefore had no reverence for it. El pitied Crystal and envied her in equal measure.

Crystal had stopped picking at her shorts. Now she was scratching her fingernails backward and forward over El's comforter with a worried expression.

"What?" El prompted.

"Do you think Nicole's seeing someone already? We were talking again, then last week she just stopped responding."

"She's probably just got stuff going on."

"That's not her though. She's not a bad texter. I *really* want to ask her sister. I feel like she'd tell me."

"I wouldn't," El warned. "Really, give Nicole some space. Try to resist the temptation."

"My dad always says 'resist, persist.'"

El stared at Crystal's broad, Valentine face. The porcelain-white forehead that wouldn't need Botox for decades, the pointed chin. What a funny foil she made to El's own sticky pink complexion and pragmatism.

"Hey, if you want to obsess—your prerogative." *And if you're miserable,* El thought, *you only have yourself to blame.*

El left her apartment at 5:20 a.m. the next morning, and even though she was in her faded NYU sweatshirt and shitty cargo pants she strolled to the M with the easy, sensual affect of an actress in a black and white movie. A breeze blew back strands of the hair she'd woken up early to straighten. For a moment she felt captivated by the idea that perhaps she was part of some great story, some mystery, that all her little actions were conspiring toward some ultimate meaning.

The ear-splitting squealing of the M put a crimp in the romantic spirit of the morning, but the train did deliver El to her stop earlier than usual. The sun was just coming up, and rather than rush to open the bakery early, El took her time, savoring the wan light. She paused before the window of a kitchen supply store, imagining what it would be like to own big brass pots and cutting boards that didn't stain. At the apartment, she and Crystal didn't even have a knife block. She was turning from the window when something caught her eye— something gold, on the pavement. She bent forward to check it out: It was a bone-shaped custom dog tag. For DANI. A Toledo, Ohio, address. And there was an inscription: *Man's Best Friend.* Huh. She wondered how Dani had come to be so far from home.

El's dawdling actually made her a shade late, but gratefully the first hour at the bakery was slow, leaving her time to get organized and to daydream, as she had so often in the past several days, about Julia's brother Tom. His social media was private, so she hadn't been able to suss out whether he had a girlfriend, but nothing had popped up on The Knot with his name, so he probably wasn't married. He had to be coming to the party. It would be weird not to come to your sister's birthday, right? Because he lived in New York—that much she'd been able to tell from the website of the investment bank where he worked.

In eighth grade she had fantasized about Tom constantly. From their Lebanese maternal grandmother, Tom and Julia had both inherited expressive, regal eyebrows. But while Julia had their Scandinavian dad's lanky light hair, Tom had also inherited his mother's and grandmother's exquisite curls: they hung dark and loose in easy waves. To teenage El, Tom had looked like a god. He might've been the inspiration for one of the deities in Ansel's illustrated book on Greek myths, the one with the long yellow spine that had stared at her from across the room . . .

Sharing a bedroom with Ansel had been the one major downside of her eighth-grade year, but it had been a matter of financial necessity. When El and her mother had first come to the city they'd been flat broke. They had stayed a week or two at a sketchy motel in Queens, El's mother calling temp agencies every day trying to find work. Then one afternoon her mother had announced that they were going into Manhattan to meet up with an old friend. El had been expecting a man, some weird ex-boyfriend, but the old friend had turned out to be a tall, freckled woman named Erica.

El's mother had laid out their situation for Erica: several months before, El's father had placed his palms on the worn wooden table in their breakfast nook and explained that he had another family. Another partner and another daughter. He had been living two lives for years and could not do it anymore. He wanted to live with his other partner. He wanted to marry her.

(Whatever El's expectations had been after this abrupt and traumatizing revelation—that she would still *see* her father, at least, that she and her mother would continue to live in Maryland, that her life would change but not *too* much—all these had been swiftly butchered. The only mercy had been her father's decisiveness. There'd been no mumbling about "I'll see you soon" or "Won't it be fun to meet your half sister." No no. Post-confession, he became the father of one child: Kirsten. El had found her online. Kirsten played soccer. She looked like El, but more angular.)

Erica had listened with her long neck bent close to her body as El's mother had explained their dire financial position. The house in Maryland had sold, but the money had gone to cover certain debts incurred during the marriage—credit cards, loans, overdue bills from the long-term-care facility where El's grandfather had convalesced for eight years. So now, El's mother had said, too desperate even to blush, she had nothing—less than nothing, because she hadn't worked in a decade. The only reason she'd dragged El to Queens was because the cousin of a neighbor in Maryland had needed a dog-sitter while he went to Singapore on sabbatical—but within twenty-four hours of their arrival in Queens, the dog had died. Their services were no longer required.

When El's mother had finished, Erica had promptly lambasted El's father and the "fuckery" (sorry, she'd said to El, sorry, but it was the only word)—the *fuckery* of the patriarchy. As El's mother knew, her own ex-husband had never paid a lick of child support. Erica had then raised her head, alien-like above that long neck, and announced that El and her mother should come live with her until they got on their feet, whenever that might be. Erica had explained to El that she would have to share a room with Ansel, her son who was El's age, did El remember him? She'd played with him as a baby. El had not remembered Ansel, and, never having shared a room before, had felt apprehensive: Would this Ansel kid be cool?

The answer had been a resounding no. Ansel, El came to discover, was terminally disagreeable. When forced to apologize, his chunky eyebrows would knit together and his eyes would go dark and cold. He had been the kind of kid neither students nor teachers could stand, and the feeling had been mutual. But there had been no one Ansel had despised more than El; perhaps he'd feared his mother would come to love a child apart from himself. Ansel had remained unusually covetous of his mother even into adulthood; when Erica had abandoned Manhattan for the Poconos in 2020, Ansel had followed her. After Erica's passing a year later, Ansel had stayed up in the mountains, but El still saw him annually: Ansel was always invited for dinner in August, for her mother's birthday, which was a week after El's own.

As for El's mother, she still lived in the 700-square-foot Columbus Circle apartment she and El had moved into after their year with Erica and Ansel. She worked remotely doing admin for a software company. She had a ginger cat named Chat and left the city as little as she could. "I should've been born here in the first place," her mother often said, and it was true.

El, however, was a New Yorker simply by default. And now that she didn't need to be in the city for her career, she'd started to wonder whether it was the best place for her. Was there somewhere better? Santa Fe? Seattle? Oslo? Rome? She had barely traveled; she'd been to New Hampshire and Massachusetts a couple times and had once attended a wedding in South Carolina. NYU had given her a grant to go to London for the summer—research for her thesis on the comedy of menace—but she had opted, at the last minute, to accept a role in a play at the prestigious Williamstown Theatre Festival where she'd (a) expected to be scouted for Broadway and (b) believed her play's director when he'd said connections like theirs were "very rare in this world" and that he was prepared to leave his wife. She had left Williamstown with no job prospects, no boyfriend and no stamp on her first-ever passport.

Being neither well-traveled nor worldly, El didn't have much confidence that Tom would find her worthy of interest. But then again, his sister had taken a chance on her in middle

school. Maybe Tom, too, would be willing to consider someone who didn't have the means to operate in his league; someone who lacked direction; someone who, these days, dragged
like exhaust behind the engine of her city.

But El didn't want to take chances: she was determined to
show up at Julia's party looking nothing like her usual depleted
self. She'd stayed up past midnight selecting the right outfit,
stalking photos from summers past by searching the profiles
of various society-adjacent girls. In the end she'd chosen a
white Rag & Bone dress she'd found at Housing Works, Tory
Burch sandals that were two seasons old but still in decent shape
and an AllSaints jean jacket that belonged to Nicole (which El
had rescued from Crystal's breakup-clothes-to-donate pile in
the front hall closet). El couldn't wait to finish work and
transform herself, but this final shift was crawling like the last
day of school, even though she would be closing two hours
earlier than usual for the holiday. After noon, there weren't
even any customers to distract her. The neighborhood had
emptied, everyone who could afford to having already skipped
town. From her cold stool she stared at the tantalizing sidewalk, at the rainbow flag across the street rippling in the sun-
shine.

At 3:45 p.m. her phone started pinging. Her remaining
NYU friends would all be meeting on Navya's roof in an hour;
she'd been planning to join them until she'd gotten the invite
from Julia. Thea texted a picture of a soda bottle: My Greek a**
is going to consume an entire 6 pack of this indica espresso shit
bc I CANNOT GET ENUF. Emma sent a video of a cat peeking

its head out from behind a weed plant. Mathias said he might arrive late. El sent a message saying she would miss them all; Navya hearted it.

El looked at the time again: *3:52*. Close enough. She walked over and flipped the sign on the door to CLOSED.

chapter four

The Jitney was hot and crowded, and El thought long-ingly of previous Hamptons journeys, watching DVDs in the back seat of Julia's parents' cool, roomy Expedition. The air conditioning on the bus was broken and those in window seats grumbled at their burden, half-standing to struggle with latches and let in the breeze. El would have traded her aisle for a window in a heartbeat. Her seat was nearest the bathroom, and even with her music on full blast she couldn't drown out the constant flushing and lock-rattling over her shoulder.

She was deeply relieved to disembark, three hours later, into the humid, humming evening. The sky glimmered blue and rose, and despite the immediate surroundings (the bus had pulled into an empty gas station), El felt a mounting excitement now that she was so close, physically, to the house she had once loved. It was a contact high. Her own history was on the air. So much had happened to her on that property, and so much had almost happened . . .

El pulled out her phone to text Julia that she'd arrived, but as she did so a white Range Rover blasting Carly Rae Jepsen rolled up next to the bus. The passenger window came down and Julia, wearing only a bikini, called out from the driver's seat: "Party up, bitch!"

Ignoring the stares of her fellow Jitney-riders, El hurried forward and hoisted herself into the car.

Julia's cheeks were flushed. Just like the teen girls in the bakery the other day, she wore her dark blond hair high on her head in a sleek ponytail, her bangs combed into curtains framing her face. She smelled so strongly of anise and vanilla it made El's throat itch.

"Eeeeeee!" Julia squealed. "I'm so pumped you're here!"

El just managed to click in her seat belt as Julia whipped out of the parking lot. They roared along the little two-lane road, and El frowned at Julia: "I'm an idiot. I didn't bring anything to swim in."

Julia waved her off. "Oh no, I'm changing I'm changing. I'm so fucking burned—is there any aloe in here?" With one hand she rummaged through the center console. "Everything's been crazy, I'm so scattered. I almost forgot to come get you and then I was like oh *shit*!"

"How many people are coming?"

"Honestly no clue. Tom invited *tons* of people too."

"Oh wow! Tom's gonna be there. I don't think I've seen him since we were like fourteen." She desperately wanted to ask whether Tom was single but restrained herself. "So what time is Anna coming?"

"Anna's in Paris." Julia's hard expression betrayed her airy tone.

"Really? For what?"

"She lives there now."

El flushed. There was no *logical* reason to feel embarrassed: El hadn't spent time with Anna in years, it made complete sense that she should be out of the loop. And yet, her inner adolescent couldn't help but feel humiliated.

"It's fucking crazy," Julia continued. "Like—okay! You *live* in Paris now? *And* she deletes her profile??"

El was about to remark that she hadn't noticed Anna's deleting her profile—then she remembered. About half a year ago, she had muted Anna. It had been right before she'd quit acting. Her acting coach had encouraged her to reach out to every single connection she'd had, so, against her better judgment, El had messaged Anna to ask whether she would mind setting up a lunch with her mother, who was on the board of The Public. Anna had never responded, and El had been mortified. There had come a point when she could no longer stand to see Anna's name in her feed. Funny, she'd forgotten all about that . . . Banished it from her mind, more like.

"She's like *off* grid," Julia continued, talking fast. "New number too. I'm lucky I even have it. Her mom gave it to me after she stopped returning my texts."

"Wait, Anna didn't even tell you she was leaving?"

"I mean we haven't been like *close* close in a while, honestly. I was running around shadowing this music video director who's the son of this guy in my building and then I was in St. Barts for a minute and just crazy busy for months and Anna was—whatever, being Anna. But yeah, no, she didn't tell me."

This surprised El. Of course she'd known Anna and Julia had made their own friends in college and after, but in her mind they had still been a regular part of each other's lives, being from the same sort of high-class background and everything; at Julia's twenty-sixth they had certainly seemed as familiar as ever. Had they simply grown apart of late, or had Anna pulled away deliberately?

As they pulled up to a red light, Julia raised her phone in the air. El, getting the hint, made a duck face and tilted her head for the selfie. Then Julia messed with the filter and, a few seconds later, El's phone vibrated in her back pocket. She pulled it out—it was a group chat among herself, Julia and a 929 number. Julia had sent the selfie along with a message: MISS YOU BITCH. El saved the 929 number as Anna New.

The light had barely turned green when Julia raced through it. "So tell me tell me. What's happening? How've you *been*? Wait. Did I tell you I'm going on a retreat? To Ios. For the summer. Tom's coming too—he fucking hates Goldman and he's gonna start law school in the fall, so he's got like three months free. But anyway it's this wellness thing, so no blue light or caffeine or any of that. I just really wanted do something centering, like I'm thinking, when I get back, maybe I want to start my own brand?"

"That'd be cool," El said. Julia always had a new plan for her future.

"Right??" She glanced at El and widened her eyes for effect. Her pupils were two dark moons.

Oh, El thought, so that explained why Julia was so hyper. She was on coke.

By the time they arrived at the house, Julia had covered a lot of ground, including:

how last night she thought her IUD had fallen out, how she wasn't sure she wanted kids but she did think, maybe, she'd make a good doula or therapist, or like a combination of the two—oh! oh shit. fuck. she forgot to buy bone broth. she and tom were supposed to be drinking all this cleansing stuff for like a *week* before the retreat and she forgot to tell carmen to buy the fucking bone broth yesterday and now the store was closed—maybe on the way to the airport—heyyy did el know those like—that like—those crunchy things, they were pink and white—neapolitan! those neapolitan things they had in the lounges at the airport in like a fish bowl . . .

El had rolled her window down, allowing the warm, whipping air to punch holes in Julia's monologue. She'd watched the scrub pines grow smaller as they'd neared the beach, watched as they shied from the long sky whose pastel became red and vivid as the sun died.

Now El was following Julia through a garden gate, past the

fat, blooming bushes of white hydrangea against the side of the house. El breathed their scent and felt herself swell with a radical joy. This place was still the Eden she remembered—private, protected, abundant. A bee shot past her and paused before a blossom, trembling. El watched it for a moment.

Julia, meanwhile, bulldozed unthinking over the manicured grass. No doubt her room upstairs was in disarray, lousy with clothes and luggage and accessories, the en suite littered with products, so many things, so much area, claimed without a thought. As they rounded the back of the house and approached the party—there were already thirty people by the pool—El thought that space was the true commodity of the rich. It was elbow room on a flight; it was peace of mind. It was wasted on the likes of Julia, who was always distracted, groping externally for her raison d'être: she couldn't appreciate the security of her circumstances. What would most people— what would she, El—trade for the restful life at Julia's fingertips? Almost anything.

chapter five

n another hour there were a hundred guests, and they looked, El thought, like parodies of themselves: starved women with Adderall nerves, dyed bright blond; self-satisfied men in Vineyard Vines, hairlines just beginning to recede. Hip-hop blasted from speakers behind the diving board. While in the kitchen fixing herself a whiskey and soda, El tried to strike up a conversation with a group taking shots. They were A.I. consultants and marketing directors for tech companies, and they tolerated El's conversation for a few minutes. When El realized they were not warming up to her she excused herself ("Have to go find my friend!"). One of the guys, who had not even asked her name, had the grace to feign disappointment ("Good to meet you!").

Julia had changed into a black dress with clear spaghetti straps and ruby stud earrings that stood out against her naturally golden skin. El found her on the patio flirting with a fluffy-haired dude who looked like a grown-up lax bro.

"El!" Julia exclaimed. Pointing to the bro, she asked, "You know Damien?"

Damien gave El the kind of once-over she'd grown accustomed to. He was wondering, because he couldn't place her, whether she was one of them—a girl from the Lycée, maybe, who hadn't partied much in high school—or whether she was, more likely, just some nobody.

"El's one of my oldest oldest friends," Julia crooned, wrapping an arm around El's shoulders and nuzzling into her. Her bangs tickled El's neck.

"Nice," Damien said, but his eyes were already scanning the party for something more interesting.

Julia put her hand on Damien's arm: "Grab a drink, babe." She guided El away, toward the pool. Someone was setting off fireworks and under their crackling umbrella Julia led El over to Tom, who had just emerged from the pool house, where people were hotboxing. His Adonis curls were matted and sweaty.

"Brother."

"What?"

"You remember El, right?"

El met Tom's eyes and her smile wavered. Briefly she glimpsed the depth of it, her need to be loved, as a climber glimpses all the miles below.

"Um, I don't know," Tom said. His gray eyes were slow and streaked with red.

"I mean—it was a long time ago," El said.

"You remember," Julia insisted. "El. From my middle school."

"I remember Anna," he sniggered.

Julia glared at him. Tom walked off, and El felt disappointment compressing the space around her body.

Turning to El, Julia asked, "Do you think Anna's that pretty? Like memorable pretty? Honestly."

El shrugged like *meh*, but the real answer was *yes, definitely*. Anna was a better-looking version of El herself, and it was hard to say whether money made the difference or whether Nature had awarded Anna the better fortune all around. They both had dark brown hair, but Anna's remained perpetually sleek where El's grew puffy in humidity; El's eyes were a staid blue, whereas Anna's eyes were changeable, so much so that El thought they might look different to every person depending on their perception (to El, they appeared green); Anna was uniquely formed, short and very slight but shapely, with intriguing breasts—El was athletic-ish, soft here and there, nothing surprising. El's attractiveness was not undeniable like Anna's. On the whole, actually, El was fairly plain besides an intangible something. Her ex-manager had once described this quality as El's "sympathy." "Something in your mouth," he'd said. "It's not bitchy, it's like a little sad. It's like you're dying to tell us something."

El discovered that the whiskey she'd drunk had transformed her embarrassment about being out of the loop regarding Anna into feverish resentment: How could Anna have failed to inform her that she'd *moved to another country*? Of course,

Anna and Julia had always been the closer of the three of them, because they'd belonged to the same world and had thus spent the most time together, but El had always believed that *if* she'd had the same amount of shared experiences with Anna, that Anna would have liked her better. Not because there was anything wrong with Julia—Julia was fine. But Anna's ego wanted a witness, someone to appreciate her barbs and sarcasm and insights, and El had always been better in this capacity than Julia, who was, honestly, just not super bright. But even as El brooded upon Anna's ghosting, she recalled the advice she'd given Crystal just last night: don't fixate on a person who abandons you. If she chose to obsess about Anna, she'd only have herself to blame when she felt like shit.

Julia wanted more coke, so with nothing better to do, and in hopes of putting Anna far from her mind, El followed Julia to the nearest bathroom and supplied her own license for cutting lines on the toilet tank.

After a few short minutes, El began feeling light-headed, the birds on the wallpaper coming into greater and greater focus. Had she ever done this much cocaine? On a big night like Halloween she'd do a couple bumps with Navya since Van usually had a hook-up, but she and Julia were now at five, six, seven lines each. After the last one El felt her hands quaking, and there was a concentrated buzz in her head that made her feel very significant, like a walking bomb. She and Julia left the bathroom and went their separate ways without a word.

El found herself outside, charging through the yard.

She gaped at the pool, a memory bubbling to mind—Shay—
Anna— She pushed it down. She walked on until she was
standing in the no-man's-land behind the pool house. There
were no lights back here, no garden ornaments, just a few dark
trees. A hundred yards away, a white fence demarcated the end
of the property. Tall oaks on the opposite side blocked a neigh-
boring house from view. El stood, listening to her rapid heartbeat, and just as she was trying to remember why she'd come out
here and concluding that she *needed* to get back inside, something caught her eye. Blood rushed to her head: she felt faint
with fear. Mere feet to her left was a guy standing still and alone.
He had a stocky build. Pale skin. He was staring at her.

"Bryce," he said softly, motioning to himself.

She ran. As fast as she could, all the way back to the house,
through the kitchen to the foyer into the front room where
everyone had dropped their stuff, their designer purses and
jackets and blazers. She looked behind her. The guy named
Bryce had not followed.

The fear was gone now and seemed laughable in retrospect.
She felt giddy. And thirsty. She went to the kitchen and discovered one of Tom's colleagues (she recognized him from the
investment bank website) sitting on a stool, draining a beer
and scowling at his phone. His face was sculpted and severe,
emphasized by heavy brows. Dark chest hair poked through
his Ralph Lauren button-down. There was something devil-
may-care about him.

"It's giving early Brando," she said, scanning him up and
down.

He glanced up, a contemptuous crease down the middle of his forehead. "Huh?"

"Marlon Brando, that's who you look like."

His face relaxed when he realized she hadn't been insulting him. "Oh shit," he said. "No way." He wavered a little on the stool as he leaned to one side to slip his phone into his pocket.

"I'm tired of standing," she said, boldly approaching him, and, though surprised, he opened his arms to make space for her on his lap. When she sat she became aware of simultaneous, rival sensations: his foreignness—his woody smell, his rubbery quad muscles beneath her ass—and his perfect familiarity. How naturally they fit together! Jesus Christ. You could spend weeks, months, years scouring apps and parties and coffee shops for someone compatible, could spend days looking forward to dates that turned into nothing. But this was a *connection*, so easy!

They spent the next hour roaming the party together, often holding hands. He introduced her to some people, douchebags with expensive watches and stunning girlfriends. El hoped they would come across Tom, so Tom could see her with one of his peers, but they never did. She was in Julia's eyeline at one point, and waved, but Julia did not seem to see her. At some point El glanced to the edge of the yard behind the pool house, but the man named Bryce had gone.

Sometime after midnight, El and her companion—she still didn't know his name—walked the path to the beach. The ocean was black and roaring. El was deflating, the buzz in her head all but evaporated; her companion, however, had been drinking beer steadily. He was ready to fuck. She wasn't wet. They didn't have a condom. He spat into his hand and maneuvered her so she was kneeling, facing the dunes. The waves were so loud she didn't hear him when he said he was about to come, so when she pushed backward into him he was forced to throw her off. She landed on her side in the cold sand and righted herself quickly, though she swayed, drunk and dizzy. She wiped her inner thighs with the bottom of her dress. With a sobering flush of embarrassment, she recalled plopping herself into this stranger's lap and mistaking his welcome for fate. Already she was thinking about how she would spin this night to Navya. This preppy guy, she'd say. Nah, just a onetime thing, but it had been fun.

In the morning El returned to the beach to look for her underwear. She squinted at the bright sand, a headache building behind her eyes. Two women were nearby, walking a drab little terrier on a long red leash: the elder of the two eyed El disdainfully. The terrier had been batting at the surf, but now it jumped in El's direction and barked.

"Control your dog," El muttered, and she trudged back toward the house to sleep a bit longer.

At ten she woke for the second time and, after a brief search of the house, discovered she was alone. Julia and Tom must have already left for the airport. Feeling like an idiot, she called a rideshare service and waited in the front hall with her bag, wishing she'd thought to search the bathroom cabinet for

Advil, until the housekeeper, Carmen, came in the front door. Though initially surprised to find someone in the house, Carmen offered to drive El to the Jitney stop.

"I'm okay," El replied stoutly.

But Carmen said she had to leave soon anyway to get to the farmer's market before it closed, and El felt it would be discourteous to refuse a second time. She canceled her rideshare and climbed into Carmen's black Jeep. As they passed green fields and one spectacular house after another, El's headache became a full-blown migraine. She girded herself against throwing up, gripping her seat with both hands as if preparing to launch herself through the windshield should worse come to worst. At a stop sign Carmen glanced over at El and said, maternally, "Almost there."

The Jitney was a nightmare. El had a seat near the front this time, but a clear view of the traffic ahead made the drive feel unbearably long. By late afternoon she was finally back in her apartment, where she had such ferocious diarrhea she actually prayed between bouts.

The rest of the day she spent in bed, napping intermittently. Around eight she stomached several palm-sized packets of soup crackers. She rewatched a favorite season of *Survivor*, mostly just listening with eyes closed.

The following day she was so depressed she called out of work. She pretended not to hear Darcy's impatience, thanked her pointedly for understanding—she was lucky to have such a cool boss, et cetera. After the call, El moaned and shrank into her sheets. She loathed herself for groveling.

Crystal poked her head in at two p.m., dressed in a cable-knit sweater and khakis. She was going up for a bit part in a procedural in which she would play a teacher who got smothered to death before the first act break.

"Break a leg," El said.

"Thanks. Need anything?"

El shook her head. Crystal tipped an invisible hat and turned to go.

"Can you close it?" El asked, a little desperately.

Crystal turned back and pulled the door shut. El stared at a spidery shadow her Creeping Charlie was making over by the window. She exhaled a long breath and sat up, encouraging her squished pillow to better support her.

"Okay," she said to no one. "Okay."

A tightness came into her throat and she realized that she could cry now, if she wanted. Instead she focused. There was some malignant kernel festering inside her. Why did she feel so worthless—Tom's rejection? The anonymity of her hook-up on the beach? Then it came to her. She had not let herself go there at the party, the whole Anna and Shay thing.

chapter six

That year of eighth grade, El spent Sundays by herself. Anna and Julia always brunched with their respective families, and El's mother always slept in, as Sunday was her one day off from her temp job at the orthodontist's office. El would've liked to sleep in too, but she couldn't. Ansel's boy smell, like vinegar and sweat, lingered sickeningly even with the windows open all night. The moment El became conscious, she'd fly out of the apartment and use one of the remaining fares on her MetroCard, fares she'd conserved by walking home from school during the week, to go downtown.

She'd ride the train to Christopher Street and walk east toward Washington Square Park, then she'd head south past the clusters of just-waking-up bars to the record store where *he* worked. Shay. They had met one day when a shard of glass had sliced through her sneaker and she'd limped to the nearest storefront for help. Once Shay had patched her up, El had inquired about a box of decals by the counter that read ORIG-INAL SOUND. That turned out to be Shay's band: he'd given El a copy of their demo. (She had discovered upon listening that Original Sound played mostly covers.) The following Sunday El had returned to the record store. She hadn't found Shay especially attractive; he was eerily tall, and his face was littered with tiny cavities, acne scars—he was no Tom, that was for sure—but there had been something compelling about him nonetheless.

Over many subsequent Sundays, El learned about Shay. He was only eighteen. He hailed from Northern California and had dropped out of college after his first semester. Max, Original Sound's drummer, was his best friend. His high school best friend had died of a heroin overdose.

Shay was not indifferent to El, but he also didn't seem interested in her romantically. Was her age the prohibitive factor? she often wondered. It should have been, she eventually concluded, but it wasn't. No, El sensed rather that she lacked some quality Shay needed to complete himself, or to become himself, the person he was trying to be.

The thing about El that seemed to fascinate Shay the most, actually, was her proximity to wealth, via her school. When she'd told him how some of the boys had been suspended for gambling with hundred-dollar bills during recess, he'd whistled. "Sometimes we play gigs for people like that. These people . . . The last reception we played, it was basically all gold, everywhere—like the bride had a crown, and the plates were lined with it, even the ceiling. Just gold vomit."

Usually El felt that she was the less knowledgeable of the two of them, but listening to Shay she had thought that, for once, he might be the ignorant one. The people who hired Original Sound to play their weddings weren't the same as Anna and Julia and her other classmates' families. His employers had to announce their wealth whereas, at school, everybody had this astonishing kind of nonchalance. Like when Claire R. had come to school wearing her mom's old sweatshirt from Princeton. All morning she'd worn it tied around her waist. At lunch, she'd used it as a napkin for mustard-y fingers. After last period she'd forgotten it beneath her seat. El had seen it there, crumpled on the ground. It was this *not worrying*, this not coveting, this abandonment of the emblem of a legacy because you *were* the legacy—*that* was real money. But El had not shared this with Shay. He believed they rubbed shoulders with the same kind of people, and she wanted to appear to have as much in common with him as possible.

It was a lucky thing when the school year ended and Julia first invited El to the Hamptons, because El's feelings for Shay were nearing a dangerous inflection point; the temptation to reach out and touch his underfed reptilian body had become incredible. Instead she watched the Atlantic from the hard white chairs Julia's family kept perennially on the beach. She ate string cheese by the pool while Julia read her *Twilight* paperbacks and Anna issued bored sighs, browning with her eyes closed and her headphones in. Thus passed every weekend for seven weeks, until one Friday in the middle of July, when Julia's parents decided to stay in the city and entrusted the girls' welfare to Tom. The cool mornings and marmalade sunsets were more beautiful without real supervision. Late one night El, Anna and Julia sat by the pool getting buzzed on some of Tom's weed and a half-bottle of vodka Julia said her mother wouldn't miss. Tom was inside, fully occupied with a pretty EMT-in-training. For a while the girls took "candid" pictures of one another, but then Anna got an invitation to a closed Facebook group of Upper East Side kids who were going to be Hill School freshmen. The Hill Schools: above Van Cortlandt Park they stood in a proud cluster, welcoming (according to Tom) mainly legacies and Dalton rejects. The public performing arts high school had accepted El early, so she hadn't even bothered to try for a scholarship to one of the Hill Schools, but she had checked out their websites to see what fifty grand a year could buy.

Julia craned over Anna's shoulder, her face illuminated by the light of Anna's phone. "Invite me!" she whined. "Do you see Brady?"

"No, he's going to Trinity," Anna said.

El groaned, which she would not have done if she weren't somewhat drunk and high. This happened frequently, Anna and Julia talking about people she had never met.

"There's Woller," Anna was saying. "His sister's such a cunt."

"Who?"

"Remember she was the Bunk 2 counselor that year?"

El particularly resented any reference to Lowile Bay, the sleepaway camp that Anna and Julia went to every August. It wasn't one of those camps where you learned practical stuff like how to portage a canoe or start a fire. (El knew how to do lots of practical things. In fourth grade her father had started taking her to camp in a state park in West Virginia. There, in the haunted cadence of a man under a spell, he'd extolled on the importance of survival skills. After the divorce she'd wondered if the survival he'd been preparing her for was a life without him in it.) No, Lowile Bay, by the sound of it, was a camp where you water-skied and played tennis and made out with people behind a boat house. It was a country club, basically, and El desperately wished her mother had the eight thousand dollars it would take to send her there, to be with her friends.

As Anna and Julia continued to lambast Woller's sister, the evil Bunk 2 counselor, El pulled her phone from her back pocket, the stiff mesh of the pool chair creaking beneath her. The day before, Shay had messaged her for the first time since their last exchange in early June. She reread the text now: close call, it said, and beneath that was a photo of some broken glass on the sidewalk next to his boot. Seeing Shay's name brought that heavy, allergic fullness back to her chest. Life had been shallow in his absence, but she'd been able to breathe.

Still—replying to him couldn't hurt.

very close call, she wrote. And then, impulsively, she snapped a picture of the pool in front of her and sent that, too, along with: that Hamptons life.

After a moment her screen illuminated: i'm in the Hamptons too. @ a reception.

She asked Shay where he was exactly, and he mentioned the name of a town she didn't know. She searched it: he was twenty minutes away. He told her Original Sound's set was done. A DJ had taken over. For the best, he said, because the bartender had been keeping him and Max and Josh, their bass player, a little too well supplied with champagne.

"What's up?"

Anna's shrewd voice broke El's concentration. Anna stood largely in shadow, though the pool light cast a thick crescent of brightness that trembled over her chest.

"Oh it's just my friend."

"What friend?"

"This guy. Shay. He's in a band. He's— They have to drive back to the city tonight but they're all drunk. It's stupid."

"Have to drive back from where?"

"Near here."

"How do you know him?"

Julia flopped down on the pool chair next to El's. "How old is he? Is he hot?"

"I met him at this record store. I think he's eighteen."

A pause, then, as Anna stared. El knew Anna was surprised that El had a secret, an apartness. El felt a moment's pride— Anna and Julia had their apartness, their Sunday brunches at The Boathouse and JG Melon; why shouldn't she have something too? But under Anna's pointed gaze El's confidence wavered, and she began to feel nervous. Anna, she felt, was calculating the shape and significance of Shay.

"Tell him to come here," Anna said finally. "He and his band can take a cab over. They can crash and drive back to the city in the morning."

El tilted her head and pressed her lips together, indicating she didn't think much of this plan. She didn't want Shay coming to the house, stepping out of the compartment in her life she'd relegated him to, and she looked to Julia for backup. "I don't think Tom would like it . . ."

Anna scoffed. "He's balls deep in that lifeguard or whoever she is." Anna turned to Julia. "I mean, Jules, you don't care."

"I mean, no," Julia said, in an almost frightened voice.

"Right," Anna said, looking back to El. "So tell him to come."

El had been expecting a cab, but it was a green Econoline van that came snaking down the gravel drive. She squinted at the headlights, holding a hand to her eyes until the van drew level with her and the engine died.

"I thought the whole point was you not driving," she said when Shay hopped out. He was wearing his usual all-black, but the pants he had on were a step up from jeans, and over his T-shirt he wore a black jacket that partially concealed his wiry frame. It was the best she'd ever seen him look.

"Couldn't leave all our gear at the venue," he said.

From the passenger side emerged a dude whose hang-dog eyes made him seem either more or exactly as drunk as Shay was.

"Max," Shay said, gesturing to the dude.

"Hi," El said.

"Hi," Max grumbled. His phone was vibrating, and on what must've been the final ring he answered: "Yeah?"

"His girlfriend," Shay explained. "Doesn't understand why we're not coming back tonight."

"Where's your bass player?"

Shay grinned. "He has other accommodations. That bartender chick from the wedding."

El tried to appear amused too. "Nice. Should— Let's go inside?"

Shay raised an eyebrow as if to say, *just waiting on you.* He held himself stiffly, hands stuffed in his pockets, but his eyes and cheeks shone with immoderate excitement. He hadn't seemed very drunk before, but he did now: trying to appear sober had betrayed him. She had never seen someone trying to downplay their inebriation, and it made her feel distant from Shay to know that he was presenting her with brand-new experiences—she became suddenly, sharply aware of the wrongness of their association; even though in some other slightly more palatable but still not good reality he might've been a senior in high school and she a freshman, that wasn't the case. Was *he* aware of the strangeness, the inappropriteness of their relationship—and if so, what was he doing here?

El folded her arms across her chest, and Shay followed her

into the house where Anna and Julia were eating Ben & Jerry's Phish Food from the container. El introduced them all.

"I thought your friends were coming," Anna said, surveying Shay.

"My friend Max is outside."

"Talking to his girlfriend," El clarified.

Anna kept her eyes on Shay. "Do *you* have a girlfriend?"

"No."

She slipped the lid back on the ice cream carton and Shay's brows gathered. "Not going to ask if I want any?"

Anna smirked.

"Should we watch a movie?" El interjected. She wanted to buy herself some time. The sensation she'd had outside of being abruptly uneasy with Shay was like an injury that she hoped might resolve itself. Maybe instead of accumulating life experience gradually, she could grow up very quickly. Tonight. Why sit around until she was ready for an adult man? Why could she not just anoint herself? Maybe that was all maturity was, a game of confidence.

Shay gave an unenthusiastic shrug in response to El's movie proposal.

"Oh right," El said. "I forgot you hate fun."

He grimaced at her. They had discussed this, how he liked documentaries but regular movies he found tedious.

"If you just want to crash I'll show you the den," Julia said. "The master's free upstairs, but that might wake up my brother."

The front door swung open and closed, and Max came in from the hall.

Shay turned to him: "We're crashing in the den."

Max nodded.

"We have beer if you guys want," Anna said.

Max didn't hesitate: "I'll take one."

"Yeah, thanks," Shay said.

While Julia fetched the drinks, El watched Max taking in the vastness of the kitchen, the stainless-steel appliances, the pristine cabinets with elegant crown molding, the gleaming bowl of fresh fruit on the marble countertop. El remembered Shay telling her once how Max lived in a shoebox apartment with his girlfriend and her grandmother. How the grandmother's smoking habit regularly triggered Max's asthma. El was now glad that they weren't watching a movie: she didn't want to see Max's expression when he realized there was a home theater in the basement.

Julia handed the guys their beers, and Shay twisted his open, looking out the kitchen window. "And there's the pool. Looks serene."

"I go out there sometimes when I can't sleep," Anna remarked.

El frowned, confused. "You do?"

"I do," she said with a laugh.

Shay, for some reason, laughed too.

"I like this," Max mused, examining the label on the beer.

"Oh, my brother *hates* it," Julia said. "I can show you guys the den?"

It was all happening too quickly. El glanced sidelong at Shay, hoping he would meet her eyes. She had an idea they would stay up, talking as they used to at the store, and when they were alone she would say, *so what do you think?* Meaning the house, Anna and Julia, the world she had so often described for him. He would say her friends were not bad—*but you can tell they're spoiled.* And he wouldn't say it but he'd be thinking, *not like us.* Their connection would be undeniable. They would kiss and she would say she wanted to, and he would be unsure, and she would lie and tell him she'd done it before, and then it would be over before she knew it and she would be the first of her friends to have lost her virginity, which was a kind of capital.

Shay didn't look at her, though. He followed Julia and Anna and Max to the end of the kitchen, past the half-bath, down the gallery hallway, through the formal living room to the spacious den at the very end of the house, where two leather couches and several wide chairs had been arranged to face a fireplace and a widescreen mounted on the wall.

"There's a mini-fridge inside the thing there with waters and whatever," Julia said.

Shay kicked off his shoes and sank into one of the couches. "Oh man." He looked up at El. "Thanks."

"Happy to help you avoid a DUI."

Shay clucked his tongue and pointed at her with his index finger and his thumb in the shape of a gun. Max had taken a seat in one of the chairs.

From behind El, Anna spoke up: "Night."

"Hope you can sleep," Shay said.

Anna smiled with closed lips. "That's so nice of you."

El nudged Shay's calf with her knee and said softly, "See you tomorrow."

"Maybe," he said. "We might have to get an early start." He glanced at Max, whose head was craned over his phone.

"That's cool," El said.

Julia was at the door. She waved.

Shay raised a hand to her. "Thanks again."

El took a few steps back from Shay and paused. "Good night."

"Good night," he said, his voice warm and contented.

El always slept in the smallest of the guest rooms. There was a full-sized bed with buttery ivory sheets, an antique dresser, a wicker chair and a secretary desk of intricate design. Her window faced the front of the house. She lay atop the comforter in a sleep T-shirt and some Juicy shorts, a loaner pair from Julia she'd never returned. El itched the spot where the tag scratched against her skin and stared out the window past the sheer curtains to where, by the moonlight, she could see the back end of Original Sound's green van.

She had been ruminating for twenty minutes about what she might've said to convince Shay to linger the following day. Usually they didn't drive back to the city until after dinner, when the bulk of the traffic had died down. She should've persuaded Shay to do the same, to hang out and lie with her by the pool—the pool—

She rolled sideways as if to dodge it, the thought that was bursting upon her now. And then, for a moment, she was still, waves of shock rolling through her: she stared at the door to her room, the knob of black porcelain. It couldn't be true. She thought of how sweet Shay had been as he'd bid her good night. And he'd come here in the first place to see her—obviously she was of some importance to him. No, he wouldn't compromise what was between them; she was sure.

Are you?

The voice in her head was dry and mocking. She'd begun to hear it after her father's ignominious departure from her life. The voice, always keen to point out when she was in danger of looking the fool, put her in mind of the courtroom scenes on *Law & Order*. She could almost see the body of the voice: a tall prosecutor with a wry, disquieting expression.

Trust your instinct, the prosecutor whispered. *Trust your instinct not to trust.*

She dropped from the bed and discovered she was trembling down to her fingertips. She tiptoed over carpet and hardwood and opened the door to the dark hallway. She felt her way to the stairs, gripping the smooth banister as she descended, the sound of her breath loud and exaggerated to her ears.

When she reached the first floor the entry light was on, and though it had been dimmed she could make out the kitchen up ahead on her left, empty and undisturbed. She glanced down the long hallway toward the den where the boys slept: she heard nothing. Could it be that the prosecutor—that her own base instincts—had been wrong? She hurried forward like a child who's checked under the bed, and now rips back doors and curtains to confirm for certain the absence of monsters. She vaulted herself toward the kitchen sink, snatched at its cool wide edge and stood on tiptoe to see out the window . . .

They were there. Two figures, groping each other by the pool, and between the in-ground lights and the moon's glow it was easy to see them: Anna, already half-naked, and Shay, his face tilted down, his expression almost neutral as Anna tugged his boxers off.

El began to shake so violently she could no longer keep hold of the sink. Her body seemed to be rejecting the rawness of the hurt that overwhelmed her now. It was claustrophobic, panicked pain. For long minutes, on the verge of being sick, she watched helplessly. Anna and Shay remained standing for a while, kissing, then Shay jumped in the water. Anna watched him, disapproving, until Shay seemed to accept that Anna was not going to follow. He trudged up the steps of the shallow end, went to Anna and wrapped his dripping arms around her, but she directed him to lie on a pool chair. Right before Anna climbed onto him, El saw that numb, neutral look on his face again.

A few minutes, then it was over. Anna dressed while Shay remained on the pool chair. He was still lying down when Anna started toward the house, and only then did El take fumbling steps back to the little guest room. There in the stillness she began to feel her real anger—not toward Anna, but toward herself. Anna had only done it because she, El, could not. She hated her own softness, her fear. Why had she not been born with Anna's iron stomach?

She slept in fits and was awake at dawn when the van started up. She watched it back down the drive, then turned her face toward the ceiling. She could make out small rough bumps, here and there, and they reminded her of Shay's pockmarked skin. For one more moment she cradled the body of what he had meant to her, and then she reached over, rummaged for her phone in the blankets and deleted his number.

chapter seven

Two days after she returned from Julia's party, El felt like herself again. She could see how returning to the East Hampton house combined with her cocaine comedown had given rise to old feelings of worthlessness. In eighth grade El had imagined herself among the world's have-nots: when Anna had claimed Shay, it had represented to El just one more win for the winners. El had long since put herself in context though, and recognized her immense privilege. It also helped to remember that Shay, now in his midthirties, probably did not possess his cute mop of hair anymore, and that whatever fleeting sense of possession he'd experienced in sleeping with a rich girl had likely evaporated in shame and panic over that girl's criminal youth during his drive back to the city or soon thereafter.

El got ready for work and hurried to the train. It wasn't until she pulled out her wallet at the turnstile that she realized the clear pocket was empty, the pocket where she usually kept her driver's license. Directly behind her a woman with a gnarled face tsk'ed, and El had to wave the woman back so she could get free and have a look around. She scanned the grimy floor and ran back up the stairs to the street, but there appeared to be nothing besides the final remains of a burrito. It was completely possible that someone had already snatched her license up and equally possible that it had fallen out at home. She texted Crystal, asking her to keep her eyes peeled.

After a couple more minutes of searching (even kicking the burrito guts half-heartedly, to see if her license had been concealed beneath), El looked at the time and knew she had to get going. She couldn't be late, not after flaking yesterday. When she caught her train, the gnarled-faced woman was in her car. El glared at the woman and received, in kind, a devastating stare of nonrecognition.

They came to a temporary halt just before the Delancey station, and with a surge of anxiety El wondered if the guy on the beach had really pulled out effectively. She was on the pill, but she wasn't *perfect* about taking it . . . Would it be worth it to get Plan B still?

Wait. That night. She and Julia had used her license to cut the lines of coke in the bathroom.

El tightened her fist around the subway pole. *Shit.* The train started to move again, and she drafted a text to Julia that she sent when they got to West 4th and her service came back:

> hey babe, you're probably already in paradise and not using your phone but juuuust in case, is there anyone like Carmen or someone at your place who could mail my driver's license back to me? Pretty sure I left it in the bathroom we were in downstairs... lmk, ty! hope you're having an amazing time!!

All throughout her shift El checked her phone, but there was no response from Julia. How did one get a new license anyway? Would she have to actually go to the DMV?

Later, on her way home, she neared a drugstore and thought again of buying Plan B, but it was so expensive, plus she had read an article alleging that some far right cybercriminals— enraged that the drug had been protected at a federal level from being deemed an abortifacient—were planning to leak the personal data of every Plan B purchaser of the past ten years. However unlikely it was that she specifically would be targeted should such a leak occur, the very thought of being harassed was enough to keep her moving past the drugstore's automatic doors.

When El reached her building she climbed the three stories to her landing, calves aching from another long day on her feet. She smelled Crystal's stir-fry as soon as she reached the door. The only drawback of Crystal's cooking was the mess she regularly left, but El never said anything because Crystal always shared her food. The weird thing was, sometimes it seemed like Crystal wanted El to lay into her, because recently she'd started badgering El with questions like, "Is there anything I do that bugs you? Like any little roommate thing?" And El had routinely said no, not wanting to be roped into that level of intimacy. Crystal, it seemed, needed a surrogate for the emotional space Nicole had long occupied—someone to be in the weeds with, wrestle with, argue with. It made El feel so un-special. And it was the same with dating too: once you neared thirty, almost everybody had experienced their Great Love, and most of the time it seemed that the person texting you and making love to you and standing in line for bagels with you was just using you as a repository for all the jokes they hadn't been able to tell and insights they hadn't been able to share with the woman before you, the one who'd been Actually Important.

"Hey!" Crystal said, glancing over her shoulder. "Almost done. Wanna watch something with me? I'm in the mood for feel-good."

"Sure, as long as it's not you know what."

Crystal's go-to comfort binge was the *Hunger Games* series. Jennifer Lawrence (as Katniss Everdeen specifically) had been Crystal's inspiration to become an actress. El had once asked Crystal whether watching *The Hunger Games* ever made her depressed, because she, Crystal, had been battling so hard in the business for so long, and Jennifer Lawrence had been much younger than both of them when she'd booked Katniss. Crystal had asked, with genuine incomprehension, why should that make her depressed? Crystal had unflinching enthusiasm for the craft and a tolerance for rejection El had never possessed. Sometimes El thought that it hadn't so much been acting she had loved—the process of it, the becoming—than the opportunity to be chosen that acting had presented. Why had it been acting she'd pursued, rather than singing or painting or anything else? Probably because, at the age of thirteen, acting had seemed the most accessible type of fame. To El the world had appeared lousy with successful actors—they were on the covers of magazines, on buses and billboards, on posters outside movie and Off-Broadway theaters. Why shouldn't she become one of them? Wasn't she due? Wasn't there some proverbial brass scale out there that weighed a life's misfortune, and hadn't she already been passed over for the role of daughter? If she counted from age fifteen, when she'd started at the performing arts high school, she had given acting fourteen years. The number of times she'd been chosen in any meaningful way during those fourteen years were so few and far between as to constitute chance. A year ago she'd been desperate enough to hire an acting coach who had frequented the bar where she'd worked, but after six months El had incurred three thousand dollars in additional credit card debt and absolutely zero new prospects. It had begun to cohere around then, the understanding that she was not built like Crystal, committed enough to withstand being consistently, if not interminably, invisible.

Settling on the couch with large glasses of five-dollar Cab

and bowls of jasmine rice and chunky tofu stir-fry, they flicked through the possibilities on several streamers before choosing a new rom-com to watch. Neither of them had high expectations, and by the midpoint they agreed that to continue would be too painful. El turned it off.

"It's the stakes," Crystal said. "When we were younger it was like, 'Will the two main people end up together? Oh my god!' And now it's like, 'If someone's not going to literally *blow up* or something, then who cares? Let them not end up together. One less possible divorce.'"

"No"—El was laughing—"you're absolutely right."

Crystal became droll when she drank. Her front teeth were stained purple with wine. "I seriously have to stop watching movies like this though. Even the bad ones make me depressed. Has anyone actually had a meet-cute in real life?"

"Probably not since dating apps."

Crystal stared at the screen, which still displayed the title of the movie they'd been watching. "Nicole loved shit like this. You would probably think of her as like a Terrence Malick person, right? No no. She has crap taste. She just learned the right things to reference at Brown."

El nodded and stood at the same time. Now that they were inching toward Nicole territory, it was time to escape.

Back in her bedroom, El opened her laptop and began to research how to get a replacement license. Almost instantly, a notification popped up in the corner of her screen:

Bryce Ripley-Batten has sent you a message.

Bryce . . . She squinted at the photo icon next to the name: A slightly stocky guy. Pale white skin. A broad forehead and fine, fawn-brown hair. *Oh my god.* Was that . . . ? It was. The guy she'd fully *sprinted away from* at Julia's party! She cringed, remembering their interaction. All he'd done was introduce himself—at the time she'd been startled by his presence, but *she* had probably surprised *him*, sprinting out of the house and into his space like that. How had he found her?

She clicked on the notification and read: Hi—found your driver's license at a party a couple days ago. Happy to get it back to you. Hit me up.

"Holy shit!" she exclaimed.

Crystal shouted from the other room: "You okay?"

"Yeah! All good!"

Quickly, El wrote back: Yay! I thought it was gone forever. My address on there is current, so feel free to send it. I can venmo you the postage?? Haha

His reply came seconds later: I live in the city. Maybe I could give it back to you over drinks?

Huh. El clucked her tongue. Did Bryce not recognize her as the coked-out girl who'd run away from him?

She clicked on his name to bring up his full profile. When all the social media companies had consolidated six months ago, they'd also combined forces on information: now you could see not just someone's picture and bio and friends, but *when* they had become friends with those friends, and in many cases *where* they had met those friends. It was easier than ever to get a general idea of where someone had lived and worked.

El scanned: she and Bryce had no mutuals, not even Julia. She scrolled through the five-hundred-plus names, just getting a sense—all people she didn't know, of course, but underneath about a third was *Connection: University of Cambridge.* So was he British? Some of the names listed a connection to an investment bank, so maybe Bryce knew Tom through that world. But then she saw, down at the very bottom, eight or nine names that all showed *Connection: Lowile Bay.*

El checked Bryce's birthday in the info section of his profile: he was her age. Okay, so he obviously knew Julia from Lowile Bay, from camp, and he'd been at her party, so that was fine. She could meet him, why not? Especially as he didn't seem to remember her unhinged behavior. She replied: Sure, drinks are good!

He messaged back instantly: When's good for you?

She decided to wait a few minutes before writing again and passed the time clicking through his pictures. She hadn't gotten a great look at him in that dark section of the yard the other night. He wasn't exactly sexy—there was a pessimistic sag about his chest and shoulders, a meaty quality to his jowls—but this was maybe excessive scrutiny. He was cute enough, she decided. And possibly British. She felt a sudden, sucking excitement in the bottom of her stomach. It had been months since she'd been on an actual date, and two full years since her last relationship. Colton, her ex, had been a junior talent agent. He'd refused to call her his girlfriend until one night when he'd come over very drunk, tearfully lamenting how the simple days of his Indiana youth were over, bike rides and TP'd houses and Little League . . . "And you're my girlfriend," he'd said bitterly, "and we don't even have a garden." This last part hadn't made much sense to El, but she'd assured him they could have a garden. There were community gardens. Or, you know, if they were to live together, they could get one of those window boxes. The next morning Colton had left early. Later he'd sent an e-mail saying it just wasn't working between them. He'd signed it, Buds forever—C., and, underneath that, Sent from my iPhone please excuse any f*$^&ing typos!

Even though she knew Julia wouldn't receive it until the end of the summer, El sent an update to her previous text. It seemed to her that, whatever this Bryce thing turned out to be, meeting him still made her more relevant to Anna and Julia's world, that invite-only dimension. She'd been introduced to a number of Anna and Julia's friends over the years, but Bryce was the first one she'd be meeting outside their company. She wrote: Crisis averted. Bryce Ripley-Batten found it?? Meeting him for drinks I think. xo

She returned to Bryce's profile and came across a picture of him in a muddied rugby uniform, his arms around two teammates. In the background of the photo stood a redbrick building with a gray roof. The scene struck El as so patrician and correct, the bright green pitch and the boyish camaraderie and the brick, it filled her with an almost chemical desire, a longing to dissolve, atom by atom, into the laptop screen, into the photo, into that place. With a start she wondered whether Bryce had been stalking her profile as she had his. Had he drawn any conclusions about who she was? He would know, of course, that she'd been at Julia's party, so would he just assume that she was somebody monied, some frequenter of the Hamptons? The home address on her license would not betray her as non-wealthy. Plenty of rich people lived in Williamsburg. In fact she and Crystal were outliers in their neighborhood, with their blessedly rent-stabilized apartment (frequent cockroaches and paint-bubbling walls and faulty toilet notwithstanding). Would Bryce be disappointed when he learned that El's net worth was about, oh, four hundred and fifteen dollars? (Her typical monthly low point, as she was between paydays and she'd just given Crystal her share of the rent.) Then, once again, she found herself remembering the day in the computer lab when Anna and Julia had plucked her out: they had seen something in her. What were the chances this Bryce Ripley-Batten would see it too? She had next Friday and Saturday off, so she sent him a message suggesting they meet one of those nights. Again, his reply was immediate: Friday is perfect.

She thought about what Crystal had said about meet-cutes and whether they ever happened in real life. And although El, as a single twenty-nine-year-old in New York City, knew better than to get her hopes up, she allowed herself a small smile.

chapter eight

So Bryce Ripley-Batten was not for her, El knew this off the bat. For one thing, the dispirited way he carried himself really was pitiful, and though in theory she might have liked the idea of a man who tried to take up less space, in practice it was just demoralizing.

He had chosen a dive in Red Hook notorious for its noise and had just returned to their table with her bottle of Blue Moon and his tulip glass of Guinness. They were the only party of two on the patio. Big groups surrounded them on all sides. He set the Blue Moon in front of her as he took a seat.

"So, Héloïse," he said. "Is your family Catholic or just really into French history?"

"Neither. My mom saw it in a baby book. I go by El."

"Oh, sorry."

"No, it's fine."

And there was a strange pause, because he'd obviously learned her full name from the license he hadn't yet returned. Neither of them had brought it up. What was a polite amount of time to wait before demanding it back? The duration of a beer? She took a long sip.

"It's pretty loud," he said, looking apologetic. "I've never been here. I don't know many bars in New York. I lived in London until about a year ago."

"You don't have much of an accent." He didn't; she'd been disappointed to discover that when they'd first said hello.

"Well, I moved from Surrey to Connecticut when I was twelve. I did go back to England for university but, yeah, I was desperate to sound like an American when I first arrived here. Show my father I was fitting in. I watched a *lot* of American TV."

"Like what?"

"*Lost*, erm . . . *How I Met Your Mother. How I Met Your Mother* was my favorite, actually."

"Yikes."

"Not a fan? Is it okay if I still like it?"

"No, sorry, you'll have to change."

He grinned, and she regretted her words immediately. It had been a first-date reflex to participate in the dance of how-intimate-will-we-become. She needed to move away from jokes, reground the conversation.

"I almost went to London in college," she said, picking up her beer.

"Almost? Have you never been?"

She shook her head. "Never been out of the country. I'd probably rather go to Paris than London, though." What was Anna doing in Paris right now? she wondered.

"Your parents, they're both from the States?"

He kept on her with question after question. In the end they covered the basics: her drama with her father ("so the take-away is all Kirstens suck"); her experience at NYU (her class-mates whose parents bankrolled their short films were starting to become successful and that was undeniably grating); quit-ting acting (you really had to love it). Eventually she began to feel guilty that she'd been talking so much about herself, and she got the gist of his story as well: Bryce's mum had been separated from his father a long time; Bryce's father was an American who, ironically, looked a lot like Boris Johnson—they weren't close; Bryce worked in finance, a career you didn't really have to love.

"But don't you work crazy hours?"

"At times. It was worse when I started."

"But, I mean, okay." Bryce had bought another round, and now that El was near the bottom of her second Blue Moon she'd begun to feel bold. Still, she teetered for a moment.

"What?" he prompted.

"You could do nothing if you wanted to, right? I mean this is like gauche or whatever to say, but you're rich. Not like, 'my parents are surgeons,' like, WASPy trust fund kind of deal. Right?"

To his credit, he didn't squirm. He just cocked his head as if to say, *I suppose.*

"So did your family pressure you to work in finance?"

"What do you mean?"

"I'm just saying, if you don't need money, why not do a job you actually like?"

"Like work at a bakery, you mean?"

"Fuck you." She smirked. "Never mind."

He wiped an invisible smudge from his glass of Guinness. "When I was younger, my sister, Brooke, died. Very unexpectedly."

"I'm really sorry. Wow."

"Probably too deep for a first—" He stopped himself. "I gravitate toward stability. That was my point."

"Security, yeah."

"Yeah. Money's good. Never have enough of a good thing."

"Totally," she agreed, but her thoughts were with the dead sister. How had she died? El imagined something medical and tragic, an aggressive tumor. And then, for the first time ever, El wondered if her own sister—half sister—was still alive. No reason she shouldn't be. But it was a really strange idea: that maybe their father had chosen Kirsten, and maybe Kirsten had succumbed to some untimely fate.

Bryce drained his glass and stood. He pointed to her empty. "Another?"

"Oh—thanks. But I'm happy to buy us this round, I'll just need my license—"

"It's okay. I have a tab open."

He walked away before she could say anything more.

That . . . had been weird. Even if he'd wanted to buy the drinks, shouldn't he have given her license back regardless? Had he just spaced out? Maybe the money talk had made him eager to demonstrate his generosity. Or maybe talking about his sister had been tough. El felt guilt stir in her gut, and something else also: A quiet arousal. A sense of possibility. Bryce had lost someone he'd loved—even before he'd confessed it to her, El had known it unconsciously. He had that worn-out aura of heartbreak. Rousing him into loving again was an intriguing challenge. The solution, the beloved: that was a part she never played.

When Bryce returned to their table she studied him anew. His light brown hair was short and neat as if he'd just had a haircut; she wished it were longer. She did, however, like the length of his scruff. And Bryce had a nice way about him. He seemed to have a sense of humor, and his teasing didn't have the mean tenor that, in other men, belied a dangerous self-hatred. She remembered that just the other night she'd been worried that Bryce, being wealthy, would not accept her, and now she smiled at the absurdity of that notion: no one had ever been less invisible than she on this worn little bench, in this loud courtyard, at this moment. Bryce's mute gaze as he settled back into his place on the opposite side of the table was so fixed she felt almost startled, as if she were back onstage and had forgotten her lines.

"That was fast," she said, picking up her fresh beer.

"Had to fight my way, it's packed."

"You had to fuck some people up?"

"Had to bring out my sickle."

"Huh, old school."

"I shun modernity."

"Man after my own heart."

A beat, and then he cocked his head. "Is it just me, or is this fun?"

"It is kind of becoming . . . fun."

He wrapped both hands around his glass. "I wasn't sure you'd show up, given how you fled my presence the other night."

So he does remember me from the party! She launched into an explanation about all the cocaine she'd done with Julia moments before running into him. "I'm not usually that crazy," she said. "That was kind of an extraordinary moment."

He laughed, then lifted his glass in a toast, his eyes never leaving her face. "Here's to more extraordinary moments."

An hour later they were both leaning against the stained wooden bar inside. Bryce settled the tab with his card and, at last, drew El's license from his wallet. A string of purple Christmas lights hung like a smile overhead. She expected him to say something sort of dorky as he handed her the license, like, *It's been a pleasure meeting you, Hélöise.* But he said nothing, and in the silence his finer qualities were magnified until they grew pixelated; it was this distorted version, these squares of blush cheek and brown stubble, that El saw when she leaned into his kiss.

By daylight he was, again, just a man. His apartment, which spanned the entire fifteenth floor of a Financial District high-rise, was spectacular: he was slightly less so. He ought to have become a friend and then an acquaintance and then a memory. But El had slept with him, and in his downy bed they had cuddled (*he* had cuddled, she had endured his breath on her back). Now they were leaving his lobby to get some breakfast and El experienced an uncanny sensation when the fresh air hit her face, a surge of lethargy that made her sigh. Maybe, she decided, she would just let this thing with Bryce happen to her.

chapter nine

After a marathon first date—two nights, one full day, and an amount of fooling around that was surely breeding ground for a UTI—El had to leave. She had to work. A sliver of early-morning light, where the bedroom curtains had been left parted, illuminated Bryce's desperate face. Did she have to go, really? She couldn't call out?

"Go back to sleep," she instructed. "By the time you wake up, my shift'll be halfway over."

"And you'll come back after?"

They had thrown her clothes in his washer and dryer the night before, and she was in the habit of carrying her birth control in her purse, so she didn't really *need* to go home. While she considered the prospect of coming back to his place again that evening, he asked another question.

"What would you want to do today? If you could do any-thing."

A loud barking suddenly drew her attention. She'd been standing by the window, dressing herself, and now she looked out to see a husky on the street below. It wore a leash, but its owner was nowhere to be seen. The dog's fury was directed at a panicked man with a baby in a carrier strapped to his chest.

"Whoa," she said.

Bryce rose from the bed to stand beside her. He squinted outside. "That dog's about to wake the whole neighborhood," he said, stifling a yawn.

She looked at him. Was he not seeing what she was seeing? Before she could point out that the volume of barking was the least concerning element at hand—certainly the least concern-ing to the father with the infant—the commotion stopped. She leaned forward and saw, through the glass, that the dog had run off. The father was nearly to the other end of the block now.

Bryce, meanwhile, was adjusting her bra strap, which she had fastened poorly. "I think this is broken."

"It's not," she said. "Just really bent." She faced him, sup-pressing a yawn of her own. The adrenaline she'd experienced watching the drama on the sidewalk was ebbing away, leav-ing her more tired than she'd been when her alarm had gone off. She threw her arms around Bryce's neck and bent, limp, into him.

"What would you want to do?" he asked again.

Her honest thought was that, if she could do anything, she'd like to go to Julia's Hamptons house and spend the day by herself. A full fridge, hotel-soft towels, pitching ocean. She stalled, as if considering the possibilities. "Mmm, what would *you* want?"

"I just want to be with you."

She rolled her eyes.

"You tease . . ." He moved closer, his boxers pressing against her underwear. She drew back, laughing to protect his ego: it gave them both cover—they could pretend his advance had been in jest. She was still sore from yesterday's fevered activity and, having only slept four hours, needed caffeine before she could even think about giving of herself again. This recognition of her own needs was novel, and she felt it, right in the moment, how good it was not to abandon herself for fear of losing a man's interest. Of course, perhaps this wasn't really bravery on her part; for the first time in her life, she knew she had someone under her thumb. Bryce would want her if she rejected him a hundred times, and that knowledge made her feel reckless.

"I know what we should do," she said.

"What?"

"Well, first, have some coffee. But then we should get pierogis."

The pierogi place she liked was deep in Brooklyn, forty minutes from her own apartment. Bryce was accustomed to taking cabs, she'd learned, but he followed her gamely into the subway, seeming to relish every jostling minute, every moment that he got to lay a palm on her thigh or scoop her legs to rest on his or meet her eyes again after they, still tired, lapsed into a prolonged, unconscious silence. El spent much of the ride feeling grateful for this unanticipated day of freedom. Calling out of work had actually been less stressful than she'd imagined. She'd told Darcy that her "bug" from the previous week (when she'd called in after Julia's party) was "back with a vengeance." Darcy had wished her the best and encouraged her to visit an urgent care should she feel worse. Darcy's boyfriend, the sous chef, had apparently neglected to do this recently, allowing a run-of-the-mill cold to become bronchitis.

According to El's phone, the pierogi spot was a half-mile walk from their subway stop. They would arrive just as the place opened, she informed Bryce. The sun was already bearing down on the city, though it was only ten to nine. El had on one of Bryce's Barbour jackets over her white tee and black leather miniskirt, but now she stripped the jacket off and tied it around her waist in a double knot.

"Want me to carry that?" he offered.

"I'm good." The sidewalk twinkled in the sunlight. El had read once that the sparkle effect was the product of some chemical element mixed into the concrete, and usually it was at odds with her mood. But not today. Today she was full of whimsy.

Bryce seemed to be feeding off her energy. He was almost grinning. "I don't know that I've ever had a pierogi in America."

"Sorry, there must be some confusion. *You* just wanted to be with me. That was your dream day. *I'm* going to be eating pierogis."

"O-ho! I'm meant to watch, is that it?"

"Yeah, basically—"

"*El!*"

She and Bryce both turned. Across the street Navya was removing her earbuds, her long brown legs accentuated by a pair of bright coral running shorts. El waved, and before she had time to download Bryce, Navya was jogging across the street, standing in front of them and smiling widely. There was the tiniest chip in Navya's right front tooth and, though it drew the eye, El had always thought there was a flattering sweetness about it.

"Nav, this is Bryce. Bryce, Navya, my college roommate—"

"—life partner, soul mate, ride or die, et cetera, et cetera," Navya finished.

Bryce's expression was pleasant, but El thought he looked troubled too. Maybe it was his inner Brit, being put off by Navya's enthusiasm. Or maybe it was just nerve-wracking to confront the best friend when you were still technically on a first date.

"Bryce and I met at that Hamptons party," El explained.

"I seeee." Turning to Bryce, Navya asked, "Do you live around here?"

"No, I'm in Lower Manhattan sadly, not a, erm—not a— Brooklyn dweller."

God, El thought. *He is nervous.* "We're on a pierogi mission," she told Navya.

"Of course! Fun! Well, I won't hold you up—have some for

me—" She gave El an air hug. "Sparing you my grossness. See you—?"

"Next weekend," El said.

"Great! Oh, yay. Call me this week, too."

"I will," El promised.

"Pleasure meeting you," Bryce said.

"You too!" And though Navya flashed another smile, El noticed that she exhaled as soon as she looked away, before she resumed her run, as if she were trying to expel Bryce and whatever he might represent.

chapter ten

The following weekend delivered that unhappy combination of cloud cover and oppressive humidity. As El neared the beer garden she pulled a clip from her purse and thrust her heavy hair into a low bun. When her phone began to vibrate in her pocket, she knew already who it would be. She had said goodbye to Bryce that very morning, stopping at her own apartment only to change, but she'd learned in the past week that if Bryce didn't hear from her every few hours he would call—maybe text, if he was really busy at work. He said he just liked hearing her voice.

Earlier in her life El might have recoiled at this level of enthusiasm, but years of failed relationships had worn her down. At least the calls from Bryce meant someone cared about her.

"Hi," she said, keeping some distance between the screen

and her face so her make-up wouldn't smear. "Can't talk long, I'm almost there."

"That's okay. I just wanted to tell you, I saw Blue Dracula!"

"What?" El was smiling now. Blue Dracula was their new name for the man in the blue tracksuit who always power-walked Bryce's neighborhood late at night. "Was his flesh burning in the sunlight?"

"Not that I could tell."

"Was he wearing his usual?"

"What do you think?"

She had reached her destination now and could see Emma approaching from the opposite end of the block. Hearing her silence, Bryce jumped in: "All right, see you in a couple hours."

"Say hi to Blue Dracula for me."

She hung up as Emma neared, her light red hair lank around her shoulders and pasty, tattooed arms gripping the strap of a bamboo tote bag. She inclined her head to El with a humorless smile. Out of the whole NYU group, Emma and El were the least close. There wasn't outright hostility between them—it was rather as though, for approximately a decade, each of them had been giving the other a second chance, an opportunity to become a more compatible friend.

"Shall we?" Emma said. She fell in step with El as they passed through a wide round door into the dark interior of a bar that opened onto a courtyard. Stout shrubs rimmed the fenced-in area. Navya, Navya's roommate Van, and two guys El didn't know had already grabbed an extra-long picnic table.

"Hello, lovely!" Emma called, opening her arms as Navya stood to embrace her.

El was grateful that she'd remembered to call Navya this past week, as Navya had asked her to do. She had given a curious Navya all the details about Bryce, and she'd apologized for Bryce's awkwardness when they'd run into her, saying, *I think he was just intimidated because I'd already talked about how important you were to me and stuff.* This hadn't been true: El had barely mentioned Navya to Bryce prior to their sidewalk encounter. But Navya had believed El, had seemed charmed by the explanation and had told El that apologies weren't necessary, that Bryce hadn't seemed awkward to her at all.

As Emma greeted the others, Navya implored El: "Sit with me."

"Let me just get a drink quick," El said. "Do you need something?"

"Sure—Bloody Mary?"

When El returned, Navya scooted to make room. El slipped in beside her and looked around: there were ten of them gathered now. Apart from Van and his two friends El knew everyone well, as they made up her and Navya's cohort from NYU. There was Mathias, Lila, Thea, Daniel—and Emma of course. Handing Navya her drink, El asked if Navya was expecting anybody else. Navya didn't think so.

El affected an English accent. "Then perhaps it's time to *toast.*"

"Nooo," Navya said, "never that voice."

El raised her beer and leaned forward to get everyone's attention. "We are here," she began, "to celebrate the *promotion*—"

Daniel flicked his dreads from his eyes and raised his own drink. The others followed suit. Lila whistled.

"—of a wonderful human being. On Friday she was an editorial assistant and tomorrow she'll be an . . ."

". . . an assistant editor. Just a different kind of assistant."

El raised her drink higher. "To being a different kind of assistant!"

Around the table people laughed and Navya said, "Still getting paid crap."

"Okay, *fine,* we're buying," Van said.

"No!" Navya protested. "I didn't mean that."

Van blew her a kiss and returned to his friends.

Navya's shoulder knocked lightly into El's. "Thank you for being here."

"It's not like it's a favor," El said. "Why wouldn't I be here?"

"You're in this new relationship, I don't know. I just appreciate you being here. Being you."

"New relationship?" Emma had been listening from across the table.

"Sort of," El said. "It hasn't been that long."

"Tell her the story," Navya prompted.

El was loathe to discuss the details of her life with Emma but felt compelled to be open with her in Navya's presence, given Emma and Navya's closeness. "I lost my license," she said. "And Bryce found it, returned it to me and, yeah—that's it."

Emma brought her lips together and made her chin long, as though puzzled by this simple narrative.

"Bryce *Ripley-Batten*," Navya said, in a much better English accent than El's.

Emma's expression became curious. "I feel like I know that name."

"Why didn't you bring him, by the way?" Navya asked.

"I didn't know this was a plus-one situation. Also he and I have been around each other kind of nonstop anyway."

Emma had become absorbed in something on her phone, so El and Navya were left to chat by themselves.

"What does Crystal think of him?"

"Oh," El said, "they haven't met."

Navya looked surprised.

"I mean mostly we're at his place," El explained. "Or, always I guess. I actually haven't seen a lot of Crystal for like—yeah. Ten days. Two weeks, whatever it's been."

"Eee . . ."

"Yeah, I know, but—"

"Yeah, she's clingy." Navya lifted the celery from her Bloody Mary and set it aside. "I saw her post that she got a cameo in some procedural."

"Wait, the teacher part?"

"I don't know what it was."

Emma leaned forward then, her face eager. "Batten—I knew I knew that name." She consulted her phone. "Your boyfriend's dad is a big pharma investor. And he lives in some absurdly like—look at this." She flashed her screen at El and

Navya, and El saw the gray face of a mansion on a verdant lawn. Emma set her phone down. "Forty million for a house. Imagine, instead of putting your money toward medical research that could actually help people, you sink it into these bloodsucking companies. Just so you can buy an island or a yacht or a fucking rocket."

El had never looked up Bryce's parents; she had not online-stalked Bryce, in fact, since before they'd met. Probably because she'd been in his company so much. And he'd offered such personal information right off the bat—about his parents' separation, his sister's death. Since then he'd filled in more of the blanks, like how love had led him to the University of Cambridge. He and his girlfriend from his Connecticut prep school had gone there together, but she'd broken up with him mere weeks into their freshman year, which had been extra tough because she'd been his best friend too. It had been the rugby club that had saved him from the blackness of his heartbreak and had given him purpose. He'd also shared just how lonely he'd been in New York before he'd met El. How disillusioned. El had empathized with this completely. She was angry that Emma felt justified in drawing unfair conclusions about kind and sensitive Bryce based on a couple of headlines about his father. But rather than make this point, El decided to make light of Mr. Batten's sins. That would irritate Emma most. "I *hope* he has a rocket," she said. "In a few years when we're getting temperatures of like 140 in the city, I'm off this planet."

Navya might have laughed had Emma not been there;

instead, Navya played the diplomat. "Batten Senior sounds like an unfortunate person, but that's not Bryce's fault. Sins of the father and whatever."

El knew that Emma would next interrogate what use Bryce made of his inherited wealth and privilege, and she decided to get ahead of it. "Well, Bryce works in finance, so I wouldn't say he's using his trust fund powers for good."

Emma looked grave. "And you're all right with that?"

"I've never had real money. I'm not sure I can pass judgment on how I'd use it."

"I disagree," Emma said fervently. "You're *more* qualified to make a judgment because you're more aware of the basic needs that go unmet by most people, and the fact that these pharma companies are just cashing in on—well, on everybody, but especially the most vulnerable in our country. Your boyfriend's family wealth was built on their backs."

"I think his mom's the heavy hitter actually. She's from some old English family."

Navya nodded in faux approval. "Nice. Little bit of colonialism thrown in there too."

"Yes, exploitation and colonialism, all the ingredients of an impressive fortune," El said dryly.

El could tell Emma was dying to continue her diatribe, dying to lecture El on how droll resignation, rather than being harmless, enabled capitalism and its attendant malignancies. The irony was that Emma had grown up in a Calabasas Mc-Mansion and possessed a sizable trust fund herself, information she kept low-key. Back in college, when El had found out that Emma's parents regularly shipped her designer clothes that Emma donated to Goodwill, El had realized Emma would never understand the less-advantaged people she felt so passionately about. El hadn't been able to imagine giving away objects of value like that, couldn't imagine not needing the cash for rent or food . . . While she and Thea and Mathias and Daniel had griped about the loans they were taking on (Navya had a partial scholarship and Lila a full ride), Emma had bemoaned the system at large. All higher education should be free, she'd say. It was ridiculous. Emma had *said* all the right things, but she'd also had her own professionally cleaned one-bedroom apartment. El had often wondered, would Emma be such a vocal socialist if she'd grown up watching while her mother debated whether to buy food or medicine with the money she had left for the week? Would Emma still want to burn the system down then, or would she want to best it, climb it, show them all? Did she actually care about injustice, or was this progressive persona just a way to punish her bourgeois parents? It frightened El to think that maybe, under different circumstances, Emma would've turned out to be the very same altruist she was now—that maybe Emma had been born good, and El herself slightly rotten.

The hour grew boozy, thanks in part to Van, who badgered everybody when their drinks were getting low. He had brought a nice camera and started taking pictures while El got acquainted with his friends, Adam and Andrew, who she learned were also painters. She and Adam flirted openly. She liked the residue of mascara under his eyes and the way he commanded her attention. They had an intense discussion about the fickle natures of the art world and the film industry, and what she liked most was Adam's composure, his cool detachment when he observed that irrelevance lurked around every corner. It didn't seem to bother him that the shot-callers were sheep; his whole attitude said, *I don't need your faith in me, I have plenty of faith in myself.* In a quiet aside she asked Navya what Adam's deal was. What did she know about him?

"I think he and Van used to hook up, like a long time ago, before Van moved in. Or maybe it was just once."

"Is he bi? I thought I caught a vibe." El felt heat rise in her cheeks. Bryce was practically her boyfriend. Was her loyalty so fragile as that?

"Maybe he's pan? Or bi, I don't know. He and this girl from my work made out at Union Pool a couple weeks ago, I know that."

"What girl?"

"Anika," said Navya carelessly.

"Huh."

"I don't really know that much about him, although I did meet his parents when Van and I went to his Chelsea show. They flew in from Mexico City and oh my god, his mom is *stun-ning,* I think she used to be a model, and his dad is unreal too, like an old Henry Golding. If my parents were that pretty I'm not sure what I would do with myself."

"Excuse me, Savita and Vikash are very pretty. Must we review the wedding pictures?"

"You are obsessed—"

Just then Daniel called out to their half of the table: "Fam, we are starting to talk food down here."

"Oh!" Navya jumped up. "I meant to get some stuff for the table."

"I'll come," Daniel said.

As the two of them walked inside together, El scooched over to sit with Mathias and Lila. Lila told a horrible story about her childhood dog running away from home the week before, in full view of her stepsister, who'd been with him in the backyard.

"Was he chasing a fox or something?" El asked.

"No! When I say 'backyard' I mean like a concrete slab with like very sad grass. No wildlife to speak of."

"How old was he?"

"Sixteen! Mathias thinks he went off to die . . ."

"Well," Mathias shrugged, "that's what old dogs do."

"Right," El said, "but wasn't he running?"

"Exactly," Lila said, giving Mathias a significant look. "Literally he sprinted down the street. Dying dogs don't do that."

Mathias seemed annoyed, and Lila deftly changed the subject to Mathias's brother Julien, a competitive surfer who had just moved to Portugal. Soon Daniel and Navya returned carrying baskets of fried pickles, Navya balancing a fresh Bloody Mary in the crook of her arm. Mathias and Lila hugged El goodbye. After they left, Navya whispered to El that Lila was expecting. No one was supposed to know, but Mathias had let it slip the other night when he'd gotten high with Thea and her girlfriend.

El ate too many pickles too fast and felt the backwash of acid in her throat. Adam brought her a glass of water, but that only made it worse. Van tried to take a picture of her as she sat completely straight taking a deep breath: she waved him away. Navya drained her Bloody Mary, hiccupped and brandished her phone in the air, where a dating app was open to the profile of a man with richly tanned skin and a Mallen streak.

"Should I invite this delicate snack to meet me here right now?"

"Yes!" Van shouted.

"Second," Emma said.

"Ooh no, no no." Navya set her phone down, discouraged. "Gemini sun, Scorpio rising."

"Nav, you *can't*," Van gasped.

"I'm not! I unmatched."

Thea made a comment about Daniel's latest short story having been published in a "fairly well-respected" magazine, which Daniel took immediate issue with: the magazine was *very* well-respected. Thea was not nearly as familiar with the speculative fiction community as he was. Rather than apologize, Thea doubled down on her position, arguing that from an *objective* point of view, speculative fiction, sci-fi, and fantasy weren't accorded equal merit with grounded literary fiction, and that wasn't *her* fault. Then Daniel rattled off names—um, Carmen Maria Machado, George Saunders—Karen Russell was practically queen consort of *The New Yorker*! There were other parties standing around the garden, waiting for their picnic table to become available. El stood, planning to use a bathroom trip as a prelude to her ultimate exit, but Navya pulled her back down by the elbow and fixed her with imploring eyes.

"I *miss* you."

"Miss you too," El said breezily.

Navya fingered a strand of El's hair that had come loose from her bun. "I know how you feel."

"About what?"

Navya pouted her lips and shrugged. "Giving up on acting."

"Oh."

"No one knows what they're doing. No one here anyway."

"Yeah."

"Don't be a stranger. We're your friends."

"I know."

"So call me again this week. I know life is life but we need to make more plans."

"Yeah. Heard."

"I'm an assistant editor now. I'm a powerful person."

"You're an enforcer."

"I see these fools like every night and it's not as much fun without you."

Am I fun? El wanted to ask. *What's fun about me?* She thought maybe Navya meant that things felt more complete with her present. Navya seemed to feel that she, El, Thea, Daniel, Mathias, Lila and Emma were the kind of college buddies who ought to grow old, or at least to middle-age, spending the majority of their free time in one another's company, roughly aligned in their liberal politics, engaged with the same kinds of art, and generally reposting and reconfirming their collective existence. There was nothing so wrong with this, and El wondered why she resisted being truly part of the group, why she'd kept her distance more and more since she'd stopped acting. Maybe it was that she had an image of herself down the line were she to surrender to Navya's vision—she, midforties, a marketing manager at an artisanal coffee company and a part-time freelance film critic, a host of intimate dinner parties (on her roof because her dining room still wasn't *really* big enough). She saw herself passing around a cheapo salad bowl from IKEA that had "really held up," feeling young and unrealized still but, oh, she would seem together, power bill on autopay, cholesterol normal, dreams not deferred but shrunken, bite-sized as the amount of carbs she allowed herself in a day . . .

On her way out she texted Bryce that she had a migraine and would catch up with him tomorrow; she would be spending the night in her own apartment. He sent the head exploding emoji. She liked it. He called and she ignored him. Too hard to talk with head pounding like this :(.

Of course, really, her head felt fine. It wasn't that she didn't want to see Bryce, but she'd been disturbed by what Navya had said—*No one knows what they're doing.* Inadvertently, Navya had drawn a line under what El knew to be true: that she, El, was completely directionless. And since El had met Bryce, she'd been too distracted to think about that fact. *I'll make a plan tonight*, El resolved. *How can I get out of this rut? What do I want to do?* Graduate school was out. More loans? No thanks. Though she didn't do it much, she did enjoy baking— hence the working-at-the-bakery idea. *I could make content—*

easy baking, baking for non-bakers. I could go into work early and shadow. Learn for free. But even as she thought this, she felt discouraged. How was she supposed to stand out in the absolute avalanche of content already out there? And she knew she'd never get up and get to work earlier than she did already. *Maybe I'll start boxing or something,* she thought. *And diet, but not in a destructive way. I'll just get really in shape and that'll be my new thing.* This fantasy cheered her all the way home, where she shot to her room, kicked off her flats and stepped over the unvacuumed carpet into bed. She visited all the profiles of all the people she would impress with her new, strong amazing body until it started to get dark and she ventured to the kitchen for food. She melted cheese onto rice cakes and washed them down with two lonely pilsners that had been in the fridge door since New Year's. She lay back in bed and her reflux returned, bubbles of acid tickling her throat. What was Kirsten, her father's chosen child, doing with *her* life? El thought about how satisfying it would've been to have become a household name, a serious actress in an acclaimed new series that her father's friends would've raved about in low hasty voices so as not to offend Kirsten at the family's annual Christmas party. El lay with her esophagus burning, willing transcendence. *Let me find something. Let me become something.* The air was stale and warm, and after a minute she got up and opened the window. It was just as hot outside as in. She didn't have A/C in her bedroom, only the overhead fan and the tiny portable bedside one that she'd used backstage during her summer in Williamstown. *Let it rain,* she thought. *Or let tonight be over.*

It didn't rain, but twenty minutes after El lay down again, she fell asleep with her clothes still on. And eight hours later, morning groped through her blinds with bright white fingers.

She had the later shift the following day, and by the time she began her commute, she'd received four texts from Bryce—a good morning; a selfie; a dreamed about you last night; a Spotify link to the Herman's Hermits version of "I'm into Something Good." She ate a moist Chewy bar and listened to the song on the train. On her break she sent back a heart, and he sent her two articles: the first, a profile of a comedian turned wellness guru; the second, an indictment of an Australian lawmaker pushing looser gun control regulation.

She had planned to call Bryce after she locked up, and assumed it was him when her phone buzzed just as she was dumping the recycling in the back. She brushed her hands on her skinny black apron and pulled her phone from her back pocket—but it wasn't Bryce after all. She swiped to answer.

"Hey, Mom." She could hear her mother shushing someone. Then came a loud meow. "Mom?"

"El? Hello?"

"I'm here."

"Can you hear me?"

"I can hear you."

"What do you think about trying the new Indian place on

Columbus tonight? It's Punjabi cuisine. People seem to like it. And I was thinking that after we could catch a movie."

El hesitated.

"El?"

"Yeah. I can do that, sure."

She sent Bryce a message that she was going to see her mother and would hit him up later. She also promised to check out both the articles he'd sent, but she'd barely made it halfway through the comedian piece when the express pulled in at 72nd Street. She and her mother met on Broadway and walked together to the restaurant. Every available table was taken, inside and out, but there was just one other party of two ahead of them, and the obliging host assured El's mother that the wait wouldn't be too long. Nonetheless, her mother eyed a couple lingering over their check and muttered, "Oh, come on . . ."

"I'll be right back," El said. She only sort of had to pee but was eager to avoid being party to her mother's impatience.

When El returned from the bathroom she found her mother seated at one of the four inside tables nearest the window, sipping from a sweating glass of sauvignon blanc and looking over a paper menu. El's chair scraped as she scooted in. After they agreed to share tandoori chicken and chana masala her mother began trying to catch the eye of the nearest waitress, and El started to feel anxious. She felt obligated to tell her mother about Bryce but couldn't understand why. Her mother had not, historically, been supportive of her romantic relationships. In fact her mother wanted her to shun dating and focus instead on personal development—sign up for an online language course; train for a marathon; visit the Fulton Fish Market in the early morning, just to see it. El knew her mother had only begun to discover herself postdivorce, knew her mother didn't want *her* to have to wait so long. But you could find yourself and find someone else at the same time, couldn't you?

The waitress submitted to her mother's X-ray glare, and once their order had been placed and their menus had been cleared away, El rested her forearms on the table and said bluntly, "So I met somebody."

Her mother straightened against the high back of her chair. "What does he do?"

"Investment banking."

"How did you meet?"

And El explained (minus the cocaine) about misplacing her license.

"El, you really shouldn't be leaving your license around like that. Do you always keep your eye on your things when you're out? And you know never to leave a drink unattended, right?"

"Mom, I'm twenty-nine. I'd be dead by now if I didn't know that."

"Don't say that."

"Anyway," El said. "His name's Bryce. I like him a lot." But this sounded strangely thin, even to her own ears.

Her mother didn't ask any more questions about Bryce, but at the end of the meal did comment that El might've brought the remaining chana masala to her boyfriend if they hadn't made plans to see the movie.

"Or you could've brought it home with you," El said.

"Oh no." Her mother touched her waistline. "I've had plenty." Then she massaged her neck as if it were bothering her.

El pulled her bag from the floor onto her lap. "You still want to do the movie, right?"

An accusing wrinkle formed on her mother's brow. "Do you need to go early?"

"No," El said, annoyed. "I was just checking because you seemed tired."

They walked to the theater, which was only a quarter full because the movie had been out for weeks. El thought she could've done a better job than the female lead, but did not mention this on the walk back to Columbus Circle lest her mother probe her about her post-acting game plan—given the fruitless brainstorming of the previous night, El felt especially unequipped to bullshit her mother and project false confidence about career stuff. At the station El hugged her mother good-bye and descended the steps: it was like wading into a swamp. Once she was through the turnstile she texted Bryce to let him know she'd be staying at her own place again. She'd see him tomorrow.

His response came: ?

How could she explain that taking a second night off was in Bryce's own interest? That she had felt phony at dinner professing how much she supposedly liked him, but that everything felt phony in proportion to the immense weight of her mother's expectations. She did not "like him a lot" in any absolute, unequivocal way, but absolute truths were very rare, maybe nonexistent. All she needed was a little space, a little distance, and she would remember that she liked Bryce plenty. She liked him fine. She liked him enough.

According to the sign in the station, the express was nine minutes away and the local just one. She opted for the local, which was so packed she didn't really have room to hold her phone in one hand and hold on with the other. She dropped her phone into her bag, telling herself that she didn't really owe Bryce a response. So she wanted to spend another night on her own, big deal. Just as she got off to transfer at Washington Square, she saw her screen light up in her bag. It turned out to be a text from Crystal, but her phone died before she could read it. She hustled to the M platform and made it just in time to hear the whistle and screech of the approaching train when, in her peripheral vision, she saw a tan shape jumping from a woman's purse and sprinting along the platform, and the woman throwing out her arms—

The train barreled in, and people parallel to the front car screamed. The woman who had thrown out her arms collapsed, her mouth open in a silent wail.

A short old man in a Mets cap swore. He was slightly nearer than El to the woman, whom he was watching with a trepidatious look.

El stepped next to the old man. "What happened? What was it?" But she knew. She had seen the collision.

"Damn dog jumped," the man growled.

In the end El had taken a taxi home. They'd had to shut down the track, and a stretcher had come for the hysterical woman, the dog owner. The man in the Mets cap had walked out of the station with El, and before they'd gone their separate ways he'd muttered, "Never seen a thing like that."

El stepped into the darkened hallway of her apartment, thinking of Lila's story about her childhood dog. El imagined its old limbs extending, stretching, gaining improbable speed, racing away from Lila's stepsister in their shitty concrete backyard. It seemed to El like there were two kinds of loss. There was loss you might see coming, and maybe it did break your heart. But then there was loss so unexpected, so incomprehensible, that the pain was the pain of your own brittle grasp on reality. A dog was not supposed to abandon you. A dog was not supposed to intentionally hurtle from the safety of your purse into the jaws of a train.

The light at the end of the hall flicked on, and Crystal stepped swiftly out of her room.

"God," El breathed. "You really freaked me out."

Crystal ignored this. "Just so you know, not a big fan of McDreamy dropping by at all hours of the night. He woke me up."

"What?"

"Thanks for introducing me formally by the way. It feels good to know you see me as such an important person in your life."

And Crystal marched back to her bedroom and shut the door, leaving El baffled. El was about to go after Crystal when her own door creaked open and Bryce poked his head out, looking sheepish.

"Sorry—I was trying to surprise you."

El waved him backward into the room. Then she saw the rose petals everywhere, scattered on the bed and the floor, and the stems wrapped in plastic in the trash can under her desk. Oh *god*.

"I just couldn't spend another night without you," he said. "And I had your address stored on my Uber account so I just . . ."

If there was one thing Bryce could've done to make himself less appealing tonight, when she was already feeling weird about him, it was this. But, okay. Okay. If this happened to someone she knew, one of her friends—if Navya or Crystal had been dating someone and El heard that that person had showed up out of the blue with flowers trying to be cute . . . Wouldn't she be jealous? Wouldn't she want someone who was that into her?

"I really feel awful about Crystal," he said, watching her anxiously.

"It's okay."

"I'm really sorry."

"Don't worry. Crystal being pissed isn't about you anyway. It's 'me and her' stuff."

There was a short pause, then Bryce said: "Can I kiss you?"

"Yeah," she said, like *of course*. He seemed relieved.

When they separated he took a seat on the end of the bed, which was made up neatly. That had not been her doing. She was certain that this morning her comforter and top sheet had been bunched up, she having kicked them off in protest when her second alarm had gone off right next to her ear.

"Have you thought about your own place?" he asked.

She sat by him and patted his head. "Ah, my little prince, no idea how the other half lives."

"Well, you can always stay with me. Every night if you want to."

"Oh yeah?"

"I mean, as payment I will expect you to narrate me to sleep doing your best David Attenborough."

"Seems fair."

Her hair was up, and he stroked stray tendrils from the nape of her neck. "I am serious, though. You could move in."

"What? Really?" *After three weeks of dating?*

"Hey, no pressure. It's a standing offer."

Maybe she should have seen this coming. A few days ago he'd said *I love you*—just once, and he hadn't said it since. They'd been in his (amazing black-marbled) shower, and she'd said it back, maybe because she'd been naked. Naked was not the time you wanted to share a hard truth with the man who, apparently, loved you.

Come to think of it, maybe saying *I love you* had been a bigger concession than moving in would be. What was the difference anyway? She was already over all the time. And no rent? She imagined herself stretched out on his Italian-made sectional in the middle of the day . . .

The following morning at seven a.m. she kissed Bryce goodbye at the door and shuffled to the kitchen. While her coffee brewed, she surveyed the apartment. The dream catcher tacked up above the sink. The dusty living room blinds. The scratched-up oak coffee table Crystal had found on the street. This apartment, El realized, had always been a waiting room. She was ready for her real, adult life. She was ready to trade in this shitty plastic drip coffee maker from her dorm room days for the shiny, high-end espresso machine at Bryce's.

But she didn't tell Bryce that she was ready to move. Not yet. She kept hearing Crystal's bitter words—*It feels good to know you see me as such an important person in your life*. She decided that, if these were going to be her last weeks with Crystal, she would try to be the best roommate possible. She regularly asked Crystal how things were going. (Crystal *had* booked that teacher cameo, it turned out, but the part had been cut.) She restocked items they were running low on: paper towels, nail polish remover. She sorted the mail, participated in a spirited discussion about whether to implore their landlord to replace the toilet, which sometimes took two flushes to do its thing. She even attempted to cook a few times. But maybe she didn't try hard enough, or maybe it was just the amount of time she was still spending at Bryce's—however involved El tried to be when she was present, she was too absent overall. The apartment came to remind El of the tiny bedroom she'd shared with Ansel: strained, sour.

At the same time, El was getting more and more used to the Financial District, which had, before Bryce, always left her with the impression of someplace dystopian, *1984*, Ministry of Love and all that. But now that she was there more often, she saw it was the same New York, the apartments were just stuffed into former office buildings and banks. There were bikers and runners by the river, sunbathers on Bryce's roof, college-aged interns hustling and sweating over crosswalks in their first professional outfits.

Navya, meanwhile, had been badgering El to come out with the group since her promotion drinks. El didn't like to let Navya down, but between work, her attempts to placate Crystal and her time with Bryce, she didn't have much left in the tank for trendy vegan restaurants and late nights at arcade dive bars in Bushwick. But then Navya texted El about a show—Thea had been tipped off that a famously reclusive indie singer El loved would be putting on an impromptu concert. For a moment El was tempted to dash on eyeliner and rush out the door. But she was at Bryce's, and they were halfway through preparing dinner. El told Navya that she had plans!!! sadly!! but to have a great time for her!! Then she put on the singer's 2021 album while Bryce seasoned their salmon and she fixed halloumi salad. She had become one of those people who put their relationship first, which ought to have made her ashamed, perhaps. But she was too consumed by how *good* it felt—like a pleasant fatigue, like succumbing to a stultifying heat.

chapter eleven

N ext Friday doesn't work," her mother said. "I'm taking Chat to the dentist."

El set down her favorite of Bryce's stoneware
mugs on the kitchen counter and ran a hand through her hair,
exasperated. Her mother had called hoping to find out what
her plans were for the Fourth of July that weekend. Did she
want to watch fireworks from a colleague's apartment on Central Park West? El had suggested, instead, a lunch on her off
day the following Friday, but that was out, apparently, thanks
to Chat. Really El had no good reason to turn down her mother's invite. She didn't have concrete plans for the Fourth. Navya and everybody had bandied around the idea of Fire Island,
and El knew she had to see her friends *sometime*, but going
anywhere overnight was such a commitment . . . She told her

mom she'd get back to her about the holiday, walked to the en suite bathroom and knocked once.

"Admission granted for foxy babes only," came Bryce's voice from within.

She opened the door. He glanced over, mid-shave, and winked, eyeing her lack of bra under her white sleep tank.

"That was my mom asking if I want to watch the fireworks from her friend's place on Saturday."

"'I' not 'we'?"

"I think it was implied," she lied.

"So," Bryce asked, "are we going?"

El's pulse quickened. Something about her mother making the cat a priority was, however reasonable, infuriating, and stirred up an old feeling of wandering the city as a lonely pre-teen while her father had been wherever the fuck with his other daughter and her mother had been so busy and unavailable and El had known herself to be in a bad pocket of life, stranded between meanings, awaiting someone who would relieve the ache because no person could survive as she had been, so un-witnessed. She took a breath. "How do you feel about moving me in that day instead?"

Bryce put down the electric razor and turned to her. The shaved face didn't suit him at all. It gave fresh expression to his slightly sagging cheeks.

"Come here," he said, extending his arms.

The instinct to buck was like the tip of a wave that rises, sullen, before pitching forward. Being held by him was like being reabsorbed, liquid erasure.

That night she went home to tell Crystal, but Crystal wasn't there. El texted her: you around? No reply.

She slept badly in her bed. Her old bed, as she was coming to think of it. She was used to Bryce's sheets now, so cool on her skin.

The morning dawned quiet and sunny. El had started packing up her bedroom stuff when she finally heard Crystal unlocking the front door. She froze, gripped by something like stage fright. She listened to Crystal walk all the way down the hall to the bathroom and turn the shower on.

Twenty minutes later, still agitated but telling herself that she just had to get it over with, El knocked on Crystal's door. Crystal appeared moments later with damp hair and an aloof expression.

"Hey!" El said, trying hard to sound upbeat. "I came home last night so we could talk."

Crystal made a face. "Okay? I'm not like obligated to be here . . ."

"No, of course. That's not what I meant, I just wanted to see you. How is everything? Good?"

"Uh-huh. What did you want to talk about?"

El summoned her courage. "Well, so, I'm moving out. Me and Bryce are moving in together. I'll obviously pay for August too, so you'd have till the end of the summer to find someone."

"Okay," said Crystal blankly.

"Okay? Are we . . . good?"

"Yup, I got it. You're moving out. But, uhm, I have to dry my hair . . ."

"Oh, sure," El said, backing out of the doorway.

And that was it. They never had it out for real. Two days later, when El was leaving with the last of her things, she passed the open bathroom door: Crystal was fixing her eyeshadow, dressed like a roller girl from the '80s. In the mirror she met El's gaze.

"I'll Venmo you for the last utilities," El said. And when Crystal didn't reply, she added: "Really hope you get the part."

Crystal shrugged. El wanted to say something more—she considered making a broad apology, but how would she word it? *I'm sorry I didn't make you a priority?* That wouldn't even be honest. Why was it her job to protect Crystal's expectations? Crystal had no idea how uncaring people could be. El's shallow engagement was nothing compared to the actual neglect of, say, a parent. Of, say, a father who chose his other daughter over you. She wished Crystal would rage at her so she'd have had an excuse to say that.

Alas, it was only her mother's anger she had the privilege of confronting. Ten days after the move El came uptown because her mother needed her to hold Chat still while she trimmed his nails. While Chat fought El's grip and scratched her forearms, El's mother asked what Bryce's parents had to say about their moving in together after such a short time. El replied honestly: that she had no idea. Bryce's father lived in Connecticut, and she was pretty sure his mother was in London—she didn't know how up-to-date Bryce kept them on the ins and outs of his life. Then her mother switched tack: "You have no rights, you know, if you're not on a lease." To which El replied that she hadn't been on the lease at her place in Brooklyn, either. Her mother was not mollified.

She left her mother's around 7:45 p.m. and took the train to the East Village, where she met Navya for dinner. Navya was working longer hours than ever before, and she and El spent much of their meal discussing the injustice of this—how Navya's company only paid her fifty-five cents more an hour than they had previously, but now Navya was expected, off the clock, to weed through all the submissions from smaller agents who claimed to have discovered the next Liane Moriarty or Gillian Flynn. Between crunchy bites of buffalo cauliflower Navya recounted the plots of several implausible novels she'd read the week before—"And you would think, no, surely, this one won't *also* have little paragraphs in italics between each chapter narrating the killer's point of view—but then you realize, oh god, yes, they all have that! And they all think it's so original!"

It wasn't until they got around to paying the check that the subject of El's moving in with Bryce came about.

"So how's living with the man? The mystery man."

"What? You've met him."

"For like a second."

"We'll do something soon, it's just hard. His hours are nuts, and then I usually only have like one weekend day off, so. Anyway. How was Fire Island?"

"Amazing, actually."

Dodging a cluster of cauliflower crumbs, El rested her forearms on the table and leaned toward Navya. "I'm so sad I missed it."

Navya mirrored her body language and leaned forward too. "You missed another Thea–Daniel showdown."

"Yikes."

"I know. Also, literally, Van is the only person I know who gets *sad* on molly??"

"Did his friends come too, the ones who were at your promotion drinks?"

"Adam and Andrew? Yeah, they were there."

"I like Adam," El said, remembering, at the promotion party, how he'd held her gaze with chilling confidence.

"I like him too," Navya said. "Although, I dunno. I think maybe he's kind of full of himself."

A pause, as the server returned with their debit cards and receipts. They both thanked him, and El spoke again while they were scribbling their tips: "I'm really bummed we couldn't do Fire Island. I do want you to meet Bryce for real—"

"Oh no, I know."

"I feel bad."

"I totally get it. I'm sure it's been crazy with packing and unpacking and everything."

Not really, El thought. Bryce had hired a moving company. She'd only been in charge of grabbing the small stuff, forwarding her mail, plugging up a few thumbtack holes in the wall with gummy patching compound.

They both stood, pushed in their chairs and thanked the

hostess in front, who didn't even glance up from her phone. As they stepped onto the sidewalk Navya turned to El with a small gasp.

"I forgot to tell you! Lucely's is closing."

The blue twinkle lights of Lucely's Kitchen shone on the corner. It was a small café, one El and her NYU contingent had frequented during college. Lucely's served a handful of Dominican staples, tostones and empanadas, and six nights a week, after seven p.m., Lucely's opened the stage in the back of the restaurant to anyone who wanted to perform—comedy, poetry, dramatic reading, whatever. El had tested out monologues there from time to time, and Daniel had once written a one-act play in which El had appeared as a young Carl Sagan. On the back of Lucely's single-page laminated menu was a picture of the owners, Lucely and Cam, and their two elementary-aged kids, Manny and Gaby. The paragraph beneath the photo explained that the café had come to be in 2014 when Lucely, a radiology assistant who loved to cook her mamá's recipes, had met Cam, a former rodeo clown from Houston looking for his next adventure. That adventure, the menu said, had turned out to be a two-hander: a business and a family.

Frequenting the café as they had in its early years, El and her friends had come to know Lucely and Cam well. They'd met Manny as an infant and had pitched in for a gift when Gaby had been born their senior year. It was true they hadn't patronized Lucely's much after they'd graduated in 2019—the virus had hit so soon afterward, shutting everything down, and by the time the café had reopened they'd been out of the habit. They all still followed the Lucely's social account, though, and El had dropped in occasionally for a catch-up with Lucely over coffee or a Presidente. Often playing nearby were Manny and Gaby, upon whom El bestowed hugs and high-fives. It was terrible to think that the café would be closing. El was seized with the angry, helpless feeling she sometimes had in the very early mornings at work, when she arrived in time to help the bakers with simple tasks—sprinkling sugar, slicing fruit—the bakers were always in high spirits, laughing and listening to the radio. Witnessing this, El wanted to scream at them: *Shouldn't we all be furious to be here?! We don't own this place! We have no stake, no power, no control!*

"That's so awful," El said, turning from the blue lights to look at Navya. "Why? They're just not making enough money?"

"Yeah. That's what Emma says. I think she's gonna try to do something to help them."

"Well, let me know. Fuck."

"Yeah. I know. It's not fair."

"Fair only comes around once a year."

"Hm?"

"My dad would say that sometimes."

Navya gave a pained smile. El knew that mention of her father made Navya uncomfortable. El gathered that Navya's own family had survived intact by mere force of will—her parents, both employed by the same D.C. marketing firm, had apparently bickered consistently about money (whether to send their children to public or private school, whether to buy a bigger house, whether and when to take vacations). Navya's two brothers were twins and seven years older. In leaving for colleges on the West Coast they'd abdicated the role of conflict mediator, a mantle that Navya had reluctantly taken up in their absence. Even when she and Navya had been at NYU, El remembered Navya frequently fielding separate calls from her mom and dad, each of whom wanted to relay their side of that week's argument. Years of training at the hands of her less-than-happy parents had groomed Navya into the person she was today—the peacemaker, the group mother, the mender of ties. It wasn't from a place of judgment that Navya regarded El's crumbled family unit but, El suspected, from a place of a fear. What was more difficult, El wondered: to grow up in a broken home or in one that always felt moments from breaking?

"Anyway," El said.

They looked at one another and hugged. Navya tilted her head hopefully. "I'll see you soon?"

"Soon," El promised.

Over breakfast El admitted to Bryce that her mother had some doubts about their fast-moving romance (though she made it sound like her mother was more ambivalent than anti). He seemed hurt, which she didn't expect, and she found herself in the odd position of defending her mother.

"She hasn't even met you yet."

He nodded between bites of blueberry yogurt. "I guess. That'd probably be strange for some mothers."

For *most* mothers, El wanted to say, but she held her tongue. Obviously he had his own distant maternal situation.

"What did you tell her about it?"

"About what? Living together? I told her it was good."

And really it was. Moving in was supposed to be harder than marriage, right? She'd read that once. But it had been okay so far. Granted, there weren't many responsibilities to divide up. An older housekeeper named Bogna came to clean and do laundry once a week. Groceries were delivered then sent up in a cart by the doorman. There were no too-loud neighbors, no surprise mold, no risk of packages being swiped.

The only thing was, Bryce seemed to fear El would vanish if he left her alone too long. Of course he still had to work, but he had told his boss, Ian, that he was having "autoimmune issues" and had started coming home at five or six to finish his business from the couch. El had balked when Bryce admitted to having lied—"I'm okay here, you can stay in the office as long as you need!"—but Bryce had brushed her off. His colleague's wife had just had a baby, he'd explained, and he'd been taking on a bunch of extra responsibility. As long as he was getting stuff done and showed his face every morning, his boss didn't really care where he finished out the day.

Bryce set his empty yogurt bowl in the sink and walked over to her. She offered her lips for a peck.

"I'll see you later," she said.

He bounced there for a second. "Love you."

They hadn't said it since that night in the shower, before she'd moved in. She didn't really like his saying it now, on his way out the door. Only because, didn't it, a little bit, have the valence of manipulation? *Love you*, like, *don't do anything to hurt me*. Or maybe it was totally benign—and this was the frustrating thing, she didn't necessarily trust her own perception. Regardless, she didn't want to hurt Bryce, or leave him feeling abandoned, even though that bounce he had just done with his heels was almost nauseating in its earnestness . . . But anyway, she probably loved him so—

"Love you too."

He beamed but had the good sense not to swoop in for another kiss. "Call you later."

After he left, El hauled a duffel bag from the hall closet to the living room. She hadn't brought much from her old place, but one thing she had bothered to lug were these: thirty or so texts, her required reading from NYU, which she'd little valued at the time but which might, now, recommend her intellectually should Bryce's parents ever come by. Her own mother's warning words were still top of mind, and El's thought was that winning over the family might help to ensure her place *if* there were ever trouble on the home front. She imagined Bryce's mother or father alighting with pleasure on the bright, artful additions to their son's rather sparse library (*The Economic Role of the State, Heart of Darkness, The Complete Short Stories of Ernest Hemingway*).

It took about ten minutes before it all looked right, and a few of Bryce's things she had to rearrange, including a red leather photo album she found stuffed way back on one shelf. She flipped through it. There were pictures of an auburn-haired woman on a terrace squinting at the camera—Bryce's mother? There was something familiar about her, a certain Elizabeth Taylor–like haughtiness. There were many pictures of a gray puppy: here running, there curled up to sleep. The final pages of the album featured a six- or seven-year-old Bryce; he was unmistakable, meat-cheeked, a downtrodden way about him even then. He and a slight little girl—perhaps several years his junior—were petting a handsome brown horse in one photo. *His sister,* El thought. *The one who died. What was her name? Also a B . . . Brooke?*

Errands composed the rest of El's day—picking up her birth control, closing her account at the $12 a month gym she hadn't been to since she'd been auditioning. Bryce texted before dinnertime: Ian on one today. Don't know my eta yet. Might be kind of late.

Got it, she wrote. I'll get us some food and put urs in the fridge.

El thought about what she wanted to eat, but in the end decided she wasn't very hungry. She ordered Bryce a black bean burger and picked at some prosciutto and berries they had in the fridge. It was ten o'clock when the front door unlocked, and El paused the documentary she was watching about the social media merger and its fallout. She stood and walked to the kitchen. Bryce was already swallowing a bite of burger.

"Thanks," he said. "But why didn't you order anything for yourself? That's why I added my card to your Seamless."

"How do you know I didn't order anything?"

Bryce shook his head, reaching for a paper towel to wipe

some avocado from his lips. He pointed to the far corner of the kitchen where El now saw there was a walnut-sized home security camera. "Saw you eating rabbit food out of the fridge. I look in every once in a while to make sure you're okay."

A moment passed before she found her voice: "You look in on me like I'm . . . a pet?"

Bryce raised an eyebrow. "Like you're . . . the woman I love?"

She saw that before her was a choice: to make this a fight or to, quickly and delicately, fold this fact into their story. So he checked up on her, so what? A violation, sure, but she remembered the toddler from the photo album, the sister he'd lost so abruptly. Maybe he wasn't even conscious of how neurotic his monitoring was. It didn't seem like it. He appeared completely unabashed.

"It's still kinda Stepford."

"I've never read it."

"Nobody's *read* it. You know what I mean." She could see that he wasn't going to apologize and decided she didn't care enough to argue. "I'm gonna jump in the shower."

"Want me to queue us up?"

"Sure. I was watching a doc but I'm ready to go back to the island."

"What doc? I don't even remember what happens this season."

"It's the Others, and Kate and Sawyer in the cage. Oh, hey—you never told me you had a dog."

He gave her a weird look.

"I said the other day I'd never had a pet and you said 'me too.' But I saw a dog in the photo album. On the bookshelf."

"Oh," he said. "Mouse. She was more Mum's dog. She actually had a litter. Mum kept one."

"Mouse? Animal named for another animal?"

"I named her. She was supposed to be mine, but—" His voice became oddly tight. "Dogs attach to whoever feeds them."

She shrugged. "State of nature."

"She loved me though," he insisted.

There was a weighty pause as he boxed up his remaining food and stuck it in the fridge. His being flustered annoyed her. She was the one being observed without her knowledge. She should say that! She deserved to make her point more forcefully than she had . . . But then, she knew what he might do. He might say that he was sorry if it made her feel uncomfortable, but that it was innocent and rooted in a desire to protect and caretake—he wouldn't use that word, *caretake*, but that was what he would mean, and she would remember that she'd rarely—never—had a man in her life who'd treated her like this, like she was something worth safeguarding, and she would begin to doubt her position, which she didn't want to do because it was a completely valid position. So maybe it was better not to bring it up at all. Let him be flustered for whatever stupid fucking reason and just move on.

"I was watching *Social*, that doc about the merger," she said. "To answer your earlier question."

"Oh yeah."

There was still that strain in his voice. She really, really wanted to ask what the hell was the matter, but what was the saying? "Do you want to be right or do you want to be happy?" She linked her arms above her head and stretched side to side.

He looked at her, his expression softening. "Feel okay?"

"Yeah. I'm excited to see the whole Dharma Initiative backstory. I like this season."

He unbuttoned the top buttons of his shirt. "I used to love the girl . . . who's the blonde again? She's one of the Others?"

"Juliet?"

"Love her. Not as much as you of course." He came over and kissed her for several long seconds. He tasted like black bean. When he drew back, he said, "I'll pop in the shower with you."

She gave him a warm, assuring look, but it was funny—when her cheeks stretched and her lips curved, she had the sensation that she was acting.

But that makes sense, said a voice in her head. *You're on camera again.*

chapter twelve

T he e-mail from Emma came that Saturday, and El read it in the bathroom at work.

GIVE LOWER MANHATTAN'S BEST DOMINICAN CAFÉ A FAIR SHAKE

Dear friends & allies,

Join us NEXT SUNDAY July 26th at noon to raise funds for our beloved LUCELY'S KITCHEN. Lucely's is a New York staple, and if you don't know Lucely, Cam and their two children personally then you'll just have to trust me—this beautiful family has cultivated an inclusive, celebratory and *delicious* environment in their café. They deserve to keep their doors open for many years to come, so LET'S HELP THEM DO IT.

Never forget the number one rule of being an ally: SHOW UP. Let's do this!!!!!!!! RSVP below!!!!!!!!!!!

In solidarity,

Em.

El RSVP'd, then texted Navya: she couldn't just make a gofundme? Navya responded with an LOL, which El appreciated because—right? Wasn't hosting an in-person fundraiser just a little bit more about Emma proclaiming herself white savior to the rescue? This bitter thought consumed El's remaining hour at work. Darcy was in a horrible mood because the sous chef had dumped her. When Darcy spotted a syrupy splotch on the counter El had neglected to clean, she berated El for *not even attempting to make an effort.*

When Pia arrived for their shift, El murmured, "Beware the Ides of March."

"Got it," Pia said, twisting their long, ashen hair into a braid. Then their eyes fell on the spot where the syrupy stain had been: there was still a smudge left. Pia immediately grabbed a rag and wiped it down. There was no question that Pia was a much, much better employee than El. Pia got along with the bakers. Pia could even make croissants and other simple pastry. Feeling shitty about herself, El walked downstairs to get her bag from her cubby and took the back entrance out, cutting through the alley to the street.

El couldn't imagine where Pia got the energy to be so focused at work and so busy outside of it. Based on offhand comments Pia had made about trips taken and concerts seen, the constant buzzing of their phone and their habitual haste to leave the second their shift ended, El gathered that Pia had a very big life. This fact notwithstanding, El did feel that Pia would've been amenable to some kind of friendship if *El* were to make the effort, but El struggled with that idea. It was fundamentally humiliating to extend yourself to someone who *almost* liked you. How many times had El encountered this— with friends, fuckbuddies, casting directors—people who nearly liked her, but something held them back. Maybe if she showed her belly, how much she hungered for connection, maybe then she'd manage to convert doubters into lovers. Maybe she would have more friends who challenged her, rather than those who simply accepted her in her limited, emotionally anorexic state (because Navya did this, she knew; Navya enabled her avoidance by always being the one to reach out). Maybe she would have made it in acting after all had she learned to be vulnerable when it counted the most. The fatal ingredient in her personality was spite. Just that one little ounce of it, the part too bitter to show her need, had it kept her from a better life?

El sighed aloud as a drop of something wet fell on her forehead. She resisted the temptation to glance up and was glad she did, because another drop soon fell on her neck. This was part of New York in the summer, the steady drip of someone else's air conditioner onto your body. It was only water, but there was something medieval about it nonetheless. A double-decker sightseeing bus sped past, and El thought, with heart-skipping excitement, that she could, if she so desired, catch a Jitney *right now* to East Hampton, take a taxi to Julia's house and probably convince Carmen to let her in for a glass of water, at least; it might be worth all that effort just to glimpse the tiered bowl on the kitchen island filled with fruit, tidy as a still life.

At that moment El's phone began to vibrate in her bag. She fished it out and saw it was Navya. She answered in a faux-peppy voice, quoting Emma's e-mail, "'Never forget the number one rule of being an ally—show up!'"

Navya laughed. "I know, I know, but hopefully this fundraiser will actually be good."

"How are you?" El asked.

"Fine. Tired. I'm just walking to grab a salad but I wanted to make sure you'd be coming to the Lucely's thing so I'd get to see you."

"Yeah, I'll definitely go."

"How's everything with Bryce?"

El hesitated. She didn't really want to tell Navya about Bryce checking on her via security camera, but she also didn't want to give just a boring report. She had always shared with Navya the gory details of her dating life. She finally decided to tell Navya about the episode she thought most likely to make her laugh. "Oh, so wait. I don't think I told you this when we had dinner. The day of your promotion drinks I was supposed to meet Bryce after but I didn't really feel like going back into Manhattan so I just went home, right? And then the next day after work my mom wanted me to come hang out, and you know how she is—"

"Oh, Deb."

"Exactly. So then after that I was also feeling kind of blah, told Bryce I'd be staying at my place again, and I get there and Crystal is like *pissed* and says something about McDreamy showing up and all of a sudden Bryce opens the bedroom door and he's *there*. He just like came to my address—he had it saved on his phone—and he shows up with roses and is like, *I couldn't spend another night without you.*" There was a beat during which El could only hear the sound of wind and traffic on the other end of the line. "Nav?"

"Yeah. Wow. That's crazy."

"It's hilarious."

"So Crystal had let him in obviously, right?"

"Well yeah, he didn't break in."

"Were you freaked out?"

"No. I was surprised. Crystal was freaked out."

Navya didn't seem to get it, so El tried to set the scene better. "There were rose petals all over the bed, like a bad movie. And I mean he felt *so* guilty for freaking Crystal out but, you know, it was cute that he missed me."

"Yeah," Navya said, and her voice was short. "Hey, you know what, I'm here and I have to order, but I'll see you next weekend. Are you bringing Bryce?"

"Yeah."

"All right. Well—have a really good day. See you soon."

El's phone beeped twice: Navya had hung up. *Well*, El thought wryly. *Really glad I didn't tell her about the security camera.*

Later that night, in the middle of *Lost*, El turned to Bryce. A revolting dribble of cereal and milk had become lodged in the stubble on his chin: she made an involuntary groan of distaste. He looked from the TV to her in surprise, and she motioned to the spot. Self-consciously he wiped himself, and she felt guilty. She, who knew keenly what it was to want someone's total acceptance and approval—why could she not give these things to Bryce, as he gave them to her? She had to do better at stifling these nasty impulses to criticize him. She thought of her earlier call with Navya and wished Navya could see Bryce now. How goofy he was. He wasn't some weirdo, he was just kind of lame. He wasn't unsolicited dick pics guy, he was unsolicited flowers guy.

To put Bryce at ease, she laid her head on his shoulder and curled her right leg over his left and told him how much she loved spending time together. He put a hand on her thigh and pulled it closer around him.

"You're like my little cat."

El suppressed the urge to roll her eyes and looked back at the TV. "I want to go to the beach."

"Do you want the beach, or do you want Matthew Fox and Josh Holloway to be fighting over you?"

"The beach," she said. "Maybe we can rent a place. Amagansett or Wainscott. Something."

"Hm." He was stroking her leg under her sweatpants, against the grain of the fuzzy hairs on her calf.

"There was a guy in college who broke things off with me because I was too afraid to get a Brazilian."

"What a dick," he said, and she could tell he meant it.

"You'd be surprised by what most dudes expect."

"Girls can be harsh too."

She was caught off guard for a second—was he referring to before, when she'd made him self-conscious about the stuff in his beard? Was he more aware than she realized? Could he sense her treacherous thoughts?

He kissed the top of her head. "Not you of course. You know there's like, the girl of your dreams? You're like the nice version of that. Like the human version, if that makes sense."

Gettable. Gettable was what he meant. That she was the best he could do. The ounce of spite in her rib cage flared. What if she walked out tomorrow, how *gettable* would she be then? But no, no, she had to relax. Being the cold and ungettable woman, tempting as it was, would get her nowhere. The high of walking away would only be temporary. She knew this from experience, having ended a fling with a guy named Jordan her senior year (the get-a-Brazilian guy's roommate, so ha-ha). It had been empowering, at first, to imagine herself missed. Watched. Loathed, even. But come one mundane afternoon, she'd looked around and realized—it was over. Jordan wasn't chasing her. She'd become invisible again.

Bryce's phone buzzed on the nightstand and he disentangled himself from her to see who it was. She paused the show but glanced at Bryce in time to see a stern look come over his face as he hit ignore.

"Work?" she asked, curious. "Actually, never mind. Have your own independent existence. Carry on." *Be nicer, be nicer* went the mantra in her head. He leaned back and she cuddled against his chest.

"You're very cute," he said, picking up the remote.

"Oh wait—are you free Sunday? Not tomorrow, next Sunday?"

"All yours."

"Okay, 'cause there's this fundraiser. It would be a good chance for you to hang out with Navya and meet everybody else. You don't have to wear a suit. It's more grassroots."

"I'm grassroots all the way. Peace, love."

"Oh my god, stop."

"You don't like it when I do John Lennon?"

"That was John Lennon?"

"You're an American. You don't have the keen English ear."

"Oh." She laughed. "So you're full-on English now?"

"When I'm doing John Lennon, yes."

"Do Ozzy Osbourne."

He screwed up his face. "Well, love—"

"That's pretty good!"

"Thank you, but you're still an ignorant American, so your opinion doesn't really count."

She laughed again and in an odd, out-of-body way realized she was having fun. *I am having fun with the man I live with in this big, expensive apartment.* She swatted at Bryce's chest playfully and had that sensation again, the sensation of acting. The camera was in the kitchen, but it felt like there were eyes on her in here too. Were these walls collapsible? Just out of sight were there a few harried producers and a director watching this take? If only people out there could see this moment: she finally had a winning role—a life worth envying.

At dawn the Sunday of the fundraiser, Bryce came into the bathroom yawning as she brushed her teeth.

"I'll have to go straight from the bakery to the thing later," she said. "So I'll just meet you there, unless you want to meet me at work?"

He was standing at the toilet with his eyes closed, his head tilted back.

"Okay?"

She watched him but he didn't say anything or even open his eyes. After a moment he started to pee. She went back in the bedroom and changed bras, having accidentally put on the one with the finicky clasp. While she was throwing on a shirt, Bryce called out: "I don't think I can come today." He emerged from the bathroom. "Ian e-mailed me at like three a.m., I've gotta get all this shit done before tomorrow. But I have something for you to bring."

He walked to the far corner of the room, where his jeans were splayed across a chair. Out of a pocket he drew his wallet and a folded-up check. He handed it to her: it was for $15,000.

"I didn't know who to make it out to, if it's the business or one of the owners . . ."

"Jesus Christ."

"Well, you said you wished you could help them more."

"I mean . . . what I was going to give looks extremely lame by comparison."

"Just make this our gift, from both of us. Unless you feel weird about it."

"No. It's great. It's just—a lot."

"Well, you know I'm here for you too, whatever you need, right?"

El was embarrassed by how even it was, the pull to tell him to fuck off and the pull to say, *Here, yes, take my loan payments, my phone bill, help me, I want better health insurance, I want to pick my doctors, because what if I get really sick? With my plan I'll be one of those people who goes into debt forever, if I do get sick it'll be because I worry, help me not to worry.* Her ambivalence must've shown on her face because he became instantly contrite.

"That was not— I didn't mean to say it like that. I love you. That's all."

She looked again at the check in her hand. "This is really cool. Thank you."

He ran a hand over his face, rubbing his eyes.

"Hope you get some more sleep," she said.

"I'm sorry you can't."

"Working girl." By which she meant only to signify her obligation to The Man, but in his half-asleep, half-animal state Bryce just registered the sexual valence, and he reached his hand around her hips and pressed his erection into her jeans. In that moment, El felt a fleeting stab of hate so strong it would've almost been worth the price of murder to satisfy it. It felt like Bryce was fetishizing the socioeconomic differential between them; it felt like he was infantilizing her for having a menial job and, most of all, for being a woman, a body to put his body onto, into, whenever he pleased. She felt awed by the sudden force of her rage—was that always there, lying dormant? Morning was coming on out the window, the sun a yolk, a big yellow amphibian eye. The world was so large, she thought, and so old—could it be that all it wanted from her was to suppress her impulses and behave?

chapter thirteen

There was a huge NYU turnout at the fundraiser. No one had changed so much. The associate professor who'd taught what everyone used to call "stupid math" was still sort of young. The woman from El's postcolonial seminar, who had married some distant Kennedy, still dressed like a member of Fleetwood Mac. The guy who used to run the outdoor program—schlepping other students to the Catskills for the weekend to camp and whatever—still gave those creeper vibes. She and he had been the kind of acquaintances who'd said hey at parties until their junior year, when he'd come up to her at a bar, barely coherent, and grinned: "So if we're friends, where are all the benefits?" Today he greeted her with a fist bump.

Most of the crowd El didn't recognize, though. They looked like garden-variety middle- and upper-middle-class progressives, but here and there was somebody completely out of place: a man whose Rolex poked out of his sport coat, a woman with a Balenciaga bag—the very rich were sprinkled here and there, perhaps parents or colleagues of those in attendance, otherwise contacts of Emma's, Democrats from Kennebunkport families, the kind who read headlines only, who proclaimed on their second Pinot that George Clooney ought to run for president. They knew nothing of policy and little of history, but of the present they understood that being an ally was the only acceptable liberal lane.

El saw Emma flitting around with Cam, whose head of tousled flaxen hair towered above them all. Navya she found at the bar, sitting beside Van. Van raised his pink cocktail to El in a salute, and El gave Navya a hug around the shoulders. Behind the bar stood Lucely, who looked her usual lovely, unpretentious self in dark jeans and a lavender sweater.

"Tell her it's okay to drink at your own party," Van said, pointing to Lucely.

"I don't want to sound crazy later when I have to make my speech!" Lucely's pitch-black hair fell around her shoulders in waves as she bent to crack open three beers. She placed these on napkins and slid them down the bar to a portly guy in a wrinkled button-down.

"Why do you have to make a speech?" Navya asked.

"I don't know," Lucely said wearily. "Emma says we should. I want Cam to do it."

"Where are the kids?" El asked.

"Sleeping over at my sister's. Every time they stay over

there Manny comes home with nightmares. His cousins show him these horror movies. For *weeks* he doesn't sleep."

Then Lucely had to step away to fix a pair of pink cocktails like the one Van was drinking, and Navya turned to El and asked, "Speaking of missing people—Bryce? I thought he was coming."

"He was, but then he got slammed with some work stuff."

"Boo," Van said neutrally.

"This probably isn't really his thing anyway," Navya said.

"What do you mean?"

"Nothing." Navya looked evasive. "I just meant he doesn't know Cam and Lucely."

At that moment Lucely rejoined them. She bent forward so her voice wouldn't carry. "Emma wasn't happy when she saw we didn't bring Gaby and Manny tonight."

El rolled her eyes. "Yeah, because what kid doesn't love a fundraiser? She was upset she wouldn't be able to parade them around."

"To be fair they're basically the most endearing kids on the planet," Navya said.

"Save the children!" Van cried.

Lucely gave a wry laugh. "Yes, maybe I'm being naïve but let's hope people will donate because they like our food and our atmosphere."

"They do!" Navya insisted. "And they will."

Lucely looked to El. "Want something, honey? I didn't ask you. Want a drink?"

"No thanks, I'm good for now."

El had it in mind to find Emma. She had considered handing Bryce's check right to Lucely, but never having been to a fundraiser before she wasn't sure if this would be rude. Who were you supposed to give your money to? The organizer, probably.

But El couldn't find Emma anywhere, nor Cam, who had been at Emma's side earlier. She had never seen the café quite this full: people were now standing three deep around the bar. Just as she was thinking of texting Navya to order her a rum punch, El felt a tap on her shoulder.

When she turned, she came face-to-face with Nicole, who was, as Crystal had feared, in the company of someone new, a short woman with strawberry blond ringlets and deep blue eyes. Nicole herself was as cool and put-together as ever, her warm beige complexion complemented by tasteful streaks of silver eyeshadow, her small nose adorned with a new diamond stud.

"I didn't know you'd be here," El said. "It's good to see you."

"This is Ange." Nicole indicated the woman beside her, who flashed El a sunny smile. "Ange, this is El—she was Crystal's roommate."

"Oh hi!" Ange fawned. "Hi, so nice to meet you."

"You too," El said. She looked to Nicole. "I feel compelled to tell you that I wore your jean jacket once. It's still at the apartment with Crystal, or it might be on its way to Goodwill by now."

"Oh, no, I got it back. I stopped over for coffee last week."
Nicole reached for Ange's hand and gave it a squeeze.

"Wow." El looked between Nicole and Ange. "Both of you?"

"No," Ange laughed.

"Just me," Nicole clarified.

Ange stroked Nicole's arm. "Babe, I think I should get in
line . . ."

"Yeah yeah, go," Nicole urged.

While Ange disappeared into the crowd, Nicole looked
pointedly at El. "Crystal's in L.A. this week, testing for a network. A drama pilot."

El felt it then, the old sensation of the grandfather clock
inside her, ticking toward her own extinction as an actress—
whenever someone else succeeded, someone in her circle especially, this clock became louder and more difficult to ignore. It
took a second for El to remember that she had already given
up. She was no longer competing.

"That's so great. I should call her."

Nicole gave El an appraising look. "Maybe. Maybe not."

Clearly over coffee Crystal had fed Nicole all kinds of crap
about El being a shitty friend, which was not entirely without merit—but on the other hand, was it a friendship if you
were someone's consolation prize? Nicole was the bad guy
here. Nicole had created the wound in Crystal, whereas El
had—by moving forward with Bryce, by pursuing her *own*
happiness—just rubbed salt in it. El could not stand to see the
candid disapproval on Nicole's face: it seemed to be everyone's
disapproval. It was Crystal playing the victim and her mother

judging her every move and Darcy haranguing her at work and Navya, whose silence and surreptitious questions about Bryce said as much as outright insults. A crescendo was building inside and—

"I wasn't asking your opinion," El spat.

Nicole raised a manicured brow in surprise. She had never known El to be confrontational. After a moment she murmured, "Good luck with everything." She passed El, turning sideways to avoid touching shoulders just as the overhead lights dimmed and colored Christmas lights around the room flicked on.

El watched Nicole's back. No doubt Nicole would report to Ange that El was *not okay*, that Crystal was *lucky* to be free of El, actually. El was surprised to find this thought didn't bother her too much. Her entire life she'd been outwardly civil, probably because her parents had argued so much before the divorce; a house could only stand so much anger and El, understanding this, had learned not to make waves. She had spent twenty-nine years marveling at the brashness of the world's fighters, playground bullies and obstinate journalists and steely world leaders. She'd always told herself she was a pacifist but deep down she'd felt like a pushover. Maybe that was starting to change.

"Howdy!"

Cam had mounted the stage in back. His big Texas accent filled the room. "Let's give a hand to my incredible wife, Lucely! Join me, darlin.'" El and everyone else gave a hearty clap as Lucely stepped out from behind the bar to join Cam onstage.

"We want to thank you," Cam continued, addressing the crowd. "Thank you for comin', for takin' time out of your Sunday—and we'd especially like to thank our friend, our *champion*, the incredible Emma Heward."

Emma was just below the stage, looking up at Cam, raising her tattooed arms, applauding him even as the room applauded her. El used the moment to sneak forward through the throng, and when she arrived by Emma's side Cam was speaking again. Emma gave her a quick sideways glance.

"Everyone who knows me knows I love an adventure. Before any of this, long time ago, I was a barrelman in the rodeo business. Now I'll explain this for all you Yanks: after the bull riders are done they gotta leave the arena, or the bull is comin' for them, so as the barrelman you're standin' in this big barrel and you gotta distract the bull so the cowboy can get out safe—and when the bull comes for you, you gotta duck down into the barrel, 'cause maybe the bull will buck you and maybe he won't. So what the hell does this have to do with our restaurant?"

"Yes, keep it moving," Lucely said, nudging him.

There was warm laughter from the room, and Cam let it ring out for just the right amount of time before resuming. "So here's the thing—at first, when that bull's comin' at you, you're scared. No way not to be. But then you get used to it. You adjust. And I know that Luce and I, and our family, we could adjust if we had to. If things don't turn around here and we have to pack it up and leave this place, leave our home, I know we'll be all right."

El heard Emma sniffle and glanced over: tears were running down her face. Emma must've felt El's gaze because she wiped her cheek quickly and refocused on Cam with a frown.

"But let me tell you somethin', folks: after enough time gettin' rolled around by bulls, you get real sick of it. We *can* adjust to anything but that don't mean we should. Y'all being here means a whole lot to us. We love our life, we love our home and we love runnin' this place. So let's see if we can tell that bull to go to hell, and make some Monopoly money! C'mon!"

Cam wrapped his arm around Lucely, and she pulled his face down and gave him a kiss. There were whistles and cheers all around, and suddenly it felt like New Year's Eve, even with the daylight peeking from behind the curtains, all the colored lights and kindled hope making El feel like the first bars of "Auld Lang Syne" were about to begin. She felt a spark in her own heart, a mite of tenderness that was almost too much. It was like swimming into the cold spot of a lake, a shock to the body and a wonder. It made her realize how unfair she had been. Emma had cried, listening to Cam. She did love this family. Her rich, woke whiteness was gross, yeah, but she did care. El thought of the check in her purse and the impact it could really make. She put her hand on Emma's forearm and asked if she could steal her for a second.

Emma looked reluctant. "Uhhh, sure."

They walked into the hallway that led to the bathroom. El opened her purse and took the check out. "So, this is our contribution. Well, actually, it's Bryce's, via me. He didn't know who to make it out to, so just let me know."

She handed the check over. Emma opened it, glanced at it and held it back out. "We don't need this. But thank you."

"What do you mean?"

"Just that. We don't need this. We have big donors here. We're covered."

"It's fifteen thousand dollars that Cam and Lucely won't have otherwise. What am I missing?"

Emma's thin lips scrunched together. "We don't need *his* money."

"This is about Bryce?"

"His family are not good people," pronounced Emma imperiously.

Something feral shot through El's body and into her hands. With one rapid movement she snatched the check back. "I'm giving this to Cam right now."

"No!" Emma said, becoming prostrate. "No, don't. I'll cover it."

"What?"

"I'll cover the fifteen on my own. I promise. I will."

"That's crazy!"

Emma really thought Bryce and his family so abhorrent she was willing to shell out fifteen grand just to be unaffiliated with them? Did she really think herself and her precious donors so pure? These people took planes; they rented SUVs; they justified disposable water bottles from recycled materials, even though, let's be honest, most ended up in landfills anyway. And how many of them had attended the Women's March but watched porn that exploited vulnerable girls? How many had

re-shared PSAs about corrupt institutions on phones manu-
factured by forced labor? How many had objected to malicious
gossip at their child's middle school but read the *New York Post?*
Who, exactly, was a pure person, again? El wanted to shout
this, but Emma would say don't let the perfect be the enemy
of the good. She would say Bryce's family was a different animal. She would say that El *knew* that, she *knew* that.

Fuck it. El was going to speak up anyway, she was going
to let Emma have it—

But someone was at Emma's shoulder, tugging her back to
the main room. Emma withdrew, leaving El hollow and nau-
seated. What had Emma been saying about her lately when she
wasn't around? About her choices, about Bryce? And Navya—
was it not just Bryce that Navya quietly objected to, was it El's
judgment also?

Ahead was the restroom. El shoved the door open and
locked it behind her. The walls were gray and stenciled with
white palm fronds. There were no windows, only a small,
honey-yellow lamp affixed to the wall by the sink. El ran the
water, intending to splash her face, and realized she was still
holding the check. On impulse, she laid the check at the bottom of·the basin. It sank in the middle, curling around the
drain, the water holding it down, strangling it like a neck.

chapter fourteen

Bryce was late. El had put on a textured maxi from Alice + Olivia, one of many recent purchases she'd made with Bryce's black card after he'd noticed a hole in her favorite sweater and insisted she buy herself some new things. The dress swished around her ankles as she paced the living room. *Where is he?* It was the eve of her birthday, and tonight the plan was to meet her mother at John's Pizza on Bleecker. Tomorrow, on her actual birthday, it would be just herself and Bryce. He was being very mysterious about what he had planned.

She tried his phone again, though it had already gone straight to voicemail twice. If she didn't leave right now, she would be late to meet her mother. She double-checked her missed calls to make sure he hadn't tried her: he had not. In fact all of her recent missed calls were from the week prior, and all were from Navya. El had made an Irish exit from the fundraiser, and Navya must have wondered what had happened to her—no doubt Navya had heard by now, though, about the argument with Emma. Eventually El would be ready to have a conversation with Navya, to accept Navya's apology for not defending her against Emma's spiteful judgment. But first El needed to feel her hurt.

She was on the verge of calling Bryce one more time when a text lit her screen: Babe I'm so sorry. I can't get away again. Ian coming down hard. Tell your mom I'm really sorry send me her home address so I can send apology flowers have fun at dinner I'll see you later on. Love you.

She replied with a thumbs-up, relieved now that she didn't have to wait around. Moments later she stepped into the shining summer evening. Taffy-pink light refracted on the windows of surrounding skyscrapers. It occurred to El that thanks to Bryce she was less burdened than she'd ever been. With a certain detachment she observed the evidence of stress and strain all around her: the concentration of a saxophone player on Canal; the exasperation of a father with a toddler melting down; the hostility of a woman with a megaphone, proclaiming the Word of God; the anxiety of a teenager on the fringe of her group, trying to be heard. And there was a sublayer too, of needs more quiet—a sign announcing a closing sale; a bus out of service; countless tacked-up posters of missing dogs.

She arrived at the restaurant right on time, but her mother

was already waiting. She apologized for being late and apologized for Bryce's absence. She promised she would bring him to her mother's birthday dinner the following weekend.

"Well . . ." Her mother sounded unsure. "Let me ask. I doubt Ansel will mind."

El tried to suppress her annoyance. "Why would Ansel mind?"

"He wouldn't. I just said he wouldn't."

El crossed her arms but uncrossed them as soon as she realized her mother had hers folded in the exact same position. Then her mother said, "Didn't you tell me that Bryce wasn't able to come to your friend's fundraiser the other weekend either?"

She *had* told her mother that. Dammit. "Yeah. It's like I said, his boss is intense. It's finance, it's not a nine-to-five."

Her mother gave her a shrewd look.

"What, you think he's lying to me or something?"

"I didn't say that," her mother said, but her expression cleared, as if grateful El had grasped this possibility. "What I would say is that, with a man, if you want to be a priority you have to set that expectation."

The host had taken notice of El's arrival and pointed at her mother. "Still waiting on one more?"

"No," said her mother, holding up her index and middle fingers. "Just two now."

As her mother followed the host inside, El caught sight of the sky. A thinning cluster of pink cloud appeared to be sliding backward, like so many dragging arms, into a vat of purple night coming from the east. With a thrill of despair El realized that by the time dinner finished it would be completely dark, and she would return downtown alone, the streets becoming more and more empty with each successive block as she left the university area behind, and for a moment she wondered if perhaps her mother had it right—that while she had no reason to suspect Bryce of lying to her, perhaps she did expect too little.

She was sitting up in bed reading a strange article about a Labrador who had been leading a pack of wolves through a series of Oregon coastal towns when Bryce finally got in. It was past midnight, and he entered their room looking careworn and miserable.

"I'll be right there. How was dinner?"

"Fine."

He disappeared into the bathroom, and to kill a couple minutes El checked on Crystal's profile. There was nothing to indicate one way or the other whether Crystal was still in L.A. or back in New York.

Bryce returned, stripped off his shirt and slipped into bed. The hair on his chest was patchy, neither thick nor thin: the unfortunate middle ground brought to mind a balding head. She glanced away until he pulled the covers over himself.

"I told my mom you'd come to her birthday thing next weekend, so don't ghost that. Like really."

"I know," Bryce said. "I'm so sorry."

"I don't need sorry, I just need you to show up." She'd spoken in the same biting voice she'd used at the fundraiser when she'd snapped at Nicole, but unlike Nicole, who had been cool and dismissive in her response, Bryce—was she imagining it? Did he seem . . . excited? Was there something perverse, perhaps masochistic, about the gleam in his eye?

"You're right. I'll tell Ian I can't keep doing this. It won't be a problem going forward. I swear."

"Good."

She had no idea what to do now. She felt like she'd summoned some power, some current from the air. Under the covers she spread her palms and fingers wide as if to lay it down, her new weapon.

Bryce, feeling her right hand encroach on his space, reached for her. He stroked her for a minute or so until his eyes widened. "Hang on, it's officially your birthday!"

"God, I'm in my thirties."

"My little sister used to say '*the* thirties.' Like, 'Mum's in *the* thirties.'"

The faint grin on his face faltered, and for a moment he looked lost. This was only the second time he'd ever mentioned his sister. She decided to spare him more unhappy reminiscence and changed the subject.

"So next weekend, *Ansel* will be at dinner at my mom's— she always does a home-cooked thing when he's there for some reason—"

"Tell me more about him."

"Well, his mom, Erica, she was kind of weird, but very nice. She and my mom met at the playground when they were both still married. Ansel and I are like six months apart."

"Erica passed away, right?"

"Yeah. And Ansel's a cop now, which is like so fitting somehow."

"Hm."

"What?"

"Nothing. I was just thinking it must've been awkward sharing a room when you were younger. He likes girls?"

"Yeah. Why?"

"He definitely had a thing for you."

"No. Definitely not. Our enmity was absolutely mutual."

"Trust me, there's nothing like a girl who doesn't know you exist."

She thought she saw real pain in his face then, and remembered about the high school girlfriend, the one who'd left him weeks into his first year at Cambridge. Reaching out, she brushed the hair from his forehead and she ventured, "What was the name of your girlfriend from high school?"

He pinched his lips. "Allegra."

"Did you guys ever have a postmortem? I mean, after you broke up and everything, did she ever explain why she ended it?"

He assumed a kind of stoic scowl.

"It's okay. We don't have to—"

"No," he said. "I forgot I hadn't told you all this." He didn't look at her, but into the shadows of the room. "The year after we split up, you remember—I think I told you—I was playing rugby. I was doing better, anyway, and I thought it was time, you know, that Allegra and I finally had a chat. So I sent her a message asking her to dinner, just friendly. She didn't get back right away, but I know she would've."

Though she didn't know why, El found herself clutching the top sheet with both hands.

"I heard later that Mel, Allegra's flatmate, went looking when she didn't come to class. Allegra was a rower, so she was always down by the river in the mornings. They say she fell. There was this massive gash on her head. They found her body facedown in the water."

"Oh my god."

El relinquished the sheet and wrapped one arm around Bryce, resting her head on his chest. For a long time they lay like that, a soft heat building between them. Eventually she felt Bryce turn, and she looked up. They kissed, and they fucked like they hadn't since the very beginning, with primordial effort, looking past each other with eyes unseeing.

El awoke naked the next morning, alone in the bed. When she reached blindly for her phone on the bedside table, her fingers encountered something bulky. She looked and saw a present in a rectangular package. Her first guess was a book or a journal, but—no, surely, Bryce would have splurged for her birthday. Was it jewelry? She tore the blue wrapping paper with the gold fleur-de-lis pattern and discovered, with an unhappy flop of her stomach, that her gift was, indeed, a book.

The Letters of Abélard and Héloïse, it was called. She read the inscription on the title page:

For my Héloïse
I love you.
Come to the kitchen for part two.

She ran a comb through her hair and brushed her teeth, chiding herself for feeling let down; Bryce had asked her what she wanted, after all, and she had told him to surprise her. But still . . . *breakfast and a book?* She returned to the bedroom to throw on some fresh shorts and a shirt. The sight of the mussed-up sheets made her think of their intense sex the night before and the conversation that had proceeded it. Morbidly curious, she grabbed her phone and searched "Cambridge University Allegra" and "river" and "death." Immediately, several articles populated about an Allegra Taylor. It was just as Bryce had described, a freak accident, "*. . . the University mourns a student who brought excellence to everything she set out to do . . .*" and so on. El closed the tab, feeling like a real asshole for not appreciating her boyfriend, who had already suffered so much but still found it in him to love and to wake her with thoughtful birthday presents.

When she stepped into the kitchen, Bryce was sipping a coffee. The long counter was bare except for El's favorite stoneware mug. Maybe they'd be ordering breakfast?

"I love the book," she said emphatically.

"Liar." He laughed.

"I really do!"

He gestured to the mug. Folded beneath it lay a piece of paper she had not noticed initially. She walked over and slipped the paper out: it was a confirmation for two roundtrip, first-class seats, New York to Paris.

"We leave at six," he said. "You said on our first date you wanted to go."

He was watching her closely, but she couldn't find the words. How could he, with all the mobility his wealth afforded, ever really understand what a huge deal this was? The idea of leaving the country . . . of going to *Paris*.

"Abélard and Héloïse are buried there," he said tentatively. "Hence the book . . ."

She cleared the frog from her throat. "A vacation to a graveyard, wow." And then—she smiled. He beamed in return, assured at last that she was pleased.

Of course, there remained one fact Bryce had neglected to consider: that El was more or less disposable at her job, and that leaving for five days without notice, especially given her lax attitude of late, presented decent grounds for getting fired. He felt horrible when El explained.

"I'm an idiot. We can just go in the fall. It's nicer then anyway."

"You're probably right, but, I don't know. Give me like an hour to think before you start changing tickets."

While he showered she sat in the living room drinking an Americano from her mug, scrolling her feed. She came across a picture of Navya that Van had posted. They were at karaoke, and Navya looked happy in a sheer-ish turquoise dress; Van had drawn a cartoon crown atop her head. With a gasp, El realized she had forgotten Navya's birthday. *That's why Navya was calling me.*

"Oh fuck me," she said aloud. She dialed Navya immediately, her anxiety heavy in her chest.

On what had to be the last ring, Navya answered in a flat voice: "Happy birthday."

"I'm so sorry," El gushed. "I'm so so sorry. I had no idea— I didn't remember about your birthday. I was just so angry about the thing with Emma, and I thought you were calling about that so I blew you off and now I missed your party. I suck, I'm sorry."

A moment of uncertain silence passed, then Navya breathed into the phone. "But it's not about my birthday, you know? Like, where are you? You're barely in my life."

"I'm here," El insisted, and she felt tears building.

"You just let this guy in, now he's like your whole identity."

El hesitated, trying to figure out what to say. "Nav, I'm—"

"I just," Navya interrupted, "I don't wanna talk to you now is the thing."

And then she was gone. El sat stunned. The distant sound of traffic seemed to amplify in the quiet, and El's feet, tucked beneath her, began to feel sore. She had waded into a tacky pool of guilt and could not extricate herself. Then she remembered that a camera was watching her. She saw herself through the camera's eye, sitting stock-still; she saw the glass coffee table and the thick blue rug, the shelf with all her stupid plays and the red photo album, the melding of her life and Bryce's—which she was entitled to, wasn't she? That was what this was about. Navya had admitted as much. It wasn't that El had forgotten Navya's birthday: it was that El had progressed to a new chapter. And maybe a small part of Navya felt baffled by this, because El had always been slightly less together than Navya. Maybe it felt unfair to Navya that her intimacy-challenged friend had moved forward first.

"Fair only comes around once a year," El murmured. She found that she could move again. She stood and walked to the en suite bathroom, resolve building in her mind. Bryce was just turning off the shower when she entered.

"Hey, so I want to go."

He opened the glass door of the shower and steam billowed out behind him. "Today? You wanna go?"

"Yeah."

"What about work?"

"I'm gonna quit."

He let out a whooping laugh she'd never heard before. His body shone pink and raw. He began drying himself brutally.

"I'll look for a new job when I'm back," she added. "I still have loans to pay." But before she'd even finished her sentence he began shaking his head.

"I'll take care of it! And you don't have to work if you don't want to. You can do whatever you want."

To her surprise, no prideful impulse inside her objected to this offer. It wasn't wholly unexpected. While Bryce had never said explicitly that he'd take on her debt, he'd said similar things. It felt sort of natural to accept his generosity. And she didn't have a trace of fretful existential apprehension, either, about what she would do with her new freedom. She had no desire to start auditioning again, no legitimate interest in grad school; she had no interest in anything, really, besides packing her bag for Paris.

She was glad to have bought so many new clothes, because the weather in Paris looked variable—some days sunny, some cool with a chance of rain. She tucked everything she could think of in one of Bryce's Mulberry suitcases with the bands of soft cognac leather across the front pockets, including her never-used passport that she'd had since she had *almost* gone to London eight years ago. Thank god it was still valid.

By 3:15 p.m. she had showered and dressed in comfortable black sweats. The doorman had a cab waiting when they came down with their bags, and the driver snatched El's from her and set it quickly in the trunk like contraband. He did the same with Bryce's (much lighter) bag and a moment later they were hurtling east through a yellow light. With a start El realized that she'd better tell her mother she'd be out of contact for five days. She labored for a couple minutes over the text, in which she assured her mother that they would be back in time for her birthday celebration the following Sunday.

Never having flown internationally El had no barometer, but according to Bryce the crowd and confusion at JFK was standard fare. She accidentally cut a horrendously long line for luggage drop-off and got yelled at by several people near the front, who were even more outraged when the person who'd taken El's luggage took Bryce's as well, because they were together. El apologized but felt no remorse, really. The world would fall apart by inches if people stopped pretending to care about doing the right thing, but as to actually doing it, or trying to . . . She was beginning to lose the thread of why that mattered at all.

She hadn't forgotten about quitting the bakery. It had been on her mind all afternoon, in fact, but she was in no great hurry; she was savoring the notion of quitting in the slightly sadistic way one savors a noxious smell, like wood polish or gasoline. Only when the plane had taken its place in line for takeoff did El actually type the text to Darcy, which she sent with no embellishments or apologies: I quit. She'd considered *I fucking quit*, but, in the end, brevity told the story best. The story being that she absolutely could not care less about the position she was putting Darcy in by leaving so abruptly.

The plane drew forward, picking up speed, and El felt herself slip a little further into her detachment. She reclined in her roomy seat with her complimentary champagne. She pulled her eye mask on, and Bryce's milky features disappeared.

For about a month in college, El had taken a prescription-strength cough medicine to treat a bad case of mono. That medicine had taken her down fast, every time—down literally, down into her twin bed, down into herself, into the heartbeat that had always seemed neutral before but the medicine had allowed her to understand that its even song was for her alone.

And there on the seafloor El had idled for hours, cheek to cheek with her truest purpose: her own survival.

Here on the plane she was distilling again, as she had on the medicine. She exhaled, inhaled. The pumping of her breath reminded her that she was her own instrument, capable and powerful. After all here she was, headed for Europe, a long way from the stagnant landscape that had been her life two months ago. She was going. She was going.

chapter fifteen

The sky had draped the city in buoyant blue. So far Paris made a most cheerful alternative to New York.

El and Bryce had spent several minutes taking the requisite pictures of the gray, pillared monument over the tombs of Abélard and Héloïse. A chest-high black fence guarded the monument from trespassers, so El had to squint to read the writing engraved on the stone:

LES RESTES

D'HELOISE ET D'ABELARD

SONT REUNIS DANS CE TOMBEAU.

Bryce folded the cemetery map in his hands and leaned forward to translate. "The remains of Héloïse and Abélard are reunited in this tomb."

The tombs themselves were carved with recumbent effigies

of the lovers. On the plane El had skimmed the introduction to the Héloïse and Abélard book Bryce had bought her, and she'd learned about a component of this illicit love story she'd never known: pre-castration, Abélard had been cooling on Héloïse, his visits to her becoming less and less frequent. He'd impregnated her, married her, then their son, once born, had been sent to live with relatives, and Abélard had stuck Héloïse in a convent, ostensibly for her protection. He'd kept his distance; she'd pined. God, men were predictable. All the mythologizing about this romance and it came down to what? Man becomes enthralled by woman, promptly seeks to tame and control her.

"Do you want to see Jim Morrison's grave while we're here? Fairly certain he's the main draw."

El pulled her sunglasses off her head and back onto her eyes. "He was a jerk, wasn't he? Let's skip it."

On their way out El overheard an English-language tour guide saying that some scholars believed the tomb contained Abélard's remains alone—that Héloïse had been moved over the centuries and her bones were likely lost to time. As she and Bryce approached the exit, El dwelled on this. All Héloïse went through in life and now she'd been *lost*? The least someone could expect from death was to be found.

Once they were back on the busy avenue, securely in the land of the living, El's thoughts turned to lunch. The concierge had recommended a crepe place in the Marais, so Bryce hailed them a taxi. As they climbed in, their driver made no effort to turn down the radio.

"Bonjour," Bryce said, raising his voice above the music. "Rue Vieille du Temple, s'il vous plaît."

The driver nodded. Bryce turned to El, alight with excitement. He'd been like this since their plane had touched down that morning. When El had seen the opulent suite at their hotel she'd been tempted to lounge awhile, maybe take a shower, try on one of the velour bathrobes, but Bryce had been keen to get going. He seemed to enjoy playing tour guide.

"Today I just want you to get a sense of the city. Tomorrow we can do Versailles, and maybe Wednesday the Marché aux Puces. Both are a bit of a trek. On Thursday—well, we have to do Montmartre. And Friday we can tackle the Louvre. It's the best district for shopping over there, though the Marais's full of great shops as well."

Their driver wove quickly through traffic, and El rolled down her window, carsick. She kept her face angled toward the street and the breeze blowing her hair behind her shoulder.

"I know we'll both be jet-lagged," Bryce continued, "but we have to try for a good night's rest tonight. There's loads to see at Versailles. When you get out there you'll understand. It's worth it to show up early."

El was just about to tell Bryce that she believed him when her gaze landed on a petite woman with a chic white purse and dark brown hair exiting a patisserie.

"Oh my god!"

"What's wrong?"

"No, nothing, I just saw someone who looks *so* much like Anna. That's in*sane*, I totally forgot that she lives here. I don't know how. I guess just the surprise—" Fingers trembling with anticipation, she fished in her purse for her phone. She had thought, just recently, that she might never see Anna again, that Anna had passed beyond her reach, but that was ridiculous! Then she remembered: she wasn't the only one with a connection to Anna. "I think you know Anna too," she told Bryce.

Bryce looked somewhat discomposed.

"You guys went to the same camp," El explained. Then, with a coy smile: "I may have stalked you a little before our first date."

"Camp . . . Lowile Bay, you mean?"

"Yeah. Anna Wallenhaver? Dark hair, my color? Tiny? She was actually voted hottest girl in my eighth-grade class."

"What school was this?"

"Eastboro Grammar."

"I thought you went to public school."

"I did, except for eighth grade, when we first moved to New York. Where'd you think I met Julia? But wait—you knew Julia from Lowile Bay too, didn't you? That's why you were at her party."

"What party?"

"In the Hamptons, where you found my license!"

"Ohhh—no, actually, I didn't even know whose party that was. A friend brought me along."

"So you didn't know Julia or Anna at Lowile Bay?"

He shrugged. "If I did, I didn't know their names."

"That's so weird. Although I guess it makes sense, you and Julia weren't friends online. I just assumed."

"But wait, hang on, I have a question. Who decided this Anna girl was hotter than you?"

"The boys. But Anna's boyfriend was kind of their ringleader and she had him by the balls, so."

"Well, there you go."

"Yup."

"Stop the steal!"

El laughed. She looked at her phone, where Anna's contact was pulled up. There was the number Julia had shared back in May and an address too.

Bryce leaned over and peeked at El's screen. "Latin Quarter. She's not so far from the hotel. Few miles. If you want to see her that's all right, I'll amuse myself for a bit."

But she heard that dejected note in his voice and knew he didn't mean it.

"Really," he said.

She clicked her screen off. "We have all week. Maybe I'll call her tomorrow, or maybe not. I don't know. We'll see." It was occurring to El that, actually, seeing Anna wasn't so pressing. The excitement of a minute ago was already fading. Ever since she had learned that Anna had left New York, El had been pining for her long-lost friend, mourning the advent of the newly concretized distance that had always existed between them. But now El didn't have to pine; there were days ahead on this trip, days on future trips. Space wasn't the only commodity the rich had a monopoly on, El thought. They also had time. And now, thanks to Bryce, so did she.

That night, as they dressed for dinner, El put on the Louboutin pumps Bryce had bought her that afternoon.

"They're stiff," she observed. "But I guess you just wear them in."

"Don't worry, you won't be walking far."

The restaurant, it turned out, was in the hotel. The wide, high-ceilinged room was bridal in its beauty, white and gold. The wine Bryce chose was nectar-light and their waiter had to circle back several times to refill El's glass. Soon El found herself smiling stupidly at the other guests. She and Bryce talked a little of Anna and Julia over dinner. Bryce was intrigued to know about the brief Eastboro Grammar and East Hampton chapter of El's life. She told him all about her outsized sense of her own lack, having worn secondhand clothes around the sons and daughters of Wall Street, about Julia's perpetual search for meaning, about Anna's salient wit. El sketched quickly what she called "the ballad of Anna and Shay," too: perhaps because he was drunk, Bryce laughed when El called Anna "kind of a ruthless bitch."

After dinner, in the lobby, Bryce suggested they visit a bar he used to know.

The dark confusion presented a shock after the bright elegance of the restaurant. Bryce ordered something with elderflower liqueur that came in a delicate glass and El had one, two of these, then several shots of tequila with the bartender, whose drawn eyebrows were like black snakes, then a third elderflower thing, which Bryce sipped before handing over. El hadn't been this drunk in a long time. She stumbled to the bathroom and looked lustily at her reflection. She had always felt possessed by heady power when she was near to blacking out.

Back in the bar, she found Bryce in the throng and kissed him with tongue. He was always probing her to do this more when they had sex, but it disgusted her, both the sensation and his desperation. She only did it now as an act of self-harm, mashing and gnawing the person she was normally, the voiceless person who opened and shut her lips, guppy-like, to prevent being wetly speared rather than simply saying, *stop it, I don't like it when you kiss me like that.*

Bryce broke away from her and said it was probably time to leave.

Chump, she thought as he moved away to settle the bill.

She wanted to mash her mouth on every single person in this bar. She wanted to drown the world. She imagined a tidal wave rising before Julia's house in the Hamptons and burying it and she could live in there, under all that pressure—pressure was air to her! I mean here she was, playing house with this man she hardly even liked. And that was the truth: what a relief to acknowledge it openly, if only to herself. Bryce amounted to a vessel, a means. *I'm on the inside now*, she thought, looking through the bar's windows to the busy street, to the many who passed like a river, to the sharp white dagger moon hanging above them all. *Inside, inside, inside.*

She woke in the dark predawn in a cold sweat. Her belly prick-led. She remembered having thrown up when they'd returned to the room. She remembered having stared in the mirror at the bar and her raw loathing of Bryce, which softened now beneath her need of a stabilizing force: she was really not well. Dangerously hungover. She needed Advil.

She felt with her left hand toward the side of the bed where Bryce was sleeping.

"Hey," she croaked.

But he said nothing, and so she rolled over fully to see—

He wasn't there.

Then she heard the whistle of the shower. She moaned and slipped from the bed, dragging herself to the bathroom. The lights had been dimmed, but she could make out his under-wear on the floor. Through the shower glass she saw him scrubbing his face and hair.

"Hey," she said, trying to make herself heard over the wa-ter. Her throat burned.

"Hey, did I wake you up?"

"No. Maybe. I woke up right before you got the shower on. Ugh." She sat on the toilet. "I feel like fucking shit."

He didn't respond. She watched him lather his arms and chest.

"Is that helping?"

"A little," he said. "I threw up too. I had to throw out my shirt."

She pressed her hands hard over her eyes until she was falling through a sea of black. "You don't have Advil, do you?"

"I'll get you some in the lobby. I don't think I can sleep anymore anyway."

She exhaled and forced out a sour pee. She gulped water from the faucet and lay back in bed. At some point Bryce woke her with Advil and she slept again, dreaming of an apocalypse in London. Anna was being held hostage at a bar run by neo-Nazis who were somehow responsible for the volatile weather, the storms and eruptions, and Anna was gentler and sweeter than El had ever known her to be and to save her El had to take a machete to the bar's boarded-up exterior and a man with a thatched haircut came up to El and started telling jokes—El was laughing and then the man said, "I learned all these from Shay," and then the man was Bryce and a helicopter was flying overhead and Anna's face was pressed to the window, looking down.

chapter sixteen

They stuck to Bryce's itinerary and went to Versailles, hangovers be damned, though they didn't get the early start Bryce had hoped for. He'd been so insistent yesterday afternoon about getting a good night's sleep so they could enjoy the palace—no doubt the wine at dinner had driven the resolve from his mind.

Versailles was bigger than El could have imagined, and they did miss some things; still, she thought she got the gist. The white marble, the galleries of painted wood, the glorious breadth of it all: the vaulted ceiling of the Royal Chapel, the stretching, symmetrical gardens which made you feel exposed. El wondered whether that effect had been intentional—whether you were supposed to feel the sun, the proverbial royal eye, upon you at all times. In the Hall of Mirrors, taking in the surfeit of gold, she thought irrepressibly of Shay and his description of the new-money wedding gigs he had once played. Bryce was quiet as they strolled down the wide hall, holding his hands together behind his back, his posture unusually straight and aristocratic. This made her consider his Englishness in a way she usually didn't, and had the pounding in her skull been any less persistent she might've asked him whether, as a boy in his mother's house, jokes had been made at the expense of the French, and whether he felt connected to a different part of himself being in Europe. But she didn't ask, and he offered nothing, and when the time came to return to the city, they'd exchanged little other than pleasantries. Dinner was a mellow affair at a nice place near the hotel where El's onion soup came with delicious browned slices of baguette. After a few bites El began to feel human again, the energy to converse returning.

"Mm," she said, dabbing soup from her lower lip. "A few years ago I could've had a night like last night and been completely fine by brunch the next morning. Now almost twenty-four hours?" She glanced at Bryce's plate. He had cut his steak but barely eaten any of it. "What's wrong?"

"It's very red. Even for me." He held up a piece for her to inspect.

"Bloodbath," she pronounced.

He lowered his fork, looking ill.

"You okay?"

"I just haven't bounced back yet."

Later, when they were nearly asleep, he rolled over and

caressed her abdomen. Without opening her eyes she moved his hand into her underwear. She lay still while he fingered her with increasing urgency. His elbow bumped into the side of her rib cage, his pointer finger jerked erratically, his slack mouth skittered across her neck. Animosity sizzled between them, she resenting his terrible work, he resenting her passive free hand beside his penis on the sheets. She felt no pity for him. She felt no pity for anyone. She came with a sincere gasp.

In the morning El woke feeling more energized, having adjusted a bit to the time difference. She suggested a leisurely breakfast at a café, a bit of do-as-the-Romans-do. It was the kind of Parisian day she had come to expect from years of media consumption, gray and mysterious. After the café they took a taxi to the Marché aux Puces, which was, Bryce told her, the largest flea market in Europe. It was like no flea market El had ever seen. There were *thousands* of vendors—high-end shops full of antiques, jewelry and furniture and art, stall after stall of knockoff purses and sneakers. Some parts of the market were covered, others open. Bryce wanted to pay for a VIP tour so they would hit all the best spots: El vetoed this, but she did allow Bryce to buy them some vintage prints to have framed for the apartment. The seller was a man with actual gray hairs coming out of his ears. He seemed to like El, and when she stifled a yawn he made her and Bryce two espressos. After four hours of shopping, Bryce convinced El to let him take her for a late tea at a private men's club in the neighborhood of their hotel. The main branch of the club was in London. Seven generations of Ripley men (his mother's line) had been members.

Bryce explained this with as much enthusiasm as he could muster. He seemed very worn-out still, as evidenced by the purplish bags beneath his eyes.

When they stepped into the private club, El's first thought was that she wished they had stopped by the hotel to change. She was wearing a midi skirt and a tailored shirt from Bergdorf's but still felt schlubby beside the other women with their pearls and tidy updos. The dining room had rich, wood-paneled walls, deep blue velvet accents and an ominous Gothic mural on the ceiling that reminded El of the tapestries at the Cloisters. She tried to look natural fixing her tea and selecting from the array of finger sandwiches on the delicate silver tray the waiter had placed between herself and Bryce.

"Do you miss this?" she asked eventually.

"The club?"

"Well, not specifically the club. I was just thinking of your life in England, all your friends."

He shrugged.

"You never really talk about your college friends," she pressed. "The rugby guys and stuff."

"Most of them are married now."

Maybe he's not really a friend kind of guy, she thought. *Remember what he said about his girlfriend from high school? That she'd been his best friend too.* It occurred to El that she held that same significance for Bryce. She was his everything. She squirmed on the velvet cushion of her chair.

They crashed hard that night, and after a sumptuous breakfast (El insisted on eating outside, though it was another cool, overcast day), they made their way to Montmartre, where they explored a house-turned-museum in which, a hundred and fifty years ago, Renoir and other artists had lived and worked. Bryce was in good spirits. Fortified by a solid night's sleep, he seemed to have shaken off the cobwebs at last, though he'd made El swear not to let him drink with such abandon in the future.

El spent most of her time at the museum wandering the spare, contemplative garden out back, and she was surprised to spy a private vineyard on an adjoining property. Seeing the vineyard made her appreciate, really for the first time, that she was in a foreign place. Everything else she'd seen on the trip she'd been expecting, thanks to Bryce. But there were surprises throughout this city—throughout the whole world!

Bryce found her in the garden after he'd had his fill of the museum, and he smiled to see her so contented.

"Let's cancel our reservation," she proposed.

"Lunch?"

"Let's be spontaneous. Let's just go and find someplace."

She saw that he wanted to object and took his hand. He stroked the thin skin below her knuckles and nodded his assent.

They'd gone just five blocks before they spotted a busy bistro up a side street that, according to a quick search, was well known for its chicken. Neither of them felt at all strange about sharing a bottle of wine; with the sky so dark, it felt like evening anyway. After their meal they resumed their walk and were just passing a newsagent when El spotted something incomprehensible: Anna's face on the cover of a tabloid paper.

She was hardly aware of Bryce as she pulled coins from her wallet and pushed them into the palm of the man who handed the paper over. She scanned the article and her fear slipped from her like a rope and fell, coiling, when she saw the photo below the fold: a tiny body on a stretcher, covered in a sheet, outside a stone apartment building.

Wordlessly El handed the paper to Bryce. In a shaking voice he read her excerpts using the Translate app on his phone. The victim, Anna Wallenhaver, was an heiress from New York . . . She had been attacked and then placed in her bathtub . . . A crime of passion, though no sign of sexual violence . . . A business owner had recently reported a man for screaming vulgarities at another young woman on the same street where Anna lived. Police said they would pursue this and every lead.

"When did it happen?" El asked, and though she felt that she'd put all her strength into articulating the question, she heard it come out as a whisper. She began to shiver.

"'Police suspect the murder occurred late on Monday night . . . possibly early Tuesday morning,'" Bryce read. She felt him watching her, but she could not meet his eye. Bitter grief welled in her chest. On Monday, she had chosen not to call Anna. And that night, possibly during the murder itself, Anna had visited her dream, desperate for her help.

chapter seventeen

Bryce mumbled that it was just morbid, but they had an entire day before them, their last day, and El could not imagine promenading around when there was a place within walking distance, an actual place where her friend had been killed. The finality of the murder was staggering. She had flicked through the channels on the hotel TV the night before and the story was being covered everywhere, Anna's name being mentioned alongside those of other wealthy female victims, Frenchwomen El had never heard of. Several of these infamous cases were unsolved, and El had wondered whether Anna's murder would go unsolved too. She'd fallen asleep with her mind in a haze, having feverishly read the English-language closed captioning on the bottom of the screen hour after hour. Bryce had not taken part in this obsessive consumption of the murder coverage. He'd put on his noise-canceling headphones and had read through his out-of-office inbox. El hadn't held this against him—the coverage had been redundant and upsetting—but she had taken comfort in watching the aging anchor with the honey eyes run through everything known and everything suspected about the circumstances of Anna's death. It had soothed her to listen to the anchor's urgency and anxiety, even if it had been a performance for the cameras. It had made her feel less alone.

That was the other thing: she was feeling again. It was as if the murder had roused all her nerve endings. She found herself grounded once more, no longer floating above her life. The summer up till now seemed like a dream. She'd woken to find herself isolated, unemployed and full of fear because if Anna could die, anyone could die. Certainly she, El, could die.

It was raining, a slow, gathering August rain. She and Bryce jumped in a taxi outside the hotel and she gave their English-speaking driver the address of Anna's building. Bryce did not attempt to hide his continued disapproval of this plan to visit the murder site. El ignored him the whole ride and instead stared out her window. In her renewed state of sensitivity she found the dripping city remote and solemn—tall institutions of white stone, imposing Roman columns, golden statues flanking bridges—all this under a powdered sky, and the people of Paris biked and zoomed past in their small, stylish cars and no one had a face that she could see. Even their taxi driver was leaning in such a way that she could make out only the dark bristly hair of his beard. She felt, like a punch, a moment's wild attraction to him, imagined him going down on her and the meat of his beard against her thighs, unpleasant but necessary. They were getting close to Anna's building now—El was tracking their progress on her phone—and she didn't know what to think anymore, where to live, who to fuck, what to do—every window on every street contained a different life—was anyone making choices, or were they just shuttled from one year to the next, buffeted by circumstance? Anna had never allowed herself to be bullied by life . . . Or perhaps this indestructible image of Anna was vestigial, adolescent imagining, because Anna's beauty and money and backbone hadn't protected her in the end, had they?

They were now just minutes away, and El could feel the change of neighborhood. Of arrondissement—Bryce had explained that Paris was divided into districts. Whichever one they were in now, it reminded her of Greenwich Village. The taxi turned off a wide boulevard and climbed a narrow street, passing galleries and bookstores and cafés. This was the area close to the Sorbonne. Had Anna been taking classes? Had she just liked the collegiate atmosphere? *Why* had Anna come here? Anna had never been an adventuresome person. Of course she had traveled . . . Lake Como, El remembered that Anna had gone there with her family in high school . . . Then there had been Biarritz, Marrakesh, the Seychelles, Bali—there'd been pictures of each on Anna's grid before she'd deleted her social media. How many times had El scrolled through those pictures? But there hadn't been much to see. It was always just Anna posing, close-lipped, green eyes challenging the camera, the background out of focus. (The assumption being, perhaps, that her audience already knew the landscape?) Anna had traveled because that was what people in her circle did, not because she was a risk-taker. And while it could certainly be argued that Paris was a requisite vacation spot for an Upper East Sider, to move here permanently was another matter. And why had she changed her number? It wasn't even a Parisian number, but a different New York number, as though she'd changed it right before she'd left.

The taxi stopped fifty yards from Anna's building: a news van was taking up most of the space on the road ahead. Bryce paid the driver and, as they stepped out, let out a black umbrella the concierge had given them. The name of the hotel was written in cursive on the umbrella's wing, and El wished it weren't. They walked, forearms brushing, toward the building, their view hindered by the umbrella. When they got close El was surprised not to see reporters or police. Maybe they were inside? She approached the building's tall green double doors. Both had brass doorknobs smack in the center. It was disorienting. Which to pull?

"We're actually going in?" Bryce asked.

El wrapped her hand around one of the brass knobs and yanked, half expecting nothing to happen. But to her surprise, the door gave way. She glanced back at Bryce.

"Guess we are."

He followed her inside. The lobby branched out right and left, though straight ahead was a courtyard full of staid little trees with white blossoms. A doorman came stalking over from the elevator bay and asked a question in rapid French. El turned to Bryce.

"Tell him we're visitors. We're meeting somebody in the courtyard."

Bryce relayed this to the doorman with a slight air of exasperation. El thought this exasperated affect, if intentional, smart—*we men understand French, and we also understand that this woman I'm with is annoying.* The doorman gave the impression of an older man, though he couldn't have been more than forty: he had the slightly dried-out look of someone ill or drinking habitually. He waved them along, and El and Bryce stepped quickly toward the courtyard, which was surrounded by apartments on all sides. Bryce looked at her, and now she could see his exasperation had not been an act.

"What now?" he asked.

Rain smacked the umbrella. Apart from the doorman they were quite alone. It was as if the building had been evacuated. Why had Anna lived in an old place like this? Why couldn't she have lived in some tacky modern condominium with heavy security? The emptiness was so huge, the emptiness of the world without Anna. It expanded like a gas from the pebbles underfoot up to the mournful sky. Where was Anna's body now? When would she be flown back to America? She'd been found in a bathtub . . . El tried to picture Anna bloated and blue, and became conscious that she was shaking her head no.

"Do you think—" She tried to find her voice but tears seemed to be stuck in her throat. "Will the funeral be private, do you think?"

"I don't know. I expect so," Bryce said. He looked all the more miserable at the sound of her broken voice, and he made a pitying sound out the side of his mouth, as if coming to an unfortunate conclusion. "Look, I know you feel responsible for this, but you've got to think it through. Even if you had called Anna the other day and you'd got together—it's terrible to think about, but all I'm saying is, whoever killed Anna probably killed her for a reason. Getting a coffee wasn't going to change anything. You weren't going to save her."

"You don't know that," El answered, her voice rising. "We don't know why she was killed. Maybe she knew she was in danger, maybe she would've confided in me." Then El had a thought so chilling her entire body tensed. "Oh my god— maybe this is why she left New York."

Bryce seemed worried at her sudden change in tone. "What do you mean?"

"If someone was after her . . ." She couldn't think clearly.

"If Anna thought someone was after her, why would she have stayed in her apartment by herself? I'm sure she knew people in Paris. And it certainly sounds like she had the means to go to a hotel."

El considered this: it was all perfectly true. She had briefly imagined that maybe Anna had been witness to some high-level white-collar crime and had become a liability, but wasn't it more likely that she'd been targeted by a random sicko because she was—because she had been—young and beautiful? Also the manner of the crime didn't really fit, if it had been a hit. Anna hadn't been shot, and there had been that strange thing about her body having been placed in the bath. On the morning news they'd had on a criminologist who'd pointed to this feature of the murder. The crime had obviously been one of opportunity, the criminologist had said, hence the blows to the back of the young lady's head. Placing her corpse in the bath had not served any material purpose; it signified the fulfillment of a ritual, the killer's process of making the murder understandable.

"Understandable?" the French anchor had challenged, outraged.

"Understandable to the killer. In keeping with the killer's own internal logic," the criminologist had replied.

They could have snuck around the building looking for Anna's apartment, but they didn't. No doubt it would be roped off, and, as Bryce pointed out, there was a chance, albeit a small one, that a detective would be in the apartment and would be keen to question El because she had known the victim. This would have been fine with El, except that she didn't have any helpful information to offer. She didn't know a thing about Anna's life in Paris.

By silent agreement, they skipped lunch. They just walked. Even though El's calves were tight she said nothing, and after about an hour they found themselves at the entrance of the Jardin des Plantes. The rain had grown gentle and El stepped out from under the umbrella, which Bryce then shook out and tied up. They made their way down a path into the vast botanical garden, passing the occasional couple walking a dog. Everything was in bloom. Green, green, green. There were rows of manicured hedges, trellises for climbing roses. All the competing scents would be heaven for a dog, though the view would be pretty unremarkable: El remembered learning, as a child, that dogs were dichromatic. They saw blues and yellows. No green. No red at all.

"I haven't been here in a long time," Bryce reflected. "Not since I was really young."

The green cast a fantastic glow on his pale face, and El was strangely reminded of how her father had appeared during their excursions in the woods of West Virginia, like a martyr who took pride in his burden, took pleasure in his terrible pain.

chapter eighteen

El fought sleep on the flight back to New York. Her dreams since the murder had been plagued by broken visions of Anna, sweet-tempered and afraid, being carried away by aircraft, by tide, by car. Bryce was sleeping okay, but El thought Anna's murder may have triggered him, too, on some unconscious level, because once or twice she'd heard him murmur the name of his dead sister, Brooke, while he dreamed.

They landed in the evening and, too grumpy to wait for a rideshare, grabbed a taxi that deposited them in front of their building at 8:30 p.m. Coming back to the Financial District apartment was not at all like coming home. El hadn't quite got used to the smell of the place, the powerful mixture of lavender and lime. She thought it must be residue from something Bogna sprayed after she cleaned.

Bryce ordered Vietnamese and they ate listlessly, absorbed

in their own phones. At midnight El took a hot shower before joining Bryce in bed. Despite having slept for a chunk of the day on the plane, he was already nodding off. El had to coach herself into closing her eyes, too (*you'll have to sleep sometime*). The nightmare seemed to come on instantly. She was in Julia's Hamptons house, in the guest room she had always slept in. It was late, the moon high. With a prickling sense of wrong, she crept out of her room and down the stairs. She tiptoed across the landing to the kitchen and saw, out the window, two dark shapes by the pool. *Anna and Shay*—it had to be. But El wasn't a teenager anymore. She wouldn't hide in the kitchen. She charged out the kitchen door, sprinted to the pool—

By the time she got close enough to see what was happening, she knew she'd made a horrible mistake. There was a dead man facedown on the pool chair. No, he was in the pool, floating. *Placed in the water*, she thought. The man looked like a stranger, but really he was someone she knew, maybe Shay or Bryce or Tom or her own father, and over the man stood his killer, a huge, furious dog with Anna's green eyes, and El knew she would not have time to run—

She woke early the following morning, thoroughly jet-lagged. God, how was it Sunday already? When she came into the kitchen, Bryce was reading through his e-mail and scraping the dregs from a container of Greek yogurt. El did not feel hungry at all. She felt gloomy and anxious.

"I'm gonna go for a jog," she said.

Bryce frowned. "It's hot already. It's like ninety-five degrees."

"I feel like I need it."

When she reached the foyer, he called out, "You have your phone?"

"Yeah."

She did have it. It was in her hand. But she looked to her right, to the long table where they kept their keys, and had the funniest impulse. As she stepped out of the apartment, the door swinging closed behind her, she glanced back at the table to the phone she had left behind.

She returned from her jog forty minutes later, red-cheeked, drenched in sweat, and found Bryce wearing the augmented reality glasses he'd been waiting on for weeks. By way of greeting she picked up his empty yogurt container, washed it out and dropped it in the recycling. She ignored Bryce when he complained about the glasses being a bit buggy and slow, and thought instead about her little deception with her phone. A thrill shot through her body.

The rest of the day she spent unpacking her Paris suitcase and watching a new dark comedy. The star was some ex-YouTuber she had never heard of. Soon, too soon, it was time to get ready for her mother's birthday dinner. She was tired, and she was *not* looking forward to an evening in Ansel's company, though maybe his presence would divert the conversation and she wouldn't have to say too much about Paris. She didn't have the energy to discuss Anna's death. Her mother had never taken the time to know Anna or Julia, not that El had gone out of her way to make introductions. Anna had met her mother just once, and El had been embarrassed by her mother's unstylish clothes, her lack of polish, her air of exhaustion. She had worried Anna would appraise her mother and assume that was how she, El, would turn out. She had worried Anna wouldn't be able to see it—the world-class actress she would become, how she would bring her mother to the Oscars and her mother would wear a black Versace dress and the red-carpet journalists would applaud her mother, recontextualize her for the world—her mother's exhaustion, her lack of polish, had all been to place her daughter within reach of the brass ring, and what a good gamble that had turned out to be! El had never really believed Anna capable of looking at her mother with this foresight . . . But who knew? What depths, what dimensions of Anna had El never glimpsed or even considered?

El was so lost in thought she didn't register at first that Bryce was speaking. She had just walked into the bathroom where Bryce was puffing up his hair with product.

"I'm sorry," she said. "Start over. What'd you say?"

She pulled mascara from her make-up bag and leaned toward the mirror.

"I just said, have you heard from your friend Julia at all?"

She blinked, and the feathers of the mascara brush grazed her eye. She winced.

"You okay?"

"Yeah." She dabbed away involuntary tears and reached for

a Q-tip. "No, I haven't talked to Julia. She's out of the country. Why?"

"Oh. I just—I was thinking you might have talked to her about Anna."

El had a sigh in her chest, but she held it in. She had the Q-tip to her eye. She stayed still and said, without moving her mouth very much, "I don't know when Julia's back . . . maybe in a couple weeks. She's at a retreat so I can't reach her."

"Was she close to Anna? As close as you?"

"Closer." El threw the Q-tip in the trash. "Although Julia did say they hadn't been that good of friends for a while."

"That's sad."

"Like she had no idea why Anna moved to Paris."

"Other than it being Paris, you mean?"

"You didn't know Anna. She was a New Yorker."

"Loads of people from New York move abroad."

"Please stop talking."

She'd said it through her teeth. Bryce looked stunned, but, no, she would not apologize. He had provoked her. She carried on doing her make-up. After a minute or so, Bryce heeded her and exited the bathroom in silence.

Half an hour later they were in a cab speeding up the West Side Highway past the glowing eyes of a hundred thousand apartments. The air in the car was stale and close, so El cracked her window a half-inch. Hot wind roared by, deafening static in her ear.

Bryce had been looking out his own window, but now he

turned toward her. Would he bring it up? she wondered. Would he tell her she couldn't speak to him the way she had?

"So what should I call your mum?" he asked.

She faced him. "Deb is good. When do I meet your mom, anyway? Your mum."

"We'll go see her sometime."

"She never comes here?"

"No. Not big on the city."

"Well, I'm down to go to England."

"Mum's in the Hamptons."

He said it like it was the most obvious thing. But hadn't he *told* her England? Or no, maybe she'd simply inferred that . . .

"Where in the Hamptons?" she asked. "East Hampton?"

He nodded, and she wondered how to respond. On the one hand she was kind of upset—he knew, because she'd told him, how much she missed the beach and wanted to go—on the other hand, he had just taken her to Paris. Now was no time to complain.

She turned back to her window and rolled it down some more. The wind became so loud that the driver glanced at her in the rearview mirror. She pretended not to notice and kept her eyes on the sludge-colored Hudson, on the sailboats enjoying the last bit of light.

At her mother's, Ansel answered the door wearing a short-sleeved police uniform. His arms were toned and lean. He actually looked strong for the first time in his life, a fact El was determined not to mention.

"Little outside your jurisdiction," she said.

"I had to drive down straight from duty."

His voice elicited in her an actual ripple of dislike.

"Hi, Mom!" she called, stepping inside. A sing-song voice answered from the kitchen.

"Hi!" Bryce called, echoing El. The singsong voice responded again, though with noticeably less pep.

Ansel stuck out his hand when Bryce came over the threshold.

"Nice to meet you," Bryce said, meeting the shake.

". . . Ansel." He said it as though Bryce had forgotten his name.

"Yes, I know. Heard a lot about you."

"Really."

"From El. Of course."

"El and I don't talk much," Ansel snapped, and he turned his back.

Bryce gave El a bewildered look. She just nodded. *Yup. That's what we're dealing with.*

A few minutes later, while they all helped themselves to risotto and salad, El's mother peppered Ansel with questions about life in the Poconos of late. How was the real estate market in his town? Had he been doing much hiking? The ticks, were they awful? She'd heard they were awful.

Ansel answered these inquiries with enthusiasm. His pomposity blossomed in the light of her mother's polite curiosity.

Somehow, with each response, he managed to circle back to his work as a police officer. More than once he brought up "Donaldson": clearly Ansel considered this Donaldson a mentor. Bryce apparently found Ansel's mini-sermons on Donaldson's commitment to civic responsibility as tedious as El did. She caught Bryce playing with his food as Ansel recounted a recent arrest Donaldson had made. The accused had been a nineteen-year-old male alleged to have committed aggravated assault against his girlfriend, and the case was complicated by the fact that the accused was also the son of Donaldson's former partner. "Now that," Ansel proclaimed, "takes integrity."

Approximately twenty minutes into the meal, El's mother turned to her slightly less honored guest: "Bryce, have you traveled much?"

"Some. When I was younger mainly."

El could tell her mother had been expecting more and jumped in: "Bryce was born in the U.K. He lived there until he was twelve."

"Mm," her mother murmured.

"Donaldson grew up in the U.K.," Ansel interjected. "Cambridge. His father was with the police."

"That's where Bryce went to college. Cambridge."

Her mother fixed Bryce with her probing gaze. "What did you study?"

"Economics. Bit dry, I know."

"No no . . ." Her mother trailed off and set her fork lightly on her plate. Then she looked at El and, with the brisk air of sorting out something unpleasant, commanded: "So tell us about Paris. I've heard the Rodin museum is not to be missed."

El took a sip of wine. "We did miss it, actually. But we saw a lot. Went to Versailles. Bryce had been before . . ."

"It was fun to see everything through someone else's eyes," Bryce said. "Really fun."

The subject of Anna could be avoided, El reasoned. All she had to do was talk about the Grand Mosque, its ornate tile and mint tea and nutty pastries, about the vendor at the Marché aux Puces who had told them about the day Notre-Dame had caught on fire, how his son had watched the spire blacken and fall. But she couldn't get the words out. The silence waxed oddly until finally Bryce, with a hesitant look at her, said, "The day before we came home, we heard some news, one of El's old friends—"

"Anna Wallenhaver." El looked at her mom.

"I remember that girl," Ansel said. "You used to have a picture of her in a frame—"

El remembered the one: she'd kept it on her night table the year she and Ansel had shared a room. El, Anna and Julia had only been friends a couple of months when the picture had been taken. They had all gone to Wollman Rink the last day of winter break, Anna sporting a golden blush having just returned from a week in Maui. Julia had asked someone to take their photo, and in the center of the rink El and Julia had pressed into Anna, tilting their heads toward hers.

"Anna was the small one," Ansel continued. "The one in white."

He was looking at El for confirmation.

"—she was found dead in her apartment in Paris," Bryce finished.

El saw her mother wince. "It happened while we were there," she added.

Ansel shook his head. "Suicides," he said pontifically. "We see them more than you think."

"No, it wasn't suicide," El corrected. "She was murdered."

Ansel pointed to Bryce. "He said *'found dead.'*"

"What a tragedy," El's mother lamented. "What was Anna doing in Paris?"

El shrugged. "I think just—living. I don't know."

"She must have had *some* kind of job."

It was really incredible that her mother was offended by the possibility of a young woman ignoring her potential, even in death.

"Purpose builds character," Ansel declared. "I can't imagine not working."

Perhaps Bryce intuited the rage building inside El and wanted to cheer her up, or perhaps he intuited nothing at all: regardless, he laid an arm around El's shoulder and said tenderly, though loudly enough to be heard, "Well, I've got *my* purpose right here."

Neither Ansel nor El's mother cooed, as Bryce had perhaps expected them to. Ansel flattened his lips together in the barest semblance of politeness. El's mother stared.

The night was cloudless, the sky a dark canvas. As she and Bryce plodded up to Broadway to catch a cab, as they got further and further from her mother's, El felt a growing unease. True, Ansel was staying the night out of convenience more than anything, but El couldn't help thinking that, now she had gone, the two of them—plus Chat, of course—could be a real family. They could play cards or watch one of her mother's favorite movies. *Moonstruck*, maybe. "Whatever you want," Ansel would say, anything to make his surrogate mother glad of keeping him around. Maybe that was El's problem: she didn't want to subjugate herself just to become more intimate with her mother. It was a mother's job to invite closeness, wasn't it? Though she and her mother were both adults now . . . perhaps the effort was supposed to be mutual? Did she only grow close to the people who held her close, by default? Or who *gripped* her close? She felt, like a phantom sensation, Bryce's arm wrapping around her. *I've got my purpose right here.*

Revulsion flooded through El. She felt that if Bryce were to touch her right now she would spit. She would scream. They had reached Broadway and he was facing the southbound traffic with his hand out. Charged with a kind of drunken recklessness, she pulled out her phone. She wanted to be in the company of someone who didn't accept her ugliness. Bryce had her on such a pedestal, and for their whole relationship she'd imagined that to be love. It wasn't, though. It was a willful blindness. It said more about Bryce than it did about her. The fledgling work ethic she'd had when they'd first gotten together had died with his encouragement. She had no inspiration now, no money of her own. And she had become so selfish, dismissing all her friends, though that part wasn't Bryce's fault . . . Still, he had made it possible. Hadn't he tried to command as much of her time as he could? Didn't he call her and message her constantly, as if supervising her schedule? Wasn't his opposition to her having a life outside of their relationship made most obvious by the fact of his indifference—no, his coldness—in the wake of Anna's death? He'd asked about it, what, once? And not even to see how she was doing, but just to see whether she'd heard from Julia, which, now that she thought about it, was just more monitoring. He didn't want her to have people apart from himself.

She texted Navya: I really fucked up. I can't believe how hard I fucked up.

To El's surprise, Navya wrote back right away: Ya.

And then Navya dropped a pin, somewhere in Bushwick. If you want to apologize in person.

An invitation! All the times El had blown Navya off, and yet here was an olive branch.

A taxi slowed for Bryce. Its light was off, but the driver asked where he was headed. Bryce told him downtown and, at the driver's nod, hopped in. Traffic was gathering behind the taxi and a black sedan honked and whipped into the other lane, speeding past the taxi through the light. When Bryce realized El hadn't followed him, he motioned.

El jogged toward Bryce and shut the taxi's door. "You go. I have to meet some people."

"What people?" he asked, his tone sharp.

"Navya."

"I thought you weren't—"

The driver raised his voice: "Hey! Let's go!"

"Go," El told Bryce. "You go."

"Are you mad at me?"

"I don't know."

Bryce's face seemed to close. He looked away from her. "Go," he told the driver.

The taxi zoomed forward, just under the wire. The light turned red, and El tore across the street and down into the subway. She felt hot and excited. Waiting for the train she found headphones in her bag, and on the ride downtown she knew exactly what she wanted to listen to: *Body Talk*. "Don't Fucking Tell Me What to Do" came on as she strode through the tunnel to Sixth Avenue to catch the M, the bass line thumping to the beat of her steps, Robyn's accusing voice in her ear:

Can't sleep it's killing me
My dreams are killing me
TV is killing me
My talking's killing me

Soon after they'd become friends, Julia had given El her old iPod Shuffle. El had never heard of Robyn before then.

She was feeling it anew through the music, the rebirth she'd experienced in the city after the heartbreak of her father's abandonment. Julia's ditzy warmth. Anna's searing charisma. Her old fantasies of becoming a star, then the loneliness and the competition of her performing arts high school, drilling monologues in her bedroom, crash diets of mustard and celery before those first auditions and meetings with agents, and nobody wanting her, and trying again . . . She thought of all the times during college when Navya had come to her performances and offered her encouragement . . . She felt feverish. Feverish and righteous. She was sure this was right, going out to Brooklyn to kiss the ring. Rejoining her old friends. All of them would feel for her when she told them about Anna dying. They would comfort her. They were the good people in her life. Even Emma—maybe being self-righteous was how Emma made reality bearable. Maybe she was more sensitive than El had ever given her credit for, and that contentious attitude was just armor.

Let go you're killing me
Calm down you're killing me
My god you're killing me

As she reached the end of the tunnel, El felt she might never go back to the apartment in the Financial District. She didn't see how she could. Her choice, she felt, was clear: stay with Bryce or get her old self back.

chapter nineteen

The bar was its own squat building, a hovel with clouded-glass windows and green twinkle lights and smokers crowding the entrance. El had to push her way through to reach the worn wooden door. She had her ID ready, but nobody was checking.

In the far corner of the bar a white thirtysomething guy was DJ'ing and trying to vibe, but he just looked like an idiot, moving his fist right to left over his face. The vibration of the music through the floor, the nautical seafoam glow of the windows plus the congestion of yelling, dancing, drinking, and people in eccentric vintage clothes gave El the impression of having stepped onto a swaying pirate ship.

She began searching for her friends, and it was Adam she spotted first. She had barely stepped toward him when he noticed her and raised his eyebrows in amused surprise. When she was within arm's reach, he touched her hip.

She leaned forward and tried to speak above the music: "I'm persona non grata, right?"

"What?" he called back.

"Persona—non—grata!"

His lips brushed her ear. "It's good to see you again."

What had she been doing, fucking around with her ponderous finance boyfriend, when there was life like this, sex appeal like this? Her clit seemed to pound along with her heartbeat. Their mutual attraction was so awake and inflamed she felt as if they were already lovers. Honesty spilled from her involuntarily.

"I think there are good people and bad people, and I might be bad," she said.

Adam moved his hand further up, from El's hip to her waist, and looked her full in the face. "There are no good people and no bad people."

He was so sure. But she had come here to be cleansed and forgiven. To become her better self, her old self again.

"I gotta find Navya."

"Let's leave," he said. "We'll get a drink somewhere else."

"I have to find her . . ."

He groaned, unhappy. There was nothing of the coward in Adam, as there was in her. She had disappointed him—not only by denying him the freedom to fuck her, but by failing to heed her own intuition and embracing her neurosis instead, her craving to be forgiven. With an admonitory look Adam backed away and disappeared into the crowd. Perhaps he thought she'd give chase. She didn't, though his silent reprimand weighed on her: he was free, she wasn't. She was attempting to live her life, again, by the rule of musts.

She texted Navya: hey I'm here

Nothing in reply, but she kept texting:

I'm kind of near the door

Walking over to the DJ

Going toward the back

Finally, she saw Navya and Van dancing together, undulating slowly to the fast song, their arms wound around each other's necks. Daniel danced beside them, on his own, bouncing over and over on the balls of his feet toward the sky like a character from a video game. El approached, penitent, and Navya squinted at El as though seeing her through a mist.

"Made it," El yelled over the music. Navya released Van, and he wandered away in a daze. "I couldn't find you," El continued. "But I ran into Adam. I'm so sorry about everything lately."

The moment she said it, she knew what a waste coming out here had been. Navya was looking at El as if El were a particularly unappetizing hallucination. She knew that expression: Navya was on something. Van, Daniel, all of them probably were. Navya hadn't actually expected her to show up, El realized.

"Hi."

The droll voice came from behind, and El turned to see Emma, whose red hair had been cropped into a pixie cut. It suited her. El thought that Emma seemed more with it than the others. Navya was looking away from El now, watching Daniel giggle at a pissed-off stranger he'd accidentally slammed into.

"Van bought ketamine," Emma explained. "Hey, d'you have a sec?"

El wondered what Emma could possibly want. Maybe to chastise her for ghosting Navya? El wasn't feeling nearly as frosty toward Emma as she usually did, but that would surely change if she had to endure anything like a lecture. As Emma made to lead El away from the music, El looked back at Navya . . . But Navya had forgotten her. She was standing very close to the clearly unnerved DJ, scrutinizing his setup.

El followed the back of Emma's head through the crowd and out of the bar where, to El's very great surprise, Emma bummed a cigarette. (How many times had El heard Emma savage the tobacco lobby?) The cigarette's original owner, a cute person in a black silk dress, seemed keen to talk to Emma after giving her a light, but Emma drew El away. They stopped walking when they came to the side of the building; behind them a short alley was partially illuminated by the jaundiced headlights of passing cars. El thought she saw something waist-high and thin skulk deeper into the alley's dark.

"I think there's a dog or something back there," El murmured, but Emma didn't seem to have heard. She was exhaling a trail of smoke toward the sky.

El waited for Emma to speak, but for a solid thirty seconds Emma did nothing but flick ash from her cigarette with a *tck tck. tck tck*. Finally Emma said, without looking at El, "So I'm kind of in a shitty situation." Emma gazed up at the subway tracks, high above their heads across the street. "It's a weird thing. You might be surprised, but I really need that fifteen thousand you offered before."

El's shock must have shown because Emma went on hastily, blowing smoke from the side of her mouth. "It's not for me. And I did cover what you offered from my own—with my own money. But unfortunately my parents got wind of a big withdrawal, and I can't take out anymore."

"Why would you need to?"

"For Cam and Lucely."

"But didn't you raise a lot at the fundraiser? What about all your *big donors*?"

"We didn't raise enough. Not with the new rent Cam and Lucely have to pay, it's not sustainable. They need another eighty grand to even consider staying. So if Bryce would be willing to part with that money I am . . . completely open to that."

"I got rid of the check."

"Couldn't you ask him to write another one?"

She could, but she didn't know where she stood when it came to Bryce. "What about your parents? They won't help?"

Emma looked severe. "They only want to help themselves."

A train barreled in and screeched to a halt across the way. Emma threw her cigarette down.

"Would it be the worst thing if Cam and Lucely had to leave

the city?" El asked. "I mean I know they don't want to, but if things are that dire . . ."

Emma lifted a finger to her eyes. It took El a moment to realize Emma was catching falling tears. She remembered now how Emma had become emotional during Cam's speech. Before El could rest a hand on Emma's back, Emma sniffed and waved her away. "Sorry."

"No, it's fine. It's really fucking sad."

Emma gasped then. Fresh tears fell. El looked around but no one was paying them any mind. She kept silent while Emma tried to gather herself. Finally, Emma tilted her head up and shook it roughly. "It's Cam," she said.

"What?"

"Cam and I are together."

The shock of it: El's first thought was that Anna's murder had made more sense than this. She tried to focus on saying *something*, something not unkind, but not a word came to mind besides *Lucely*. Did she know?

Emma was watching El now. "I haven't told anyone. Neither has Cam. At least I don't think he has . . . He's close to his brother, but he never sees him . . ."

"So Cam's not leaving Lucely?"

"No," Emma said, her voice curt. "I don't want him to."

"Then why— I mean, wouldn't it be better for everybody then if they did move?"

Emma let out a short, derisive laugh, as if El were the one who ought to be embarrassed. "I don't know why I thought you wouldn't judge me."

El felt the nervous, bowel-stirring unease of conflict in her gut. "You judged me for dating someone with a sketchy dad—"

"*Quincy Batten*, a monstrous corporate predator—"

"But now you want his money—"

"The thing about you—" Emma began, but El talked over her.

"—so you can continue your affair with the married guy with two kids! Okay, sure. Tell me what I'm like."

"You never think outside yourself," Emma spoke swiftly, her voice cutting the night. "It's so tedious and uninspiring to be around a narcissist who offers literally nothing and just *takes*. Navya's finally starting to see how limited you are, thank god."

El's voice shook with adrenaline as she shot back: "So I'm a narcissist because I'm—whatever you're implying—some kind of an apologist for capitalism, but it's okay for you to commit adultery because you're a selfless socialist?"

"'Commit adultery'? Who the fuck *are* you?"

"Who the fuck am *I*?"

It was terrible and electric to be so angry. For several long moments, they were one breath away from violence. The idea of hitting, or being hit, hung in the air, a dense, crackling cloud. El stared into Emma's surly brown eyes, waiting, breathing rapidly through her nose—and then El moved. Spun, away from Emma, and marched toward the subway. Twice El looked back over her shoulder, but Emma was not following. El didn't notice until she reached the platform the thin pool of sweat that had gathered between her breasts and the stinging red marks on her palms that her nails, balled into fists, had made.

When the train came she flopped into the nearest seat, trembling. She imagined the fight she and Emma had almost had: Emma punching her. Her seizing Emma's spindly forearm, pulling it close and twisting it down and kicking Emma from her, hard, in the side, down the alley. Leaving Emma to the wild thing that lived down there. El closed her eyes. Brooklyn had seemed like such a good idea, such the obvious solution to the problem of Bryce and his gilded cage, the isolation of her life with him, the person she had become inside of that life. How pathetic she had been to ascribe Navya the responsibility of fixing her, making her "better"—Navya had her own life to worry about. That, El thought, had been the very point Navya had been trying to make, that friendship was supposed to be reciprocal, and El didn't pull her weight. *A narcissist who offers literally nothing*, Emma had said. *And just takes.* Talk about hypocritical! How *magnanimous* Emma must think herself, encouraging Cam to stay with Lucely. But she wasn't magnanimous enough to break off the affair! Did Emma, El truly wanted to know, ever consider the effect a marital rupture would have on Manny and Gaby? No, Emma's parents were still together. She couldn't understand. And then El thought of Kirsten's mom, the woman her father had left her mother for: Had Kirsten's mom known about the double-life thing all along? Had she ever considered El? The Other Child? Had she *magnanimously* encouraged El's father to stay with El and her mother for those first thirteen years of El's life? Had El's father only stayed so long because his oh-so-generous mistress had told him to? They said the opposite of love was indifference, but maybe it was pity.

El opened her eyes, stirred by the anguished howl of the train's wheels on the track. So what now? Where was she going? She thought of Ansel on the pull-out sofa at her mother's, curled up, no doubt, with the stupid cat. Going back there was *not* an option. There was no alternative: she would have to go home. And home, for better or worse, was Bryce.

chapter twenty

The violence of the night, though unrealized, had left El completely drained. She stepped off the air-conditioned subway car and into the humid Fulton Street station wishing she could evaporate. It was after midnight, but the heat and the fluorescent light made it feel much earlier.

In the deep woods of West Virginia, El thought, it was so black right now you couldn't see the hand in front of your face. She had experienced it, once. On one of the final camping trips with her father she had woken to the sound of scuffling behind their tent. She had sat up and listened but had heard nothing besides the emergent trilling of crickets. Her father had not stirred. For all his talk of survival skills he had not been very attuned to movements of the night. The thought had come to her then: Would he notice if she left the tent? What if she were to walk off, wander until she found a new family, a new life . . . ? A house appeared in her mind, ramshackle, two-story, white, a tractor in the yard—would there be new parents who didn't argue as hers did? What was *in* the world? In school, someone had done a presentation on the Florida Keys. There were four states between West Virginia and Florida. How long would it take to reach the clear water, cornflower blue? She envisioned a job on the beach—she was pulling a rope, pulling a boat in and tying it up, she was working behind the counter of a dive shop, she was living on her own and no bickering voices interrupted her dinner and beside her porch were weeping trees with thin arms that dangled like apologies . . .

She had unzipped the tent slowly and pushed herself out, feet first. She had groped for her hiking boots and once she had stuffed them on she had reached back into the tent for her flashlight. Squatting, she'd zipped the tent back up, legs burning from the day's hike.

It had been colder than she'd expected. She and her father had pitched their tent on the edge of a clearing and after walking to its center she had switched the flashlight off.

There had been no stars nor moon to see by. It had been true darkness, such as she had never encountered. Her fantasies about what possibilities might exist for her had become futile in the face of it. There were no places in the world, and no world. And no El. She had not been able to see her body. If it hadn't been for the crickets it would have been easy to imagine herself dead. Her grandfather, who had long been in a care facility, had recently died. At the wake she had overheard her father's sister saying that she was angry. *I'm furious with him, to be honest. I'm so angry at him for dying I could kill him.* But you couldn't be angry, El had realized in the darkness, at something that *wasn't.* If her aunt had been angry she had been angry with herself, with her ideas of things, with her Nothing, all the Nothing ideas and stuff in her head. Just like El had been yearning for what was Out There, which was also Nothing. There was no white house, no dive shop, no other set of parents. El had known she would never forget this fact: she would always remember what it was like to stand in Nothing, not existing.

El glanced at the six-seat wooden bench facing the subway tracks and considered parking herself until she could figure out a better plan than going back to Bryce, whom she did not want to confront right now. The tête-à-tête with Emma had taken everything out of her.

"You don't actually want to stall down here," she told herself quietly. She made her way down the platform and into the huge station. "Good," she said, her voice low. "Now what's wrong? What's so wrong with going home?" If anyone were listening, they might think she had an earpiece in. She sounded as if she were counseling a child. "You had a bad experience at dinner. You felt suffocated and you overreacted. Bryce isn't the enemy. He's an adult. He wants adult things. He wants to spend time with you because he loves you. He shows his affection, and you've never had that before. It's okay."

She carried herself out of the station, directing herself thus. When she emerged she felt more sedate. Still exhausted but well enough to walk home. What a mess the night had been . . . But it was all right. Would be all right. She would tell Bryce that between the news of Anna's murder and the evening at her mother's she had been totally shaken up and she'd been rude and had taken it out on him and she was sorry. He would understand.

Because she'd been rehearsing this conversation, imagining him, she didn't think it strange at first when she noticed a young man similar to Bryce in her peripheral vision. Light brown hair, discouraged posture. He was tucking his wallet into his back pocket and it seemed as if he, too, had just emerged from the station. She wouldn't have given him a second look if it hadn't been for the SUV that tore through the crosswalk, through the yellow light, and El caught just a glimpse of the commotion inside: the terrified driver was shouting over his shoulder at a well-groomed black-and-white spaniel who appeared to be scraping at the windows in the back seat, fighting to get free. Everyone in El's vicinity watched the SUV pass—everyone except the young man. His eyes, she could feel, were on her. She turned her head toward him just as the light changed and those around her began to move forward. *It couldn't be Bryce, could it?* She had never known him to take the train. She craned her neck but could not get a good look at the man. She began to cross the street but stole a few feet to the right before she glanced around again. This time she saw him clearly. *It is Bryce.* Walking with the crowd a safe distance behind her, hands in his pockets as though nothing were amiss. She considered shouting his name, but then thought better of it. If she confronted him right now he would make an excuse as to why he'd been riding the train, maybe even convince her that their proximity had been coincidence. She couldn't let that happen. She had a suspicion, and she had to know whether that suspicion was correct. She had to let Bryce follow her.

chapter twenty-one

t was almost like being in Paris, she thought, as she turned the corner onto William Street. Like they'd just eaten lunch in a café and she'd walked ahead to stretch her legs while he settled the bill. Like he would catch up any minute.

There was a hush along the empty street. The quiet might've been coming from the buildings themselves, straight-backed as courtiers, flanking her on either side. They watched her. Judged her. Wasn't it time to turn and face Bryce? Surely she had proved it to herself by now: without a doubt, he was following her. For a quarter mile he had kept pace, walking directly in her wake, making no attempt to conceal himself. She had glimpsed him in the glass reflections of passing windows, each time daring him to meet her eye. But he just kept staring ahead. In profile he looked like his usual self—a bit more serious, perhaps. Or more neutral? There was something fraternal or condescending in that neutrality.

El didn't realize it until she was reaching for the door of their building, but she had begun to shake with anger. Isaac, one of the evening doormen, had risen to meet her. He pulled the door wide before she could step all the way in.

"How's it going?" she murmured.

"Not too bad, not too bad," Isaac said.

As she walked to the elevator bay, she looked around and saw that Isaac had remained by the door. She pressed UP and the elevator swung open just as she heard Isaac and Bryce exchanging greetings. She stepped into the elevator, to the right, out of sight. Feeling for the second time that night as though she could fight someone, she held down the OPEN button.

After a moment Bryce stepped onto the elevator. He smelled like the night. He turned to her, nonplussed. As the doors kissed shut, the world seemed to shrink to the space between them, to this sleek, paneled room with its strange, pale, anodyne lighting. Which play, which movie, which scene was this that she found herself in now? Where was the adoring man she knew? Who was this bizarre stand-in with the silent, tepid look?

She had balled her hands into fists again, unconsciously. The marks on her palms smarted. She relaxed her right hand and tapped the four-digit code for the fifteenth floor with her index finger. The elevator shot upward with a mechanical gasp. Breaking eye contact with Bryce, she faced the doors. She litigated in her mind, practiced for their inevitable argument

upstairs: *Why* had he followed her? *How* had he? She antici-
pated some noble justification—like with the home security
camera, he'd just been looking out for her, et cetera, but she
would say that chivalry was misogyny by another name. Wasn't
he even going to apologize? Oh, he was? Did he know what he
was apologizing for? Was he sure? Because why did he have
that stupid, calm, self-satisfied *look* still?

The elevator opened onto the little fifteenth-floor annex
and Bryce lingered, letting her go first. She had her keys ready
to open the apartment door. How many times in her life had
she held her keys like a weapon, coming home late from some
bar? It occurred to her that it made more sense to fear now
than it ever had before. *CSI* notwithstanding, it wasn't strang-
ers who were most dangerous to women, but partners. *My
partner stalked me tonight*, she thought. But the thought landed
lightly, like a leaf on water. She didn't feel its weight; she didn't
feel afraid. She felt potent. For months and months, for years
even, before Bryce, before quitting acting, she had been confused at a core level. Was it healthier to see the world as basically cruel or basically kind? Should she live in a less busy
place? Date more? Or less? Or try EMDR? Should she train
for something—an Ironman? Should she change her look, despite her manager's discouragement? Quit hard alcohol? Donate to an important cause every month, even if it was five
bucks? Which one? Play chess in the park with those really
good guys and learn important lessons about failure and patience? And make a short film out of it? Switch to tea? Die,
rather than live in this perpetual state of flux? This last had

always been faint, ghostly faint. But it had been persistent. Yes, for years she had been in despair. But now, now, she felt absolutely, unequivocally alive. And zealous. And indignant. *My partner stalked me tonight*, she thought again as she twisted the key in the lock. *What the absolute fuck.*

She dropped her keys on the hall table and kicked off her shoes so hard they made scuff marks on the cream wallpaper. She led the way into the kitchen, ready for battle. Bryce walked after her. She listened for regret in his steps but heard none. She was ready to fire at him, but when she saw his face the strangeness of his expression gave her pause. It was that tepid, even, fraternal thing still. He looked ready to offer her communion.

"I can save us some time," he said.

She folded her arms tightly, unnerved.

"I put the tracking on your phone this morning, before you woke up. I kept thinking about your friend Anna—I got really worried and—I'm not justifying it. I followed you to Brooklyn, to that bar. I don't know what happened. I stayed outside. I just saw you talking to somebody and getting upset." His face contracted and for a second he looked like someone else completely, not the doting boyfriend she'd known all summer nor the mild-mannered impostor who'd followed her from the train. He looked wounded. Sick. Like someone sitting in darkness, suddenly exposed to light. When he spoke again his tone was hard. "So fuck them. Fuck *me*, fuck *them*, fuck your mother, fuck fucking *Ansel*. You're the most important person. You're the best person. Fuck anybody who's ever offended you, you know? Fuck your dad and his choices and fucking *Kirsten*. Fuck your mother's stupid ugly cat."

She let out an involuntarily and completely inappropriate shriek of mirth. She felt her blood pumping fast.

"I saw its stupid face on my way back from the bathroom at dinner. Fucking most depressing cat I've ever seen in my life."

She was laughing again. What was happening? Blood was pounding in her ears.

"I hate what you hate, including myself right now. If I could divide myself, I would. The me who followed you— forget him. He would be gone. Lobotomy. I'd just be the me, here. The guy you come home to. The guy who's on your side."

She'd gotten hold of herself, but her swift pulse reminded her that the stakes were still high. Bryce had been honest, and now she would have to be honest.

"Sometimes I feel like two people too. A big part of me doesn't love you at all."

Never, never, could she have imagined saying something so raw of her own volition. But she hadn't been plied with alcohol, and she hadn't been prodded by some couples counselor. She was standing in the kitchen with her partner spelling out the truth of her very complex feelings toward him. She felt an unexpected surge of pride in her breast. She thought about the person she'd been when she'd started this relationship, how she'd first said I love you in the dark marbled confines of the shower because she'd been afraid to hurt Bryce's feelings— now here she stood, undaunted. Well, not undaunted. Telling the truth was uncomfortable, but it also felt inevitable. Maybe . . .

maybe she loved Bryce more than she thought. Maybe being willing to confront her clear-eyed hostility *was* love.

Bryce appeared to be handling her honesty well. He was looking into her eyes, his shoulders, for once, relaxed, his expression peaceful. And then he did something unthinkable. He reached into his jacket and pulled out a black suede ring box.

"The only reason I would ever ask you to marry me, the only reason I would ever think I'd deserve you, is that I know I'll never go anywhere. I'm not like other people that way. Once I love I don't change my mind. I think people who leave and people who play games and raise the bar and raise the bar for someone to jump over, I think all those people are scared. I'm not over here waiting for you to feel some different way about me. I love you exactly as you are. What matters is that I love you unconditionally and you deserve that."

There was a thumping in El's ears, furious, compact—she felt like someone very far out in space, or very deep underwater—she couldn't go all the way back now. There *was* no way back, as she'd seen tonight. No old life, no old friends waiting in her rearview. She could love Bryce and dislike him too and coast on his golden ticket. And who on earth was in a position to judge her? *No one.*

chapter twenty-two

L ying in bed she stared at the ring. A natural pink diamond, Bryce had said. Six carats. Inside the stone were
flecks of salmon and glittering white, and on the inside
of the band was an inscription: *My extraordinary girl.* An hom-
age to the toast Bryce had made on their first date: here's to
more extraordinary moments.

She was still exhausted from the events of the night, but
she couldn't shut down her mind. It had to be three a.m. by
now. She resisted looking at her phone to check.

Over her shoulder Bryce slept soundly, as he always did
after sex. Tonight's coupling had been quick and quiet. She
had accepted his proposal by motioning for the ring box and
had put the ring on herself. When they'd kissed she'd felt in
that touch the infinity of herself, herself and herself and herself, she'd felt that no one would ever understand this decision

to marry Bryce, especially if she were to tell the whole truth—how he'd stalked her, how only hours ago she'd thought of leaving him. She'd felt comprehensible only to herself, and this had made for powerful sex: her being so connected to the tide of her own pleasure had gotten Bryce off even more.

An ambulance whined in the distance and El, weary and resentful, snatched her phone off the nightstand. It was *four a.m.* Fuck. She rolled onto her back and stared at the unblemished ceiling. She thought of Shay, how she had lain awake that early morning at the Hamptons house staring at the ceiling after he'd left. She thought of Anna. Outwardly their relationship had not changed after that night—Anna had remained the principal, the luminary, El the understudy, the disciple. They had been two poles of a constellation: Julia had hung between them, soft and indistinct. It wasn't until college that El realized something *had* changed between herself and Anna on the night of Shay's visit, and that Anna had known it all along.

In December of El's sophomore year at NYU, Navya and Emma and Lila and Daniel and a few of the others made plans to fly to Miami for Art Basel. There was a rumor that Ariana Grande would be there, and Daniel's roommate Peter had booked a chic Airbnb in the Design District. But even if El stuck to a diet of Smirnoff and Ritz crackers when she got to Florida, she still wouldn't be able to afford the trip: the airfare alone was insane. Lila and Daniel were just as budget-conscious as she, but Lila's full-ride scholarship and part-time Starbucks gig afforded her a rainy day fund, and Peter's parents were paying for both Peter's and Daniel's tickets. El was too embarrassed to tell her friends that she had no means to make the trip work, so she told them that she had plans to visit a girlfriend in Boston, otherwise she would've come to Miami *for sure.*

The day after she told this lie El decided to see if she could make it a reality. Both Anna and Julia went to college in Boston, and El texted Julia first because it wasn't at all intimidating to ask a favor of Julia. As it turned out, Julia was also going to Art Basel. This left Anna. Feeling nervous, El composed a text in which she assured Anna that it was "absolutely no big deal whatsoever" if Anna couldn't host her, if she was busy, had plans, that was "absolutely fine." To El's surprise, Anna called her moments after the message went through.

"You can come," Anna said, panting slightly. "I do have events all weekend." She was clearly on a run, and the wind made her almost impossible to hear. El turned her volume to the max while Anna continued: "They don't normally let us bring plus-ones, but they're getting all this shit lately about being exclusionary. I don't think anyone will say anything. If they do I'll just tell them you're a friend from the city."

El understood "they" to be the people in Anna's final club. All El knew about Harvard final clubs was what she'd gleaned from *The Social Network.* They were basically frats and sororities, but more elitist and gloomy? Or maybe David Fincher had just made them look gloomy. She wondered if by "events" Anna had meant parties or something else. Recently this girl in Stella Adler had complained to El and Lila about NYU culture, about how she wished they had a little more of that *regular* collegiate life—beer miles, tailgates. The girl was from some big college town originally, Madison or something. Between bites of falafel, she had told El and Lila that she craved "that juvenile atmosphere" because she was such an "introspective performer" by nature and needed her "cocoon" to be "disturbed" once in a while. When El and Lila had left the girl to get to their next class Lila had muttered, "Fucking Adler kids."

The bus to Boston was tediously slow because the roads were covered with ice, and El's area smelled mysteriously of sauerkraut. When they pulled in at South Station, it was dark, bitterly cold and windy. Suppressing the urge to look up the weather in Miami, El hastened into the station with her backpack over one shoulder. The building was huge: it took several minutes for her to locate the subway (the "T") to Cambridge. When she emerged in Harvard Square twenty minutes later, she had a text from Anna with the address of a dorm and a see u soon. There were kids—young people El's age, or maybe younger—hanging around the Harvard T-stop in the cold. They weren't talking or laughing but standing together, backs to the wind, hoods up. By their feet were bags, plastic bags and a few ragged duffels, and one of them had a turquoise-and-black-striped blanket around her shoulders. A boy with thin skin and high cheekbones was smoking. He and El met each other's gaze as the wind picked up again, whistling and sinister. It suddenly seemed very stupid to have been worrying about missing Art Basel.

Harvard was just as lousy with red brick as it was in the movies. El kept to the side of the street with the shops and restaurants until she came to an intersection with a Dunkin' Donuts on the corner, where she turned right. She walked down a sloping road then turned again. Here, finally, was Anna's dorm. Unlike at NYU, some insane percentage of Harvard kids lived in dorms: now El understood why. She didn't have much to compare it to, but the premises put her in mind of colonial-era book reports and British novels. To enter you passed under a regal gold and black gate. She texted Anna here! and, because it was freezing, didn't wait for a response, but followed on the heels of a couple guys who had just swiped themselves through a pair of heavy doors by waving a pass.

It was still cold in the foyer of the building. El's boots, some off-brand UGGs from DSW, were soaked through at the toe, not almond-colored anymore but penny brown. It was beginning to dawn on El how *weird* this all was—she and Anna hadn't spent more than a few drunken hours in each other's company for years. They texted sporadically on the group chain with Julia, but that wasn't exactly quality time. And *Boston* was weird too. El had been in it no more than thirty minutes, but it gave her a hard, discouraged feeling. It reminded her of being little, of leaving her grandfather's care facility, dreary fading light as she and her mother and father walked to the parking lot, her father's long strides putting hasty distance between himself and the smell of antiseptic and grease and skin.

El's anxiety only intensified when Anna came down the stairs into view: her sleek hair was twisted in a comfortable knot, and she wore a loose black *Titanic* hoodie with long sleeves. In red typeface, on the arms, were the words COMING SOON. As ever Anna was cool and effortless. El hated her own stupid backpack with the straps that dangled past her hips and her wet boots and the bumps in her ponytail—

"On y va," Anna said. *Let's go.* It was the only French expression El knew outside of "bonjour" and "merci": in middle school, when the Honors French teacher would supervise recess, she would say this to encourage them all back inside after the bell rang. Anna turned around to head back up the stairs. El hurried after her.

They climbed two flights before Anna shepherded El down a hallway to a white door that had been left slightly ajar. There were no tacky laminated nameplates on the door, no messages scribbled on a mini-whiteboard. In fact, El thought the door looked freshly painted compared to the others on the hall; El could absolutely picture Anna demanding a new coat from whoever maintained the building.

With a light push on the door Anna led the way into her room. It was spacious, with a boarded-up but beautifully maintained fireplace and a window seat padded with downy cream pillows.

"Bathroom's there," Anna said, pointing to El's immediate right. "My room and Daph's room are past that. You can sleep here, it's our common room. Gwen used to be in here."

She said this as if El were supposed to know all about Daph and Gwen. El wanted to know what had happened to

Gwen (she "used" to be here? where had she gone?), but El knew better than to try Anna's patience with questions.

"So you have an event tonight for your club?" El asked.

"Yeah, and tomorrow. You brought a dress?"

"Going-out stuff. Not a dress though."

"You can borrow."

"Cool."

"Jules told me you texted her too."

El heard the accusation in this but ignored it. "Oh yeah, but she's away. Art Basel. Some of my friends are there too."

"Mm-hm."

They both dressed in black. El brushed out her hair and wore it long when she saw that was Anna's plan. It felt excruciatingly like middle school to be sharing a mirror and to see a better version of herself in Anna's reflection.

"I'm ready," Anna said in her way that meant *you're ready too.*

El patted silver eyeshadow onto her right eyelid and unzipped her backpack to grab her wallet. "How far are we going? What shoes do I need?"

"Not far. I don't know if my heels will fit you. Borrow my Hunters if you want." Anna nodded to the closet beside the fireplace, and inside El found a pair of short red boots. They were a little big—she couldn't really fill them. But her stained shoes were a no-go.

"Shot?"

El turned. Anna was pouring from an icy bottle of Grey Goose.

"Sure."

El walked over, and Anna handed her a frosted shot glass. El paused for a split second thinking she and Anna would cheers, but Anna had already thrown her shot back. Hastily, El did the same.

"They usually have crap alcohol at these things," Anna said. "So be prepared." She took the Grey Goose bottle into the other room, and El heard a freezer door open and shut.

Anna reemerged in a white puffer coat. She was pushing a sleek purse into her pocket with one hand and answering a text with the other. "Somebody wants to meet you."

"Who?"

Anna didn't answer but continued to text, walking out the front door. El followed, her hair long and heavy on her back, her feet in tights shifting softly in the red boots, and she had a passing, abstract thought that she was just a body. How fragile to be a body. Fragile to have fingers and ankles. Fragile to move in the world—all the possible accidents. This body, this narrow piece of meat, was all the protection she had.

The "someone" who wanted to meet El turned out to be a junior named Ryder, though other people seemed to know him as Snack. El thought he looked like a thirty-year-old actor pretending to be a college kid. The first thing she noticed was Ryder's black leather necklace. It reminded her of a snake.

The event was a mixer between Anna's final club and Ryder's, where the mixer was being held. It was an old house, a proper, preppy house, and might've felt intimidating if it weren't for the surfaces littered in Solo cups and the swarms of people, damp and dewy from hours of pregaming.

Ryder had met them by the front door. He had greeted Anna with a jocular, eyebrow-waggling look and El with a warm smile. Kendrick Lamar played from a common room Ryder had led them past. A few of the girls within had glimpsed Anna and cried greetings.

They were now in another wide room with a bar. More people greeted Anna. Anna greeted only one of them in return, a tall waif in a black dress of her own.

"This is Quen," Anna said. To the waif she added: "El is visiting from the city."

"Are you from Manhattan too?" El asked.

"The Main Line," Quen drawled.

Having no idea what this meant, El opened her mouth in an expression of delight and hoped that that would suffice as a response.

Ryder returned with cups of tequila. Anna didn't drink from hers but looked around the room dispassionately. To differentiate herself from Anna, El downed her tequila and approached the bar for another. She didn't look at Ryder to gauge whether he was impressed with or intrigued by her: not looking allowed her to imagine that he was. When she had her next drink in hand and turned back to the group, however, they were gone.

All around El were cliques of well-dressed people with distinctly popular energy. Country club popular, that was, not

NYU popular—or not Tisch popular; to be Tisch popular was to have been a child star or to have successful producer parents. Even at El's performing arts high school, this CW drama version of the cool kids had not really existed. Sure, there had been some kids in head-to-toe Ralph Lauren, smoking Cloves and wearing headbands, but they had by no means reigned over everyone else, except perhaps in their own minds. Here at Harvard, though—maybe it was just that Anna belonged to the final club scene or maybe El was conflating final clubs with Skull and Bones, Yale's secret society that counted three presidents among its alumni, but El got the feeling these people really did lord over everyone else. She was starting to feel self-conscious, about her split ends and her lack of a cute purse and, most of all, about her virginity. At NYU she felt largely okay about being a virgin, because lots of people were. She had still lied about her level of experience, though: she'd told her close friends that while she hadn't *done everything*, she'd done plenty of everything but. In truth El had given exactly one blow job in the tenth grade, and the experience had been so smelly and overwhelming that she hadn't done it since. If her friends at NYU had ever suspected her of lying, they'd never made it known. They were all, even Navya, slightly too independent and self-involved to care much about her sexual résumé. But these final-club-type popular people were another matter: their very power rested on their being better than you, and so they had to know you. The real, scummy you. The *liar*.

El found Anna and Ryder in the room where the music was loudest. No one was dancing besides an extremely drunk person with dark stringy hair that came past the shoulders of his suit. Everyone was drinking at each other, talking loudly. Anna had been saying something to Ryder when El approached.

"So what do you think?" Anna asked El.

"Feels like any other party." This was not true of course, but El had known a blasé response would amuse Anna, and she was right.

Anna's eyes glittered. "That's funny."

El drank her second tequila, then two beers. She noticed that Anna continued to abstain but danced with Ryder as the party grew. People began arriving who were not in dresses and suits. El guessed these new people were not in a final club, but other Harvard students who were let in after a certain hour just to be bodies.

Soon the room was over capacity. El couldn't walk without someone bumping into her arm or brushing her leg. Four drinks were giving her a clearer sense of the weekend's purpose. Being out of town, her friends gone, it was time. Who better than Ryder to lose her virginity to? She wanted to be rid of it, as Anna had wanted to be once upon a time. It seemed poetic justice to take something from Anna too: Ryder didn't seem to be Anna's boyfriend, but certainly he was someone to her, as Shay had been someone to El.

Quen drew Anna into conversation, and El seized her chance. She approached Ryder with her best come-hither eyes. "Oh hey."

"Hey." He gave her an approving look. "I'm fucking hungry, are you?"

"Kind of, yeah."

Together they left the music behind and walked past the bar toward a staircase where two guys were standing guard. The guys moved aside for Ryder, and one of them said, "Snaaack" and pounded Ryder as he and El passed.

Halfway up the stairs, Ryder glanced over his shoulder. "Only members up here."

"Oh, am I cool?"

"You seem cool."

They came to a narrow hallway on the second floor. Most of the doors were closed. Ryder led the way to an Xbox den with a small fridge and a microwave. He opened the freezer and groaned.

"Somebody ate my—ugh. Okay, we might have to order or run to 7-Eleven. Unless you want to hang out for a while?"

"We can hang out," she said.

They walked back to the hallway, and he brought her up to the third floor. Here he opened the door to another man cave, this one less lived in. El was the first to sit on the blue love seat. She noticed that Ryder had left the door open very slightly. The hallway was dark.

He had pulled a weed pen from his pocket. El beckoned, and Ryder passed it over.

"Anna's just a friend, by the way."

El took a long hit and shrugged.

"Seriously," he said.

"I believe you." She passed the pen back.

"Where do you go to school?"

"NYU. Tisch."

"That's cool," he said, exhaling a thin white fissure of smoke. "You do film?"

"Acting."

"Do you write too?"

"No, not really."

He took another hit. "I do, sometimes." He put the pen back into his pocket.

"Like books, or plays . . ."

"More ideas. Philosophy. Maybe it's a book ultimately. Not that it would be very commercial."

"*A Book for All and None*," she said, quoting Nietzsche, and she was gratified to see his surprise and the way he opened his arm a little wider around the back of the couch, as if to pull her closer.

"Are you comfortable?" he asked, more quietly.

"Uh-huh."

He came forward, and his scent and his force struck her simultaneously. Before she knew it, she was on her back having the black ribbed-knit minidress she had borrowed from Anna pulled up and over her demi-cup bra, the combined smell of tequila and pine in her nostrils. But this, the initial impact, was the only surprise. Once they were half-clothed, Ryder's kisses and caresses, though intent, became extremely predictable. (To compensate for her slim experience, El had consumed a decent amount of amateur porn.)

He attempted to snap off her bra with one hand, failed, and while she intervened he kissed her neck. He "fingered" her for approximately forty-five seconds before raising the idea of a blow job. Reciprocity and all that. The whole time El kept thinking about that slight crack in the door. Her preoccupation with it distracted her from any nerves about performing her second blow job ever. She did wonder, three or four tedious minutes in, whether they were going to have sex after all—not to do it now seemed a waste. From between his legs she glanced up, and he opened his eyes.

"Do you have a condom?" she asked.

"You're not on the pill?"

He moved past his disappointment without comment, reaching for his pants on the ground and extracting a plastic blue square from his wallet.

El remembered being at Anna's brownstone years ago, and Julia telling them how if you rode horses your hymen could break before you ever had sex and then you wouldn't bleed the first time. Julia had learned this from her cousin who was competitive in some kind of horse thing, horse-jumping. El hoped against hope that her hymen had broken somehow—she had never been able to stomach a tampon larger than the width of her pinky, which seemed an ominous sign. What if she bled on this blue couch? Would there be a lot of blood, or just a dot? Somehow, in all her conversations with her friends about sex, no one had ever mentioned blood.

Ryder had pulled her legs up toward him. At the critical moment he looked at her with a rough gratitude. She wondered what it would be like to be loved by him. *He has the capacity for tenderness*, she thought. *He just doesn't have any for me.*

The black rope around his neck beat against him as he moved. El felt that something momentous was happening and also nothing at all. She reminded herself to make sounds—not as garish as the ones in the videos she'd watched. Soft sounds. He leaned down, close over her face, and finished at a sprint.

By some stroke of intuition, El turned her head at that precise moment and squinted at the crack in the door. A figure stood there. El could only see a sliver, but she knew it was Anna. Just as surely as she knew this, she knew other things: That Anna had been aware of El's presence all those years ago, watching her with Shay. That Anna had known that this—El and Ryder—would happen tonight, here. El saw that her scheme to seduce Ryder had been Anna's scheme all along. El felt herself detaching from Ryder's sticky body and sinking deeper into the sofa cushions, into the abyss of her stupidity. Of *course* Anna would have resented her voyeurism and would have been determined to pay her back in kind one day. El was ashamed— hotly, fiercely ashamed of herself for walking into the trap. For not seeing. Because Ryder's nickname made perfect sense now. *Snack.* It was his move, to get girls upstairs. *I'm fucking hungry, are you?*

Bryce had begun to snore, but El didn't roll over to nudge him. She lay immobile in the predawn darkness, her phone under her hands. Forty-five minutes had passed, and still she wasn't tired at all. She wanted to get up, have her Americano and abandon this morbid reflection—to put her complicated relationship with Anna to rest, at least for the moment. But some other part of her wanted to stay where she was and relitigate it all. To defend Anna's memory. What if it *hadn't* been Anna in the doorway? What if Anna hadn't known Ryder to be a creep? And even if she had, hadn't it been El's choice to sleep with Ryder anyway? And hadn't El really been the one in the wrong that night, seeking to even the score with Anna—because it wasn't actually true that Anna had "stolen" Shay, was it? Shay had taken advantage of Anna. He was the bad guy. And Ryder was the bad guy. Anna and El were victims, both of them.

Or maybe, said the prosecutor in El's head, *you're all bad.*

chapter twenty-three

The end of summer brought searing temperatures, and with the heat wave came chaos in the news—a hack by international parties unknown had compromised the socials of millions of Americans, including some prominent celebrities and members of Congress. Meanwhile, the White House held a press conference to address a heartbreaking phenomenon scientists could not yet explain: all over the country, dogs were running away, abandoning their owners in record proportions. The numbers had been growing steadily for months. People were encouraged to keep their dogs inside as much as possible, out of parks and kennels, in case there was some new contagion, some virus or disease that affected the brain, prompting tame dogs to revert to their wilder inclinations.

El read about these events from the high-performance tablet Bryce had bought for her. The thing about the dogs made sense—there'd been so many missing posters lately, plus there had been that husky barking madly on the street at the father with the baby, and the one that had jumped in front of the train, and the one going nuts in that SUV the other night. Then there had been Lila's story about her family dog running away . . . It was with a strange twinge that El remembered she and Lila were no longer friends. Lila was, without a doubt, taking Navya's side in everything. How far along was Lila now? In sixth months or so, she and Mathias would be parents. Maybe it was the notion of friendship that brought it to her mind, but El suddenly recalled one more dog-related episode: months ago, before she'd ever met Bryce, she had come across that Ohio dog tag with the inscription *Man's Best Friend*. This struck El now as a strange thing to have had engraved. It was sort of grasping, wasn't it? Sort of insistent? *Your biological destiny is to be my helpmeet.*

El had already checked her social media to make sure she hadn't been hacked, but she double-checked now and, out of boredom, updated her security settings. There was no actual reason for her to care about getting hacked. Her private messages were all tame and uninteresting, and if the hackers found her debit card information, so what? She was hardly using it anymore. Bryce had made El an account holder at his bank, and she'd recently received a heavy black metal card in the mail, just like Bryce's own. She had begun, at Bryce's urging, to shop for the wedding: he had stressed that money was no object when it came to her dress or anything else—his only request was that the ceremony itself be small, as big weddings made him anxious. El had no issue with this ask. Her mother was her only real family. Who else would she want to invite, realistically? The cord had officially been cut with Navya. The day after El had seen her at the club, Nav had sent a text. Something about having seen things clearly while she was high, seeing what El had become, El had the wrong kind of energy, Navya was getting older and didn't need it in her life, she needed positive, giving people, she thought it would be best for both of them if she let go. Let El go.

El had not replied.

Crystal continued to be a ghost. Maybe she had landed that pilot in L.A. after all. El didn't really care anymore.

To her estranged friends and to grim news articles, El found she was indifferent. Anna's murder, on the other hand, continued to haunt her. Every night without fail El had horrible, Anna-themed nightmares and she'd wake, pulse racing, at dawn. In the deep blue mornings she would lie on her side with one eye open, touching the waffle-shaped depressions in their lightweight summer blanket, counting by multiples of five to calm her nervous system: *five ten fifteen twenty twenty-five thirty thirty-five forty forty-five fifty fifty-five sixty sixty-five . . .*

It only aggravated El's anxiety that Ansel kept sending updates about the ongoing investigation into Anna's death. He'd recently sent an article about the police having questioned Anna's female neighbor and the neighbor's boyfriend; this boyfriend had once taken a picture of Anna from behind as she'd unlocked her front door. With the article, Ansel had sent a message: Picture it. Boyfriend takes photo. Anna gets angry. Picks an argument? Or girlfriend is jealous. Kills Anna? Either scenario possible.

El now carried Mace when she went running. When she was out on the street and a man came too close behind her, within potential grabbing distance, she moved to the side and waited for him to pass. It wasn't rational, this new hypervigilance—the world had been dangerous before Anna died, El knew that. But it *felt* more dangerous now. The danger seemed closer and, at the same time, more unknowable. El longed to escape the city, but whenever she asked Bryce about going to his family's property in East Hampton he begged off, saying it wasn't the right time yet.

On the very last day of August, El bothered Bryce about the Hamptons again. He was buttoning his shirt, a pastel blue one she had never liked, in front of the full-length mirror by the bedroom window. She hovered behind him.

"There can't be a better time than now. It's almost Labor Day! I'm sure your mom expects us to come sometime anyway, now that we're engaged."

"I just know she's not in a good place. When she doesn't call for a while I try to give her space."

El wanted to say something sarcastic. The guy who always had to know what she was doing, who had stalked her out to Brooklyn and all the way home, *he* was trying to give someone *space*? Was he *capable* of that? But she held her tongue. She had too many questions about his mother. He was always so vague about her.

"What do you mean she's not in a good place? Not in a good place how?"

"She struggles with certain—phobias."

"Is it agoraphobia?"

Shirt buttoned, Bryce turned around and brushed past El, fetching socks from the dresser.

· "She just has trouble with people," he said, taking a seat on the edge of the bed and crossing his left leg over his right. She watched him pull a thin plaid sock over his wide foot. "She's medicated, but she still goes through rough patches." He looked over his shoulder at El. "I actually haven't gotten to tell her about the engagement yet."

"Oh." El wasn't disappointed, she was just realizing that if Bryce hadn't told his own mother they were engaged, maybe he hadn't told anyone. And she hadn't told anyone . . . Did no one know they were engaged besides the two of them?

"I'm sorry," Bryce said, and he looked it.

"No, I understand. Obviously, I understand."

There was a pause in which Bryce put on his other sock and El stared in the direction his right toe was pointing, at the dust-free baseboard by the dresser. Bryce's voice broke the quiet.

"I mean I would tell my mum this second if I thought she could process it."

El bristled. "What does that mean?"

"What does what mean?"

"You're implying that it's bad I haven't told *my* mom already."

"I'm not saying it's bad," he said, lifting his hands in the air in a gesture of surrender.

"But you want me to tell my mom we're engaged."

"I guess I don't understand why you haven't."

"And I don't understand why we can't go to the fucking Hamptons. We don't even have to hang out with your mom, we can just relax on the beach. Summer's almost over, let's just go!"

"I don't want to fight," he said, defeated.

"We're not fighting!"

He stood up. "I'm making myself a coffee. I'll make you one too."

Frustrated, El hid in the bathroom while Bryce busied himself in the kitchen. She washed her face and put collagen patches under her eyes. When Bryce finally called out that he was leaving, she shuffled to the foyer. They both leaned in for a grudging kiss but somehow barely grazed each other's lips. "Jesus," Bryce said. He grabbed her face between his hands and pulled her toward him, planting a smacker on her mouth and both her cheeks.

"Ahhh!" she squealed, shooing him out. "Be gone, or I'll start yelling about the beach again!"

She held their door open as he stepped into the annex in front of the elevator.

"Talk to you later," he said, smiling.

"If you're lucky you will."

"Cheeky cheeky."

When he was gone El plopped on the sofa to drink the

Americano Bryce had made her and to read about a Love Islander who, it turned out, was distantly related to one of her suitors. Then her phone lit up with a text: it was Julia. Calling you, it read.

Of course, it was the end of summer—Julia was home. El's phone vibrated in her hand, and she answered right away.

"Well, worst fucking homecoming ever," Julia said.

"Yeah," El murmured sympathetically.

"I turn on my phone and that's the first thing I see. A message from my mom: 'Anna's dead.' Like what the fuck? No one came to get me? Obviously *missed* the funeral."

"I didn't go. I didn't know where it would be, or when. I thought maybe it would be private or delayed because of what happened."

Julia didn't seem to be listening. "So I'd tell you to come over but I'm a fucking wreck and I'm at my parents'—they're still renovating the kitchen at my place. Some friend of Tom's is crashing here, too, and I can't fucking *breathe*." El heard the squeak of metal and the scrape of traffic. There was a street-facing terrace outside Julia's childhood bedroom and El imagined Julia out there, staring west toward Central Park, looking radiant after her cleansing summer in Greece. There was a long, silent beat.

"It's so fucked up," El said.

Another moment passed, then Julia inhaled. "By the way, you didn't meet that guy, did you? That guy you texted me about—Bryce Ripley-Batten?"

"No."

It was instinct to lie. A hardness in El's brainstem warned her that it was very important in this moment not to make a false step. To stay very still.

"Okay, good," Julia said, and she sounded relieved. "'Cause he's a fucking creep."

chapter twenty-four

The words looped in El's mind: *he's a fucking creep, he's a fucking creep*. She had to bring herself back to the moment so she could listen, because Julia was still talking.

"—to camp with us. Me and Anna used to go to this camp, every summer—"

"I remember," El said quickly.

"Yeah. Anyway Bryce was ob*sessed* with Anna."

"Like what? How?"

"Just like, he was always watching her? There was a rumor that he tried to intimidate this guy Jason, 'cause Jason liked Anna. Anyway like a year or whatever ago I found out Bryce had bought the house next to ours at the beach. His mom lives out there. She's got dementia or something. Carmen met her nurse once."

A picture rose in El's mind, a picture of the beach as it had been months ago, the morning after Julia's party. She had gone to retrieve her underwear, and she'd seen two women walking together. The elder of the two had given El a disdainful look while her dog with the gray fur had barked. El's eyes traveled to the red photo album on the bookshelf in front of her. She was putting it together now, the haughty woman who looked like Elizabeth Taylor, who'd been vaguely familiar to her—that was Bryce's mother! And the puppy in the photo album with the drab gray fur . . . *Mouse*, Bryce had said. *She was more Mum's dog. She actually had a litter. Mum kept one.*

"I only saw Bryce one time," Julia was saying. "I actually think it was the only time I ever spoke to him. I was out by the pool and he came from behind the pool house, like he'd hopped the fence between our properties, so that was *weird*. And he like, says hi and that he wants to meet up with some old camp people and that he's lost Anna's number and did I have it. I didn't give it to him obviously. This was before Anna moved."

The lie, Bryce's lie that he had never known Anna and Julia, reverberated in El's mind, shrill as a whistle. She did not want to know this: she couldn't understand. And yet, *she could.* Her father had lived two lives. Anyone could have two lives. What had Bryce said when he'd proposed to her? *If I could divide myself, I would.* He had described himself as two people, as the unsavory guy who had followed her and as the good, safe guy she could come home to. *The guy who's on your side,* he'd said.

"Then what?" El asked. "Did Bryce ever get in touch with Anna?" Her throat was so dry her voice was coming out about an octave lower than normal.

"No idea. Four months later, Anna was in Paris. No reason, just, I'm moving. Her mom gave me her number when the old one stopped working. But I overheard Dad talking a little after that—he and Anna's family attorney are both members at the Links—and *Dad* said there was some kind of big dispute settled out of court and it had to do with Anna and some guy."

When El said nothing Julia added, "So maybe Bryce did something, like harassed Anna or something."

"Right," El managed.

"*Or*, you know, Anna just fucked around with the wrong married asshole. I could see her suing for emotional damages just to spite somebody."

Yes! El thought. *Yes, that has to be it. Bryce had nothing to do with Anna.* But getting involved with the wrong guy and suing him? It didn't *feel* like Anna. Those were the actions of someone hot-headed. Anna was cold-blooded to a fault. Then El remembered the theory she'd briefly entertained in Paris, that perhaps Anna had known someone was after her. Terrible dread filled El's chest.

"So." Julia sighed. "I'm doing a thing for Anna. Like a memorial I guess. I asked her parents, but they'll be staying with friends in Zurich for a while. So it'll just be people you know. I'll get you deets. It'll be soon—before L.A. I have a friend who's a producer, wants to collaborate blah blah blah.

He's brilliant actually. And *mature*. Possible endgame, I don't know. We're definitely good creatively. Anyway, I'll see you there."

El managed a gravelly goodbye.

With the curtains fully drawn back, sun flooded the living room. El's instinct was to hide, to find a dark place—wildly she thought of pictures she had once seen of a village in the Russian Arctic. She wanted to escape herself and her dread, escape the ideas thundering in her temples, demanding contemplation.

Bryce had known Anna. And Julia. He had gone to Julia's beach house last summer to talk. He owned the house next door! So his story about coming to Julia's party as a plus-one, not knowing whose house it was—that had been a lie too. Why had he really come to the party? To look for Anna? Then he'd met El . . . El, the poor man's Anna. El tensed with fresh horror—what if Bryce had only reached out to her to get to Anna? But no, that wasn't right. Bryce had been surprised, in Paris, almost *upset* to learn that El had gone to private school for a year with Anna and Julia. So Bryce had rediscovered Anna, through El, by coincidence . . . Although that only brought El's ruminating to a darker place.

Of course Julia had not made any connection between Bryce and Anna's death, but Julia didn't know that Bryce had been in Paris when Anna had been killed. And hadn't the murder happened—hadn't it been the very same day that El had *told* Bryce where Anna was? She had showed him Anna's address on her phone, or he'd peeked over her shoulder to look . . . *Latin Quarter,* he'd said. *She's not so far from the hotel.*

But the police would know, El thought, her head pounding with sharp pain. *If* Bryce really had harassed Anna in New York, stalked her or something, the French police would've spoken to Anna's family. Her family would've told the cops whatever they knew. Right? So Bryce couldn't have come under suspicion, because no one had questioned him.

Then again . . . El considered what she knew about ultra-wealthy people and her heart sank. Wealthy people were private to a fault. Their schools, their clubs, their matters most of all. It was very possible that Anna's family had told the French police *nothing* about whatever had taken place in New York. And there was this, too—when she and Bryce had been in the courtyard of Anna's apartment building, hadn't it been *Bryce* who had shot down the notion of Anna's flight from New York being connected to her murder?

El thought about being in the hotel and watching the TV coverage about the murder. Bryce hadn't wanted to watch. And the night . . . the night of the murder itself . . . when El had woken up, Bryce had been in the shower and he'd said . . . she had thought nothing of it at the time . . . that he'd had to throw out his shirt . . .

The vomit was out before El could move or even bend toward the ground. It spilled out, down her chest, into a puddle between her legs. It was bile, a swampy green.

The sun was on her face, her neck, her knees. She lay there, roasting and quaking in her sick and her uncertainty. There passed several minutes of complete silence. There was only the pain in her head and the frozen brightness of the room. And then a thought emerged from the stillness: she had to talk to someone who knew Bryce better than she did.

chapter twenty-five

The only available automatic at the rental car place was a slightly smoky Dodge Charger. The Charger looked like a long black snout, and the gear shift was stiff and jaunty in El's unpracticed hand. She had hardly driven before. Shortly after the move to New York her mother had sold their car, so there had been no vehicle with which to practice save the one at the discount driving school where El had taken a handful of lessons the summer after high school. She had passed her test on the second attempt and in the years since had driven only out of necessity. And right now certainly qualified as a necessity. She'd thought about taking the Metro-North and then a taxi, but she felt safer having her own car. She didn't know what to expect: it would be good to have an exit strategy.

Bryce's father lived in a hamlet several miles outside Green-wich, Connecticut. El had found his address easily, just like Emma, who, all those months ago, had searched him online in order to prove to El what sort of disgustingly rich and selfish people her boyfriend's family were. After finding Mr. Batten's house on her computer, El had wiped her search history. She had left her phone in the apartment just in case Bryce was still tracking her location, and she'd deleted her call history and Julia's "calling you" text on the off chance that Bryce got home before she did. She'd rented the Charger with cash and paid the extra fifty bucks for a GPS.

El had no idea if Mr. Batten would see her—did he even know who she was? As far as El was aware, Bryce and his father were not close. Still, Mr. Batten would know more about his son than she did. He had to. Someone had to have answers for her. Bryce's mother was off-limits of course—El couldn't disturb someone who was sick, someone with dementia or agoraphobia or whatever it was Bryce's mother actually suffered from. Plus, visiting the Hamptons posed too much of a risk: if Bryce's mother's nurse did know Carmen, then word of El's visit could somehow get back to Julia, and El was determined that Julia not know any more than she had to at this point. Was it any of *Julia's* business that Bryce had been in Paris when Anna had been killed? No. El was the one living with Bryce. She was the one engaged to him. Julia wasn't in any danger.

And also—was Bryce even dangerous? He'd wanted to get in touch with his camp crush as an adult, so what? And Anna had blown him off, and he'd gone about his life, but then, Memorial Day weekend, he'd probably been visiting his mother when he'd heard the party going on next door, at Julia's. And he'd just wandered over, hoping to catch Anna there . . . Instead, he'd met El. And when he'd learned, months later, that Anna was El's friend, he'd lied about knowing Anna because he hadn't wanted to seem like a freak or hadn't wanted El to feel jealous. Guys lied about that stuff all the time. Was she stupid to be doing this, being all secretive, going to consult Bryce's father? Should she just scrap the plan now and turn around? She actually looked for a place to get off the highway. The next exit was Harrison. Two miles. She glanced at her GPS: just 9.8 more miles to Greenwich. She hesitated, her palms damp on the wheel. She was almost at the Harrison exit. She was in the middle lane. Should she get over? Car after car had been overtaking her, and now that she'd slowed to forty-five miles an hour they raced by, some beeping angrily as they passed. *Should I get over?* She nearly signaled, but fear stayed her hand. A new thought had come to her, that not one but *two* of Bryce's past love interests were dead. There was Anna, and then there was Allegra, the girl he'd dated in high school, the girl who'd broken up with him at Cambridge. *But you read about Allegra*, El told herself. *She wasn't murdered. Her death was an accident.*

Allegedly, whispered the prosecutor in her head.

It was impossible for El to be sure if she was building a case against Bryce because the case was there, or because he had lied about knowing Anna and lying struck a deep father-chord with her. El had taken a lot on faith in her relationship with Bryce, had trusted him and his good intentions even when his behavior had set off faint alarm bells. Had she been a sucker this whole time? Had she ignored every warning sign because she'd been so desperate to believe that the fairy tale could happen to her, that a guy—a provider and, okay fine, a father surrogate—could waltz in to give her all the validation she'd so long been denied? Or was this panic she felt now a hysterical reaction to some stupid lies her boyfriend had told, because the little girl inside her saw everything in black and white and couldn't tolerate the idea that a man could disappoint you without being wholesale terrible and beyond redemption?

El watched the Harrison exit come and go. She moved her hands to the top of the wheel and squared her shoulders. Seven more miles to Greenwich. She was already here. She was doing this. She was going to talk to Bryce's father just to know, just to make sure, that her fiancé was the person she knew him to be: generous, steadfast and protective certainly, but not— she couldn't even go there again. *A fucking creep*, Julia had said, but what did Julia know? That had been Julia's impression after speaking to Bryce, what? Once in her adult life?

Mr. Batten lived in a hamlet on the coast, so as soon as El took the Greenwich exit she began to make her way southeast. With the noise of the highway behind her, she turned off the air and rolled down her window. The first homes she passed were modest, by Batten standards anyway. They were nice middle-class houses with wind chimes and tomato gardens;

they put El in mind of her childhood in Maryland. But the further El drove, the more the road broadened and smoothed. Front yards were replaced by high gates and cottonwoods. Driveways grew long. The GPS directed El to make a series of left turns, and finally announced that her destination lay five hundred yards down a wide, quiet lane. There were no people at all, and yet El felt watched as the Charger inched down the street.

She halted before the gate of Mr. Batten's mansion. This was the one, no question: there were no trees planted to obscure the house from sight. It stood gray, tall and stately as a castle. How were you supposed to get into this place though? There didn't seem to be a buzzer or an intercom.

The sun blazed overhead as El stepped out of the car. Shielding her eyes with her hand, she squinted at the top of the gate to see if a camera had been placed there. She couldn't see anything but waved with both arms above her head just in case. She felt stupid, but she wanted to get someone's attention. She didn't want them thinking she was some random person who'd gotten turned around. She waved for probably thirty seconds, but the gate didn't budge. She put her arms down. It had never occurred to her that he might not be here, but of course Mr. Batten would have other homes. She jogged down the side of the gate, hunting for a sign of life. A gardener. Landscaper. Somebody. The back of her neck was already soaked in sweat. She thought about what it would feel like to turn back to the city without answers, to face Bryce without reassurance from someone else . . . It was unthinkable. If she'd had her phone, she could've found out whether any other Batten residences were public information. Shit.

Maybe she would have to visit the Hamptons after all. Risk it. Talk to Bryce's mother if she could . . . Except, Bryce probably paid for his mother's nurse. Wouldn't the nurse be obligated to call Bryce if El showed up and started asking sensitive questions about him, her employer?

Arf! Arf! Arf Arf!

El swiveled. A bloodhound half her height was bounding down the lane, brown ears flapping. It was coming right for her, teeth bared.

She threw herself toward the Charger, her hand grasping at the stinging hot metal of the door handle. She launched her body in through the passenger side and shut the door a *second* before the hound reached her. It jumped for the window, its deafening bark piercing the air again and again.

Fighting tears of panic El crawled to the driver's seat. She turned on the car as the dog beat its paws against the window, slobbering, rabid. She hit the accelerator, but the car wouldn't go.

"What the fuck!! FUCK!!"

She accelerated again and the car revved, unmoving. Then she realized—she was still in park! The moment she put her hand on the gear shift, the gate before her swung open. She sped through unthinking, and she imagined that she heard the dog whine as she drove out of reach. Somehow it struck her as a cry of sympathy, of despair. She threw the car in park as the gates closed, and whipped her neck around to look through the back windshield, but the hound had disappeared. Her heart knocked against her chest. It was probably just the high stress of the moment, her neurons firing at random, but the name "Dani" flashed across her mind. *Dani? What is Dani?* And then she remembered that had been the name on the Ohio dog tag she'd found on the street. Dani was Man's Best Friend.

Gingerly, she turned forward and bent below her sun visor so she could take in this gray monstrosity of a house. There were three stories, and the two windows on the uppermost floor were small and thin, like eyes. She'd been so distraught when she'd pulled through the gates that she only noticed now a long, low building to her right, also of gray stone—the term *carriage house* came to mind, though she didn't really know what that was.

Someone had seen her. Someone had let her through the gates. Had it been Bryce's father? *It was probably just a member of his staff,* she told herself. *Don't get too excited.* But she couldn't help feeling a bit encouraged. This had to be the place to get answers. Wasn't there always a beast to encounter before entering a castle full of secrets?

She got out of the car and approached the rose-colored front door. Why was no one coming out? She climbed the three stone steps and paused for a moment, thinking. Nobody knew where she was. She had no phone. She'd paid for the Charger in cash. She'd seen no one driving up to the house. If something happened, who would find her? She thought about her namesake, Héloïse. Her body lost to time.

Someone coughed behind the door, a deep, guttural cough. Instinctively El leaned back, and the door swung open to reveal a middle-aged man in a very bad way, bald and yellow and sick. He looked into El's face with fierce impatience.

"What the hell do you want?"

chapter twenty-six

El had lots of practice with hiding nerves: all she had to do was think of this like an audition.

"Hi. I'm El. Sorry to just drop by—I'm a friend of Bryce's."

She thought her tone had been even and convincing, but the sick man was just glaring at her, not saying a word. She remembered, the first time they'd met for drinks, Bryce saying that his father bore an uncanny resemblance to Boris Johnson. Either the man before her was not Mr. Batten, or Mr. Batten had been very much changed by whatever was ailing him. His fair-skinned face was full of fine wrinkles, like a piece of paper folded over and over on itself. There was *something* Boris-like about him though, she supposed . . . She hadn't seen a picture of Boris Johnson in a long time, but recalled that his blue eyes were closely set, and this man's were too.

"You're Mr. Batten, aren't you?"

"Who else would I be?"

With a scowl Mr. Batten turned around, though he left the door open. Had he meant to, or was this confusion, memory loss? She watched him begin to make his way down a long hall, and she decided to interpret the open door as a grudging invitation. She stepped quickly over the threshold.

It wasn't difficult to catch up with Mr. Batten. In fact, soon she was walking with tiny steps so as not to overtake him. He used a cane and coughed every couple of feet, wet strangling coughs. There didn't seem to be any staff around, medical or otherwise, although some rich people probably preferred their employees out of sight, out of mind. Still, there'd been no other cars out front. None that El had seen anyway. Maybe that carriage house was a garage?

Mr. Batten led her to a room at the back of the house, a den with three walls of floor-to-ceiling bookshelves. The fourth wall had tall windows overlooking an expansive yard. In the far distance, between a pair of oak trees, El could see a glimmer of green ocean.

In the middle of the room was a sitting area, where a brown leather chair stood beside a fancy-looking oxygen machine. Mr. Batten lowered himself into the chair, and El took a seat on the olive-colored couch opposite. Above them, a wide old fan spun slowly.

"Am I okay here?" she asked, indicating the couch.

"To what? To *sit*?"

Between the lines on his face, the gurgling wetness in his

throat and the snap of his voice, Mr. Batten brought to mind an ancient crocodile. This was a difficult man. She would have to become her most winning self if she wanted him to tell her anything.

"I'm sorry to bother you, again."

He narrowed his eyes at a spot over her shoulder. "Never seen it before. That bloodhound."

"Yes, that was wild! Thank you for opening your gate. It just came out of nowhere."

"Probably a stray . . . Could be it's the neighbors' I suppose. People want to rescue these animals, they should just be put down."

"I'm sensing that you're not a dog person."

Honestly, she wasn't much of a dog person herself. (Though one time Colton, her ex, had told her that she reminded him of a dog. "I remind you of Georgia?" she'd asked, referring to his family's dog whom she'd seen approximately seven thousand pictures of. "No," he'd said. "Not Georgia, actually—she's like a very specific personality. Very independent. I'm just saying in general. You know how dogs are usually just like, *right there*, all the time? Like I get off work, I get out of the shower, and you're there waiting for me. It's cute. You know what I mean." And then El had said, "No, I *don't* know what you mean," but, really, she had known. She followed. She was a follower. Loyal, submissive, dependent. Colton had felt that dependence, that need of hers, had fed on it, for a time.

Mr. Batten coughed again and the glottal sound made her flinch. He pounded on his chest twice with a stiff fist and cleared his throat loudly. He looked at El, enunciating each of his words with force, like a tired fighter landing jabs with the last of his strength.

"Where is Bryce, if you're such great friends?"

"Bryce is my fiancé actually."

Mr. Batten leaned forward with new intensity. "He—"

The coughing resumed abruptly, and this time it didn't stop when Mr. Batten pounded on his chest. El leaned forward, ready to help, but Mr. Batten ignored her. With a practiced hand he hit a button on the oxygen machine, and with the other laced the machine's skinny plastic tube around his head so it stuck in both nostrils. A few deep breaths and the coughing slowed.

After a moment El said: "He didn't tell me you weren't well."

"He didn't tell me jack shit about you. But—" Mr. Batten set his cane against an ornate end table with a grunt. "Not much of a surprise. Like pulling teeth to get him up here. He finally showed, few weeks ago. Both times he was—" Mr. Batten whistled twice in succession. She understood him. Bryce had been in and out. "Then he calls and says he's not coming anymore."

Last month . . . She thought back. When would Bryce have had time to visit Connecticut? He was always with her when he wasn't working. Maybe he'd skipped work, or—no, oh *shit*—the fundraiser! And the dinner, before Paris, with her mother. Both times he had bailed last minute, had blamed Ian, his boss . . . Then she'd put her foot down, saying she expected him to show up going forward. He'd given her that awed, excited look like that had been exactly what he'd needed to hear. So she'd given him an excuse to stop visiting his father ... But why hadn't he just told her about his father being sick? Conflicting feelings about dad was certainly territory she understood. Why had he lied, unless ... ?

Unless he didn't want you to find out more about him, hissed the fiendish prosecutor in her head. *The father knows something.*

Mr. Batten was looking her over. "Why are you here?"

She could picture Mr. Batten in a boardroom. Even this frail he had a commanding air. She decided that it would be best, now, not to be coy or charming, but to ask directly for the information she wanted in the least inflammatory or accusatory way possible. Because she wasn't accusing, really. She just needed confirmation that the wild narrative in her brain was wrong. That, aside from a couple minor lies, Bryce was just a slightly jowly, excessively rich, codependent romantic. That he was more or less the person she knew.

"I just have some questions," she said.

"That so."

She took a breath and forced herself to meet Mr. Batten's sharp, bloodshot gaze. "Bryce recently took me to Paris, and while we were there an old friend of mine was killed. It was all over the news and Bryce pretended not to know her, my friend, but it turns out he did know her. They went to camp together when they were kids. Her name was Anna." Pausing, El searched Mr. Batten's face for signs of shock or recognition, but he wasn't moving a muscle. "Anyway, Anna—last year, she had some kind of out-of-court legal situation involving a guy, before she moved from New York to Paris, and I had heard that Bryce may have been trying to get in touch with Anna around that time . . ." El faltered. "So I thought maybe you'd be able to confirm that Bryce had no, you know, legal trouble recently I guess with . . . anyone."

Mr. Batten looked grieved. "Didn't I just tell you that I can barely get my son to see me? What makes you think I would know about his legal business?"

Great. Now she'd upset a vulnerable man, and he didn't even have the answers she needed. Of course he didn't. This whole plan had been a bad gamble. She felt ashamed—she needed to go—

"Bryce ever tell you about Brooke?"

Mr. Batten's chair was bathed in sunlight, and his close-set eyes appeared pale and glassy as they bore into her. There was something prophetic about that look, and even though El was not sure what Bryce's dead sister had to do with anything, she felt uneasy.

"Well?" Mr. Batten urged. He was leaning forward again— too far, she felt, with no cane to support him.

"All Bryce said was that she—that Brooke had passed away."

"Did he say how?"

El tried to remember. "No. Well, I think he said she died suddenly. Unexpectedly."

Mr. Batten's nostrils flared, and he took a long tug of air before removing the oxygen from his nostrils. He held the plastic tube in his hand, on his lap. It looked like an umbilical cord.

"My sister-in-law, Claire, had a daughter a few years after Bryce was born. Claire was an addict. Blew through her entire trust before she was thirty. We—Bryce's mother and I—agreed to take in the little girl. Brooke."

The hairs at the base of El's skull were actually tingling. Whatever story this was, El didn't want to know it. She wanted this ailing multimillionaire to keel over right now before he could get the words out. He'd given all that money to blood-sucking drug companies, right? He deserved it. She glanced at the umbilical cord in his lap. His silly tether to life. *I don't need to know this story. I can still leave.* But it was happening, Mr. Batten was speaking, and, whatever the protests in her mind, she couldn't bring herself to walk away.

"Couple years passed. Claire didn't come back. Never so much as a phone call. But Brooke got plenty of attention— Bryce and his mother, they *doted* on Brooke." Mr. Batten sniffed, as if there were nothing so pathetic as loving an abandoned child. El found she liked this man less and less. "When I split with Bryce's mother I moved here. The three of them stayed in England. Then—I don't know how long it was exactly—Bryce was older, eleven or twelve, and Claire got her act together. Showed up saying she wanted to take Brooke away with her to Italy, where she was living with a boyfriend. Bryce's mother said we needed to fight it—she asked me to fly over, I did. We hired a lawyer. I was prepared to pay a lot of money for the right judge to hear us out, but after all that hassle Bryce's mother changed her mind. Realized maybe she didn't have a right to stand between a daughter and her mother, so okay. Claire and Brooke would leave. I was there the morning they were supposed to go. It was cold as shit—that house, always freezing. The English, that's how they are. You could see your damn breath in your own bedroom. Anyway, I wake up and I hear someone screaming outside. I run out and it's Claire. She's all the way down the hill at the edge of the pond and I see Bryce there, and the closer I get I see this huge hole in the middle of the ice."

El could see it. The screaming mother, the frozen ground, the young boy with the drooping shoulders and the pouting face, staring at the hole in the water.

"Bryce's story was that Brooke had tried throwing her toy across the pond, but it landed in the middle. Brooke ran out to get it, the ice cracked and she fell in." Mr. Batten shook his head. "Bryce's mother didn't believe it. She said Brooke loved that plastic horse—carried it everywhere. She would never have thrown it."

"So Bryce's mother thought . . . that Bryce threw the toy? Intentionally?"

"I only heard her say it once. She was hysterical. Said ever since he found out she was leaving, Bryce would watch Brooke, stare at her with this menace. I don't know. Brooke was a little kid but Bryce was just furious apparently that she would leave him, so. His mother thought Bryce had a hand in what happened. Naturally I couldn't leave Bryce with her. Brought him back to America with me. His mother was never the same. In and out of institutions. She has full-time care now."

Outside, the shining grass on the lawn blew back and forth. It was overgrown. That seemed unusual for someone so wealthy . . . When Mr. Batten spoke again, El had to force herself to turn back toward him. She didn't know if she could handle whatever else he had to tell her, but what was the alternative? She'd had the option—on the highway, even moments ago—to abort this mission and choose ignorance; she had chosen, instead, to find out everything. She had asked for this.

"My hours were long back then, when Bryce moved in. But I didn't want him with the nanny all the time, so I sent him to a camp for the summer. When Bryce came back after that first year—I do remember it, only because he taped them to the wallpaper—he had these pictures, all of the same girl. She had dark hair, like yours."

El felt her breath catch. Mr. Batten looked at her, stern.

"I couldn't say who she was."

"Do you still have the pictures? Are they here?"

"What, you think I've kept a shrine to my son's childhood for twenty damn years?"

"Can I ask another . . ." She felt rudderless, drained, but she had to ask this final question. "Did you know Allegra at all? She went to Cambridge too. She was Bryce's girlfriend in high school. She died in an accident. Allegra Taylor?"

"I've never heard that name." Mr. Batten leaned back in his chair and took a wheezing breath. He laced the umbilical cord around himself again. "This machine's the only thing I can't seem to quit. Fired all my staff. Threw the meds down the drain. That's why I wanted Bryce to come. I don't care for him, but he's my son. Thought he'd be the last person I ever saw. Almost was." He tucked the oxygen back in his nose. "Guess it was lucky for me that dog wanted to rip out your throat."

On the drive back to the city, El contemplated running for it. Making one last cash withdrawal from Bryce's account and driving to Canada, or to JFK. She could fly anywhere, start over. For years she'd been treading water in Manhattan. This was her chance to break away.

Highway traffic had slowed to a crawl. An older model, the GPS didn't display live updates, but it was safe to assume there'd been an accident. El brought her window down, but there was no breeze to feel. She cast about for something distracting, but on either side of the highway thick clusters of trees stood sentinel, blocking anything else from view. Her pulse quickened. She willed the traffic to move, but eight miles an hour was the fastest she could go without ramming the sedan two feet from her bumper. Her throat felt tight. She took several hasty breaths. She was sure that if she could just keep moving, she would be fine. It was the slowness creating this panic: the motionless trees, the creeping traffic, the dead air. And then, all at once, El knew she couldn't run away. Because once she got to Cape Town or Dublin or Rotterdam or Oslo, she would have to be still again, and the panic would return. She would be lying on her new mattress, preparing to sleep, or on her way to work, swaying with the movements of a bus, and she'd realize she had no idea who she was. She couldn't live an anonymous life again. Before Bryce, she had practically been a floating object, tethered only in the most threadbare way to other people. In the last three months she had made some decisions, at least. Maybe they'd been good and maybe they'd been bad, but they had been the decisions of a *person*. A person she wasn't prepared to abandon.

What she really ought to do right now was get off at the next exit, buy a cheap phone and drive back to Mr. Batten's. Demand that he repeat all the things he'd told her. But what *had* he told her? He'd known nothing about Allegra. He'd known that once upon a time his preteen son had been majorly obsessed with a girl who was probably Anna. He'd told her that Bryce's mother, a woman who'd clearly suffered some kind of breakdown, thought her son had conspired to kill his younger cousin—this was disturbing, no doubt, but to go to the police about Bryce, El would need something solid. They wouldn't charge a rich guy like Bryce without hard evidence, which she didn't have, because maybe Bryce *hadn't* done anything. That said, didn't she owe it to Anna to find out if Bryce's mother had been right? If Bryce had it in him to kill?

Traffic had now reached a complete standstill, and El shut her eyes and put her head to the wheel. She wished there were a way to talk to someone about all this, to get an objective perspective without having to do anything official. Mr. Batten had spoken candidly about his son, but that didn't mean he wasn't biased. The problem was, there were no objective people to talk to. She didn't know any attorneys or anyone in law enforcement—

And then it hit her. She *did* know someone.

chapter twenty-seven

El got off the highway at the first opportunity and headed
west, taking back roads until she reached Interstate 80.
According to the GPS she would arrive at Ansel's town
in the Poconos in ninety minutes. She couldn't call him without her phone of course, but her plan was to find the police
station and pray that he would be on duty.

As she drove, she thought about how she would phrase her
problem. El had no intention of telling Ansel that she suspected, or feared, that Bryce had had something to do with
Anna's murder. Ansel would no doubt feel obligated to report
something like that. And El felt that she'd already gotten the
full story about Brooke. In fact she probably had more information about Brooke than had been made public: no doubt
the family had kept the details of the little girl's death quiet.
What El did want to dig into was Allegra. El felt somehow

that if she could be sure that Allegra's death really had been an accident—if she could confirm that there had been nothing suspicious about it at all—then she could feel largely at ease. Without Allegra, then Bryce's association with two other dead people, Brooke and Anna, felt incidental. Without Allegra, the drowning of a little girl who had lost her toy—regardless of who had thrown it—felt like a tragic, isolated incident, and the murder, almost two decades later, of a beautiful heiress felt like a wholly separate tragedy, for which the most logical explanation was the simplest one: some guy with easy access had killed Anna in a rage. Someone like the neighbor who'd taken Anna's picture or the random asshole who'd been harassing women on Anna's block. El wasn't sure what, if anything, Ansel would be able to intuit from the publicly available information about Allegra's death, but he was the cop. That would be for him to determine.

She could not really believe she was willingly seeking Ansel's help. Pompous, grating Ansel. But she knew how seriously he took his job as a police officer, and he wasn't stupid. Speaking of which . . . how would she explain her interest in Allegra Taylor? Or her being out in the Poconos with a rented Dodge Charger and no cell phone? She zipped past an exit for a campground, and the solution came to her: she would borrow from Julia. She would tell Ansel she had gone on a creative retreat where electronics were not allowed. That at the retreat she'd had the idea to write a screenplay for herself to star in, one that would feature the true story of a girl, a University of Cambridge student who had drowned. If he asked where she'd heard about the story she'd say she'd come across it back in college, in the *Daily Mail* or something. That all seemed plausible.

It was four p.m. when El passed a WELCOME TO PENNSYLVANIA sign. Incredibly her gas tank was still one third full, and with less than an hour of her drive left she could definitely make it without stopping. She was desperate to get to Ansel and complete her mission. Skittering clouds flashed across the sky: it was as if someone were turning the lights on and off. She was in the mountains now, and the freeway was no longer flat but full of hills and curves. With every incline, every additional mile, a frantic pressure built in her mind. She moved into the fast lane, flying past trucks and RVs and commuters, feeling as if she were speeding through a tunnel. *Just go. Just get there.*

She nearly forgot to slow down when it came time to exit the freeway, taking the off-ramp much too fast. She pumped the brakes as she turned onto Main Street. This was a small town, one that obviously catered to tourists, skiers probably and fall foliage enthusiasts. There were souvenir shops, inns and ice cream parlors. Standard businesses, too—a hardware store, a pharmacy. But El was scanning for the police station. The GPS had directed her to the edge of downtown, but she didn't see anything that looked like a station. What the hell? And then she saw a patrol car coming from behind what she'd taken to be a medical practice, a one-story building with mostly drawn shades. She looked more closely and saw a small plaque on the building's façade, identifying it as the police department.

There were several parking spaces out front, none of which were occupied. The officers obviously parked out back. She opted to leave the Charger on a side street and walk over so as to be less conspicuous. She shut off the engine and grabbed her purse from the passenger seat, stepping onto the sidewalk in front of an Irish pub. Clearly it was happy hour: strident voices and Springsteen emanated from inside, and as El passed she happened to glance in and see some off-duty officers including— *Ansel.*

She backtracked and hurried into the pub. Her entrance attracted attention, probably because she was the only woman present besides the bartender. She beelined for Ansel, and his face reddened when he saw her, with shock or with hostility she couldn't tell.

"What're you doing here?" His tone was brusque, and he glanced over his shoulder at the other officers. He'd obviously been standing on the outskirts of the group, but now the other men were looking in his direction.

"I wanted to talk to you about something," she said.

The cop closest to Ansel, whose name tag read GUSSEN, cackled in a most suggestive and unattractive manner.

Looking embarrassed, Ansel set down his beer. "Let's go outside."

He led the way and held the door for her with his shoulder rather than his hand. When they stepped onto the sidewalk he gave her a wary look.

"Something wrong? Your mom—?"

"My mom's fine."

"Good."

"It's a nice town," she said, nodding to Main Street. "I can see why you like it. I've been in the area for a few days, actually."

"Why?" he asked immediately.

She fed him the story of the "creative getaway" she'd been on, and when she got to the part about the case of Allegra Taylor and her desire to know as much as possible about Allegra's death for "research" purposes, he became noticeably less tense. It pained her to flatter him, but she did. She had been so impressed by his professionalism at her mother's birthday dinner. She knew she wouldn't be able to uncover the information she wanted without his help.

Ansel cleared his throat. In light of her praise he seemed to regret having ushered her so rudely out of the pub. "Sure. I can look into the case," he said. "You said the woman was at Cambridge, and this was about ten years ago?"

"Yeah, about that."

"Have you asked Bryce whether he knew her?"

Shit. She had forgotten that she'd mentioned Bryce having gone to Cambridge.

"I haven't asked Bryce about it, no. Only because I just came from the retreat and I haven't had my phone. But he's talked about college a lot and he's never mentioned Allegra, so I doubt they knew each other."

She had no problem telling this lie. On the off chance that Ansel came across Bryce's name in connection with Allegra's death, she could maintain that Bryce had never raised the subject with her. But really she was banking on Bryce's name not coming up; she was here to confirm his innocence.

"Okay, well, give me some time and I'll give you a call with what I find out," Ansel said.

Why didn't I anticipate this? Of course Ansel didn't understand her urgency, why she needed him to look into the Allegra matter *now*, before she returned to New York. "Do you . . ."

"What?"

"Do you think you could look into it while I'm here?"

"What do you mean? I thought you'd be on your way home."

She grappled for a justification. "I thought it might be nice for us to . . . hang out a bit."

He looked at her like she had lost her mind.

She had been imagining some small, sad bachelor pad, but Ansel had taken up residence in his late mother's two-bedroom cabin. He explained that when he'd followed his mother to the Poconos initially, he'd rented out the top floor of an elderly couple's home in town; only when Erica had developed ovarian cancer had he moved in to take care of her. It had been five years since Erica's passing and Ansel, El observed, had not redecorated much. The whole place still felt like Erica. She had been an artist of miniature oil paintings and, in later years, miniature sculpture. She'd sold her art on Etsy and to small galleries. Every unsold piece seemed to be on display in the cabin. The carpeting in the kitchen and living room were a color El thought of as Erica Blue, a kind of deep teal. Only the bathroom felt absent Erica's touch. Facial hair (hopefully facial hair) was wedged between the taps on the sink; the toilet seat was up and lightly stained. That once-beige bathmat had not been washed maybe ever. It had taken Ansel sixty seconds to give El the grand tour, and now he gave her a searching look.

"Do you want a beer? When are you thinking of driving home?"

"Not sure yet. I'll take a beer."

Ansel gestured to the squishy sofa in the living room, indicating that El should have a seat. He walked stiffly to the kitchen, the wooden floorboards creaking beneath his socked feet: he had taken off his boots when they'd come in. El hastened to remove her sneakers, too, stood up and set them by the door. She had just sat down again when Ansel returned with two glasses of dark brown ale.

"It's a stout."

Quiet rung out as they both took long sips. They were miles out of town, surrounded by woods. Back at the pub, as soon as Ansel had suggested that El follow him home, she had been inclined to protest. She had assumed they would just walk over to the police station to research Allegra's death. But she'd just secured Ansel's cooperation and hadn't wanted to jeopardize it, so she'd agreed to his plan. This hushed intimacy was almost unbearable though: she could literally hear the tick of the clock coming from Ansel's bedroom.

Ansel set his glass on the steamer trunk between them and checked his watch. "It's quarter to six, so it's almost midnight in the U.K. On the way here I called my buddy, Donaldson, great guy—"

"You've mentioned him," El said, cutting him off. She remembered well the endless discussion of Donaldson at her mother's birthday dinner.

"Right. So his father was a police officer in Cambridge. Retired, now, of course. Donaldson gave me his number, but that call will have to wait till morning."

El had not expected this, but it was coming back to her now. At her mother's, Ansel had said that Donaldson hailed from Cambridge originally. She did *not* remember him saying that Donaldson's father had once been a cop . . . Well, that wasn't so surprising. She made a point of tuning Ansel out as much as possible.

"I'll find out whether his father's familiar with the case," Ansel said.

"I'm sure he will be. It got a lot of attention."

"But this was 2016, wasn't it?"

"Fall or winter 2016. Possibly spring 2017. I forget exactly."

Ansel looked doubtful. "Yeah I don't know. Donaldson's father is up there. Late seventies. Early eighties. He may have been retired by that time."

El felt like saying, *Well then, why even bother reaching out to him?* She held her tongue though and took another sip of her stout. It reminded her of roasted nuts and made her want to belch. She set it down on the trunk.

Scrutinizing her, Ansel asked, "Why do you want to write a movie about this, anyway? An accidental death? Doesn't seem to me there's much to say."

"It's not about death. It's about lost potential in death. About people disappearing into the identities we project onto them in their absence—victim, girlfriend, mistress, heiress." She had no idea where all this was coming from. When had bluffing under pressure become so easy? She also realized that she believed everything she was saying.

"'Heiress,'" he repeated. "Sounds like you're thinking of your friend. You should do a story about her. That one's a mystery." He unfastened the top button of his uniform. "I'll take a look at some of the background on Allegra when I get back. I need a shower." He raised his eyebrows and slapped his hands on his knees before he stood up. El noticed for the first time that he had finally tamed his brows, which had always been thick and unruly. Maybe the intervention of a girlfriend? Had Ansel ever *had* a girlfriend?

As he reached his bedroom, which was a mere ten feet from where El sat on the couch, he turned and asked awkwardly, "I—assume you're staying the night?"

El hesitated. "Uh, I guess that depends on what you find out tonight, but, yeah, if there's a chance you'll learn something from Donaldson's dad in the morning, I guess I should stay."

"Even if you did leave now, you wouldn't make it back to New York before dark, and you're not a very good driver."

"Hey, thanks a lot."

El thought she saw the corner of his mouth twitch before

he shut the door to his room. When he was gone she leaned back on the couch and rubbed her eyes. Bryce was going to *completely* freak out when she didn't come home. She was actually worried that he might call the police—or her mother. The cops wouldn't do anything, though, not until it had been twenty-four hours. As for her mother . . . she would cross that bridge when she came to it. She didn't want to alert her mother to her whereabouts preemptively, just in case Bryce *did* call her mother: she definitely wanted to avoid Bryce showing up at Ansel's in the middle of the night as he'd once shown up at her old apartment. She reached down and massaged her lower back, which had begun to throb. It had been a tense day.

Her belly ached, too, and she realized she was starving. Apart from these few unappetizing sips of beer and the morning Americano she'd promptly thrown back up, she'd had nothing to eat or drink all day. She walked into the kitchen, poured herself a glass of water from Ansel's Brita pitcher and sucked it down. His fridge was full of healthy food: coconut water, spinach, carrots, hummus, tofu, turkey, a Tupperware full of what appeared to be chickpea patties. She noticed a tin of protein powder beside a blender on the counter too. This all helped to explain the change in Ansel's physique that she'd taken note of the night of her mother's party. Ansel had always been scrawny thin. As a young adult he had lived off candy and soda. Now, though, Ansel's lean form had some bulk. *Why am I thinking about this?* she wondered with a jolt. She pulled the carrots and hummus from the fridge, snatched some whole wheat crackers from a cupboard and began to eat.

Fifteen minutes later Ansel emerged from his room with wet hair, wearing a plain white T-shirt and dark sweatpants. His laptop was under his arm and he set it on the grain-wood kitchen table where El had been chowing down. He pulled open the fridge, took out the Tupperware and threw the patties inside into a pan with some olive oil. As he turned a knob on the stove he said, "You're welcome to shower too."

Okay, this she had not thought through, either. If she'd been on a retreat, she would've had a bag with changes of clothes, toiletries . . . It would be weird to take a shower and then come back out with her jeans on.

"Could I borrow something to sleep in?"

She saw him tense, his back to her.

"All my stuff is dirty."

"Oh, uh-huh."

Her chair scraped as she pushed back from the table, and she put away the hummus and crackers. The carrots she'd finished. She bunched the plastic bag in her hand. "Where's your trash . . . ?"

He pointed under the sink. She opened the cabinet and tossed the bag in. "So it's okay if I just grab sweats or something?"

"In my bottom two drawers—you can take whatever from there."

She wasn't sure what else to say, so she didn't say anything. There was only one shower, the one in the bathroom off of his room, and as she began to undress in front of his bed she got goosebumps on her arms. This was *so* weird. If you had told her just last night that she would be getting naked in Ansel's bedroom . . . He was being considerably less heinous than usual, however. No doubt she'd surprised him by being more agreeable herself. She was determined to remain agreeable until he had provided the reassurance she needed about Bryce.

She washed her hair with his 2-in-1 shampoo (judging by the absence of real conditioner, she guessed that he did *not* have a girlfriend, or at least not one with long hair), and beneath the sink she found a clean towel next to backup rolls of toilet paper. Drying herself off and shivering—the sun was beginning to wane and the cabin was not very insulated—she opened the bottom two drawers of his dresser and fished out a pair of basketball shorts and a police academy sweatshirt. She put her bra back on because her nipples were cold but balled her dirty underwear into the pocket of her jeans. She hadn't seen a hair dryer, so she wrapped her body towel around her head and returned to the kitchen, where Ansel was bent over his computer.

"Anything interesting?"

"Allegra Taylor had a head wound."

"Yeah. She fell and knocked herself out. That's how she drowned."

"I've read in several places that she was on a crew team and that she fell outside one of their boathouses, but if that's true, why weren't any of her teammates close by? She wasn't found for hours."

"I'm not sure."

"A woman in my engineering program at Fordham quit

the crew team because she couldn't manage work and practice. Rowers are intense about their training. Hold on—" He clicked on the keypad a few times and then sat reading. "Okay . . . The Cambridge teams train six days a week. So maybe Allegra was by the water on her day off . . . But why would she be?"

"Any reason, right? Maybe she left something down there, at the boathouse or training place or whatever."

He looked somewhat persuaded. "I still can't find an estimated time for when she fell . . . What else did you want to know about her death?"

El felt a knot in her chest relax. "Any details are good. It's helpful to know that she was probably alone down there—that makes sense—"

"There's a picture of the body if you want to see it."

A bead of water had escaped her towel and was now trickling down her neck. She shivered, pulled the towel from around her head and dried herself off. A memory of Bryce scrubbing his body in the shower on the night of Anna's murder flashed in her mind. She felt her heart racing. "How is there a picture of the body?"

"Some bystander took it, most likely. Before a perimeter could be set up."

She walked around the table and stood next to Ansel. They both smelled like his almond bar soap. He looked up at her. "You want to see it?"

She wasn't sure that she did but nodded anyway. He clicked on a tab that had been hidden behind a Reddit forum about untimely deaths. El held her breath while her eyes raked over the picture. The photographer had been pretty far removed from the action and had shot with the wrong shutter speed, but the subject of the picture was still visible: a slight, dark-haired young woman laid out on the pavement, sopping wet. Her face was ghastly, mangled by a devastating wound to the temple. El shuddered, overwhelmed by the eerie feeling that she was looking at Anna: in frame and in coloring, Allegra greatly resembled Anna. She resembled El.

Ansel closed the JPEG and El turned to him.

"I should've prepared you," he muttered.

She took a seat beside him. "I'm all right."

She stared at a wide groove on the table for several long seconds. When Ansel spoke again it was with cautious optimism, as though willing himself to believe that she really was fine.

"Well—some other things I found out about Allegra: She was studying business. Her roommate, Mel, seems to have been her closest friend, although Mel wasn't on the crew team. And Allegra was an American, I'm sure you know that."

"Yeah, I don't need any information about her life before college."

She didn't want him looking into where Allegra had gone to high school; this, she realized, had been another oversight in her plan. Ansel didn't know where Bryce had gone to high school, but there was a chance that he could put together Bryce and Allegra having been acquainted prior to Cambridge.

"I don't know what exactly you're going to need for your

screenplay, but I can probably reconstruct Allegra's last few days if you give me some time."

El realized she had learned nothing that implicated Bryce beyond the fact that he had a thing for slim brunettes. Ansel seemed confused as to why she wanted him to look over a set of facts so ordinary. Well, this had been the best-case scenario. She felt a tension easing at the base of her skull; she had not even realized that she'd been scrunching her shoulders together. She was really very tired.

"I think I need to sleep." She sighed.

"The second bedroom's pretty nice," Ansel said. "I actually only moved into Mom's room six months ago."

He still called his bedroom "Mom's room": El knew a deep grief for him. She nearly said something about what a fine person Erica had been, but she was so fatigued by the day's events her compassion died in her throat. Instead she adopted a false, cheerful voice: "Thanks again for letting me crash your night."

"I don't mind."

Their eyes met briefly. El looked away first.

"See you in the morning," she said.

When she climbed into bed the sun had not even fully set. The sheets were staticky and her mouth was mealy from not having brushed her teeth, but none of it mattered. She turned away from the window, buried her face in the crook of her left arm and thought about Allegra Taylor's body. How could that be the conclusion of a life? Her own breath was warm on her arm. She concentrated on the feeling for a long time before she fell asleep.

Everything was darkness, but the chorus of crickets and the aching loneliness in her gut told her where she was: West Virginia, her father's woods. She extended her hands and felt around, taking cautious steps forward and nearly tripping over a gigantic root. She groped her way around a tree trunk and spied her first glimpse of light, bright red sparks from a fire in the clearing up ahead. The clearing where they'd set up their tent. But where was the tent? She couldn't see it. Where was her father? And then she realized that it had been more than a decade since she'd camped in these woods, more than a decade since she'd seen her father. As she drew close to the clearing, she began to wonder at the nature of the fire. It didn't spark and snap as fires do. It bubbled. Seethed. She got too close, and a stray ember struck her high on her forehead. She gasped automatically, but after a moment understood she hadn't been burned. She touched her face and realized with horror that the red sparks were not fire, but blood. There was a great gash on her face—she was going to die, and someone, a man, was speaking—she cast around for the man but she could not see anyone—blood was spilling into her eyes—

El startled awake to discover she had kicked off all the covers. Both her hands were on her face and her left eye was sore as though she'd been rubbing it. For a moment she was disoriented, then remembered—she was in Ansel's cabin. But what time was it? The short plaid curtains on the windows had not been drawn, and it was still dark outside.

"I understand."

She sat up. The voice had come from the other room. Ansel was awake, talking to someone. *Bryce? But how did he find me?* She stayed still, listening.

"Yes—yes, thank you."

It was Ansel's voice again. He was alone. On the phone. An early work call, maybe. She leaned back against the headboard, but almost immediately slid out of bed, massaging herself and wincing: her lower back was in knots. With no phone and no clock she couldn't tell for sure, but she guessed it was before five a.m. Even so she had probably slept seven or eight hours. She wondered if Bryce had slept at all . . . Maybe she should've just driven back to the city last night—Ansel hadn't discovered anything revelatory about Allegra Taylor. There was still the matter of Bryce having lied to her about knowing Anna, and of course he'd concealed the manner of Brooke's death and his mother's suspicion that he'd orchestrated it. The question was, were these lies she could live with?

"I appreciate it, sir. You as well."

El had forgotten to take off her bra last night and lifted Ansel's sweatshirt to examine the red impressions the underwire had made on her skin. Ansel's call seemed to have ended, and she opened her door with a creak and walked to the sitting room where Ansel sat on the couch staring at his laptop, apparently lost in thought.

"Hi."

Without preamble he replied: "Allegra Taylor's death was not initially ruled an accident."

Her feet were bare, and the wood beneath them felt uneven and cold.

"I couldn't sleep last night, so I waited until it was nine in the U.K. and then called Donaldson's father and left a message. He just got back to me."

She thought about sitting in the bulky, rustic armchair in front of her, but she couldn't bring herself to move. "So, what? What did he say?"

"That he wasn't assigned to Allegra's case, but he was still with the police at the time. He told me everything he remembered. But this has to be off the record, what I'm about to tell you. So I don't know how much help it'll be if you're looking for screenplay material."

"Let's hear it," she urged.

"All confidential."

"Yes. I get it."

"Apparently Allegra's death was suspicious from the beginning—the inspector thought so anyway. And the pathologist's assessment lines up with that too. The blow to Allegra's head was so severe, the pathologist suggested that she'd probably been pushed. And certainly Allegra falling forward onto the pavement and then tipping facedown into the water seemed ridiculous, in the pathologist's opinion. Her theory was that somebody placed Allegra's body in the water."

Placed. The word triggered something in El's brain. The French newspaper. Anna had been *placed* in her bathtub.

"The homicide angle was investigated," Ansel continued. "To a point. But the chief inspector put a stop to it in the end."

"Why?"

"Optics, probably. In the absence of concrete evidence, they took the easy way out."

"But if they were looking at Allegra's death as suspicious, for however long, how did that angle never leak? That doesn't seem—"

"Maybe it did leak. It just didn't get published."

El frowned.

"We get higher-profile things out here sometimes. Say some linebacker shoots his girlfriend, chances are a publicist is gonna swoop in and do damage control. And as much as I hate to say it"—he grimaced—"some cops can be bought. Wealthy people, wealthy communities, they don't want scrutiny. Money controls the story."

"So you think somebody with money murdered Allegra Taylor?"

"It's possible."

No, El thought desperately. "Couldn't it have been a passerby? Somebody on a bike who knocked her off balance? An actual accident, you know? Manslaughter. And maybe *Allegra's* family paid to have the story squashed."

"Allegra's family doesn't have money. I thought you said you were familiar with her background. Her parents own an antiquarian bookstore in some tiny town in Connecticut. She was at Cambridge on scholarship."

"Oh, right." She felt light-headed. *Allegra Taylor was murdered by someone with money.*

"This isn't about a screenplay," Ansel said.

She thought about protesting, but when she met Ansel's eyes, she realized he would not believe her. She settled for a half-truth. "It is and it isn't. I just—I haven't been able to stop thinking about this story. I don't know why."

"I do."

El waited, her mouth tightly shut. She tried to steady her racing heart by taking a couple deep breaths through her nose. Ansel's eyes on her were intent.

"There are some definite similarities between Allegra's case and your friend Anna's. Head wounds. Discovered in water. They even look alike. It's easier to focus on Allegra, someone you didn't know." He rose, moving toward her in the dim light. "I don't think you were at a 'getaway,' either. Where's your bag? You didn't even bring in a toothbrush."

El stared at him.

"Last night you said that you wanted to spend some time together. And I saw the way you looked at me when I opened the door at Deb's apartment." He was so close to her now, but his face was half in shadow. She heard him swallow. "I always thought you didn't like me."

When he kissed her she could feel him trembling. More than anything she felt surprised that Bryce had been right: Ansel was infatuated with her, and probably had been since they were kids. His lips were thick and soft, his unsteady fingers on her neck light and virginal. He felt completely different from Bryce, whose mouth was small, whose movements were controlled, whose tongue was penetrating. And yet there was something uncanny in Ansel's kiss. It made her think of that first night with Bryce, how she had allowed herself to be swept up by his ardor. Her internal compass had been broken then: she had not known what sort of future she'd wanted. Bryce had simply been an alternative to her dreary, pointless days. And now, months later, she was again dysregulated, again disconnected from herself, because she had just learned it was possible, very possible, that her fiancé had killed three people. Ansel did not know this of course, but he had intuited her confused, chaotic state of mind, and into that confusion and chaos he had pushed his erection. He was pressing against her now, backing her against the wall of the cabin. His kisses and caresses were still tender, but he was everywhere. On her ass. On the front of her shorts. It would be easy to let it happen again. To be erased. She remembered yesterday, recognizing that she did not want to run away and did not want to abandon herself. But she had not known everything yesterday. Her situation was grim. What if she told Ansel the whole truth and entreated him to protect her from Bryce? Could she make a life up here in the woods?

Ansel eased her out of his sweatshirt, and as it passed over her head she shut her eyes. There materialized, behind her eyelids, a velvety grayness that made her think of a stage curtain, and from her subconscious sprung a Stella Adler dictum she'd heard many times in school: *Your talent is in your choice.* She sunk into the clay pool of her motivation. Who was El? *Why* was El? And therefore, out of all possible possibilities, what would someone such as El choose to do with all the information she now possessed? Her mind hurtled into the future. There was a life she wanted, a life that waited for her . . .

With a single hand she guided Ansel's body backward. Standing before him in her bra she looked baldly into his transfixed face. "I'm leaving, and you're gonna forget everything we talked about. If for any reason that becomes difficult, the next thing that'll happen is I'll tell my mother how you tried to force yourself on me. You know you're like a son to her, but she is *my* mother. So if you want her in your life I'd keep my mouth shut. Oh—and I didn't like you. You read that right."

And then, ignoring his stricken face, she walked back to the guest room to collect her things.

chapter twenty-eight

As she rode the elevator to the fifteenth floor, El wondered whether Bryce had stayed home from work. It was a quarter to eight now, long past when he would normally have left for the office. She imagined him striding back and forth with her phone in his hand, wondering if perhaps she'd gone for a run yesterday and left it behind. Wondering if she'd been injured, assaulted, kidnapped. Knowing what she did now, she knew calling the police to report her missing would never have been an option. He would not have wanted to draw attention to himself. And then another thought occurred to her: What if there were more security cameras in the apartment? If there was a secret camera in the bedroom, Bryce might've seen her erase her computer and call history yesterday. Hm. The prosecutor in her mind pointed to the tottering pile of evidence that implicated Bryce as a dangerous criminal—a serial killer, in point of fact, someone El should avoid at all costs. *Run!* screamed the prosecutor. *What're you thinking, going back to that apartment? You should be terrified!*

And El was terrified. She was. But she was exhilarated, too, and caution seemed irrelevant in the face of that exhilaration: finally, finally, she understood what it was she wanted, and she was going to allow herself to have it, fear be damned.

She stepped out of the elevator into the annex and walked toward the front door. Her fingers twisted the knob and her toes just crossed the threshold when Bryce came sprinting from the other room. He looked horrible, his cheeks discolored and blotchy, his eyes pink and strained.

"You're okay!"

"I am." She set her purse on the foyer table. She looked in his face. There was no suspicion in it at all, just concern.

"What happened?? You're not hurt?"

"No. Although I guess—I did almost get attacked by a bloodhound yesterday."

"What? Where? Did you go to a hospital? Why didn't you call me?"

"No, I wasn't attacked. I was *almost* attacked."

He reached for her. "Jesus, I'm so glad you're all right."

She allowed him to hold her for a moment before pulling back. "I'm getting in the bath."

"Wait, where were you last night? I went to your old apartment, you weren't there."

El was momentarily distracted. "You went to Crystal's?"

"She wasn't around. People are subletting. But please, just tell me, where were you? Were you with your mom? I tried Navya from your phone and it kept going straight to voicemail, so I tried her from mine—she sounded angry, especially after I pressed, but she insisted you weren't with her."

"I wasn't. And I'll explain. But don't come in the bathroom for about twenty minutes, okay?"

"Why?"

"I have a call to make."

"El—"

"Nothing happened to me. I'm good. Okay?"

"Fine," he said peevishly.

She slipped past him and wondered, as she crossed into the bedroom, how she looked to the eyes of Bryce's cameras. At the same time she knew it did not matter. For the first time in her life she understood the distinction between herself and the appearance of herself. *This* had been her roadblock with acting. She had committed half-heartedly to every role because she'd been afraid that real commitment would mean the negation of herself, a self she had not even known. She'd never had a real grasp of her identity. She had largely defined herself by who and what she had *not* been. She had not been Kirsten. She had not been Anna. She had not been rich. She had not been chosen. Only now did she understand something affirmative about herself: that when the conditions were right, she could be vicious.

After her call, she undressed. In self-exposure she felt her smallness. She was less than a mite in the eye of the galaxy, and her life's trajectory didn't matter all that much—except that, somehow, it did. She couldn't help but matter to herself. The highest law was self-preservation.

Bryce appeared in the bathroom doorway, looking unsure. "Hey, baby."

The last twenty minutes had been agony for him. She knew that. She relaxed her neck onto the towel behind her head.

"I talked to Julia yesterday," she said, and her voice was cool and polished as marble. "She's finally back from her retreat." Bryce stiffened in her peripheral vision, and she exhaled, allowing her eyes to flutter shut. "She thinks Anna might've left New York because of some weird legal thing. An issue with some guy."

His reply came low and grave: "Wow. What—kind of issue?"

"I don't know," El said, opening her eyes again. "I was just sort of listening, letting her process. I didn't get around to updating her about me or about us or anything. She's just in that grieving fugue state." El ran a hand over the surface of the bathwater, watching the ripple it made. "Oh." She turned to him. "And I went to see your father. I didn't know he was sick, or I wouldn't have just dropped in."

Bryce stared at her, mouth parted, unblinking.

"I thought he should know me," she went on. "I had just

spoken to Julia, so the whole thing about Anna dying was on my mind, and I mentioned it to him. And he remembered her! Or someone a lot like her. I think you *must* have known Anna."

"O-oh," Bryce stuttered. "Maybe."

"But I understand, it was so long ago. Anyway, your dad wasn't up for much, but we talked for a while. Talked about Brooke . . ." She paused, relishing the fragile silence. This was the only tub she had known never to leak. There was no sound but the concavity of sound, the negative sound of held breath. And then, finally, she released the last of her ammunition: "You've had so much loss to deal with. I never really took it in, about Allegra? God, I mean, how insulting it must have been when the cops interviewed you after her death."

This last remark had been guesswork, but she saw instantly from Bryce's expression that she had been correct: the police had questioned him about Allegra. He was beyond speech. The muscles of his neck were bulging, inflamed.

"On the drive back I got to thinking about your family, just both your parents and their health and everything, and I had a thought. Your mom—maybe she'd be happier if she had actual treatment, you know? Inpatient care. Just being out in the Hamptons by herself has to be so difficult. So isolating. And with just one nurse—that feels like too little. I mean it sounds like she's *really* struggled with some pretty wild delusions since Brooke died." Bryce didn't move, but his eyes swept over her body in the water. This was what she had hoped for. To remind him, most powerfully, of her humanity. Her flesh. "You know

I'd love to get out there soon if she's gonna be gone. I've been dying to escape the city, you know that."

Bryce's eyes flicked to the engagement ring she had deliberately set on the counter. When they landed back on her, they were desperate. And El could see Anna, her green, hard gaze narrowed at the pathetic man who, as a boy, had haunted her steps at camp. Easily, El could imagine Anna saying something angry and disparaging. Could imagine Bryce absorbing the words—*Fuck off, creep*. El could almost *feel* the heat, the implosion Anna's rejection had ignited in Bryce.

She rose out of the water and reached for a towel, bringing it to a tidy knot around her chest. She motioned for Bryce to hand her the ring. He did so, keeping his eyes on her all the time. She slipped the diamond back on.

"Told my mom about the engagement, finally. That's who I was just talking to. Of course she freaked."

Bryce seemed to be trying to master himself. He was trying to work out her angle, she could tell.

"So what did you say?" he asked. "I mean—what did you tell her?"

His voice was jagged, uneven. He thought she was going to break up with him.

"I just told her, if you don't want to, don't come, but the wedding is happening."

He flushed.

"Mrs. Ripley-Batten," she said, her voice soft. "Pass me that?"

She pointed to the La Prairie jar on the counter beside

him. He handed it to her, and she took a thick dollop of cream in two hands and spread it from her knees to her ankles. When she straightened up and caught sight of his perplexed expression, she was seized by an overwhelming urge to giggle. Instead, she held out her hands to him. "Feel how soft."

He reached for her with tentative fingers, but grazed, accidentally, the surface of her diamond, and pulled away. As his eyes traveled up and met hers she thought he looked a little . . . *afraid.*

chapter twenty-nine

The life El had set about manifesting for herself lay just ahead, winking and sparkling like some edible spring. If she were to stretch out her arms . . .

Almost. That was what she'd been repeating to herself the past several days. *You're almost there.* But before she could step into her destiny, she had to lay the past to rest. She would be going to Anna's memorial, and she would be bringing Bryce with her.

El was not afraid, anymore, of Julia finding out about her relationship with Bryce. Actually, she was sort of—*excited* was the wrong word—*impatient*, that was what it was. She was impatient and hungry for Julia's reaction. It struck El, as she zipped up her black Alaïa with the empire waist, that this was a very Anna-like thing to feel.

She and Bryce were supposed to be uptown in half an hour.

According to Julia's e-vite, Anna's send-off was to be at the Frick. El knew the Frick was a recently renovated museum in an Upper East Side mansion, but she had never been there. She looked it up and read a bit of background that made her lip curl. Henry Clay Frick had been a ruthless tycoon, and he'd commissioned his Beaux-Arts pantheon of extravagance with a mind not only to house a great art collection like Vanderbilt's, but to outshine Andrew Carnegie's spectacular home in the same neighborhood. El was satisfied. It was the perfect place for Anna's memorial, cold ambition sheathed in elegance.

Yesterday, when El had informed Bryce that they would be attending the memorial, he'd barely made a sound. Ever since she'd confronted him about Anna and Allegra and Brooke, Bryce had been extremely docile, slipping silently from room to room, careful not to disturb El if she was reading or sleeping or watching something on her tablet. He ordered El's favorite foods for dinner. He kept his distance, showering by himself, not crowding her in bed. El knew he was watching her, waiting for signs of abandonment, waiting for her to take off the engagement ring and rage at him, call him a murderer. She sensed that he both dreaded and craved this sort of sensible reaction from her. Her present nonchalance put him on edge. She was haunting to him: a strange, incalculable body in his space.

"You look nice," he said quietly, when she entered the kitchen in her dress.

"So do you."

He smiled with a wince.

They caught a cab and made good time until Midtown, when they were swallowed up by rush-hour traffic. The meter and the brake lights of other cabs and cars glowed red. The sky above smoldered, deep purple. It felt like they were stuck in a bruise.

El rolled her window down, but it was no good trying to see—there was a Suburban in front of them. She put the window back up and leaned, resigned, against the seat. Then something cold touched her fingers.

It was Bryce. With his clammy hand on hers, he asked, "Why did you want me to come?" It was obvious in the way he looked at her that he thought her cruel.

Maybe you are, hissed her inner prosecutor.

So? she challenged, and the prosecutor blanched.

"Well," El began. "Anna was my friend, and we both knew her. Why wouldn't I want you to come?"

"Right." He nodded. "And obviously, I didn't—"

He stopped himself.

She waited.

He nodded again and looked away. She sighed with satisfaction as the taxi pulled forward.

Of course everything was different—the tone, the decor, the music—but somehow, the vibe of the memorial reminded El of Julia's birthday party back in May. It took El a moment to realize this was because most of the attendees were her and

Julia's own age. She had only been to one memorial before, her grandfather's, and everyone there had been old.

Who were these people? Had they been friends of Anna's? She didn't recognize a single face. Maybe they simply constituted the right crowd, people who didn't remember Anna per se, but they'd shared an AP Calc tutor or had crossed her path on spring break senior year in the Bahamas. They'd been sitting two tables away at Daniel the night Anna had blown out candles on her tenth birthday. Maybe these people had responded to Julia's invitation to demonstrate solidarity for one of their own, or maybe it was just a slow evening, the half-week lull before Labor Day.

El noticed there were no smiling pictures of Anna mounted on easels anywhere, possibly because there were no smiling pictures of Anna in existence. There was only ever that lethal smirk, that knowing glimmer of her eye.

El and Bryce had walked the length of the great marble entryway and El had not spotted Julia yet. Servers circled with trays of hors d'oeuvres and drinks.

"There's got to be a real bar here, right?" Bryce looked faint and El took his arm. "Don't you think?" she prompted.

She didn't need a drink particularly, but the bar felt like the right place to look for Julia. They made their way into a smaller drawing room with red walls and ornate fireplaces. And, aha: the bar. It was partially obscured by a crush of people. Tom was on the outer edge with his and Julia's mother. They were both nursing gin and tonics, not speaking. El pointed them out to Bryce.

"Julia's family."

"Hrm," he grunted.

It seemed a hundred years ago that she had lusted after Tom and had felt shrunken by his indifference toward her. The person who'd experienced those things amused her now. She contemplated saying hi to Tom and his mother without offering her name, just to put them in the uncomfortable position of failing to recall it, and she might've done this if Julia hadn't walked in right then. Julia was leaning on the arm of a tanned man in his forties; she seemed to be listening intently to what he had to say. El walked straight toward them, and Bryce detached from her, following a step behind.

"Julia," El called.

She watched Julia turn from the tanned man with an irritated expression, though her face broke into a wan smile when she saw El. They embraced, and Julia immediately introduced the tanned man. "Neal, El, El, Neal."

"How are you?" Neal said in a sad, rhetorical voice.

"We're leaving for L.A. tomorrow," Julia told her. "Neal's the producer I was telling you about. He says I have an intuitive sense of story."

"She does." When Neal adjusted his stance, El noticed his socks were key lime green. "And who's this—"

El half turned and realized Neal was smiling at Bryce, who had been lurking in the background. Julia had not noticed him before, but now that Neal was motioning Bryce forward—

It must have been instinct. Julia's arm flew out in front of her, as if to shove Bryce away. She glanced at El, alarmed.

El stared coolly back and saw the moment when it happened, when Julia realized that Bryce was her date. All at once Julia's astonishment faded. She looked at El fearfully, as if El were a ghost.

Neal frowned at El and Bryce.

"W-we—" Julia stammered. "We're going to get drinks."

El held Julia's gaze. "Good luck with L.A. I'm sure you'll be great. If I've noticed one thing about you, it's that you have an intuitive sense of story."

Julia's eyebrows contracted and her lips came together to form a sticky pink pencil. She was disturbed by the lilt in El's voice, the hint of a laugh, the notion of El's teasing her.

El remembered how, the first time she'd spoken to Anna and Julia in the computer lab, they had called her funny. It hadn't really been true then, though perhaps what Anna and Julia had identified was El's potential. El was not dry and direct and confident yet, but she had the capacity to be. Anna and Julia had acquired her in this unrealized state, and El understood now they had never expected her to mature. Her purpose had been ornamental. She'd been a sort of existential prop, a version of Anna and Julia had they been plucked from the vine too soon, stuck with the sour lot of being merely very lucky as opposed to unthinkably fortunate. Beside Anna and Julia, El had been green and small, and they had been more red and more rich for their proximity to her. *That*, El thought, was *extremely* funny, because all these years later, and in spite of them, she was finally fulfilling her storied potential. And then, all of a sudden, El was laughing. It was a laugh that had been building so long it came out as a husky cackle, a bark. Julia's pencil mouth contracted into a round O, and Neal had to pull her away.

Still laughing, nearly retching, El reached out and snatched a glass of champagne from the tray of a waiter who had been trying to sneak by. She raised her glass to Bryce, who had taken several steps back: "Here's to more extraordinary moments."

She grinned at his horrified look and drained the drink in one.

chapter thirty

The house was a handsome chestnut brown. Balconies stuck out from every window above the first floor. Hedges and oaks grew tall around the perimeter. As her new BMW rolled down the long drive, over the blue-gray gravel, El breathed deeply out her open window: she could almost smell the hydrangea from Julia's next door. It was only Labor Day, but the air already had a hint of cool. All the summer renters would be leaving for the city, returning to their firms and private practices with heavy sighs and sprinklings of new freckles; they would stock up at Fairway and remember what it was to eat cherries on the beach, to feel slightly mischievous burying pits in the sand; they would shop online for their kids' back-to-school supplies and complain, why was it only a few years ago the school technology was good enough, but now there was a *special* kind of laptop to order, did their kids think they were rich just because they'd spent a few weeks in the Hamptons, did they expect everything to come easy, did they expect to be supported forever, unpaid internships and workshops, shouldn't some limits be set now, shouldn't they just say here's ten bucks, a Composition notebook and a Duane Reade protractor won't kill you. Only owners would still be out here beyond tomorrow, El thought. Owners like her. Bryce had already initiated the paperwork to have the house put in her name.

And he would never come out here. She felt sure that he would never seek her company, never touch her, again. Oh, he would marry her, but he would shun her otherwise. Her presence in his life signified his absolution, but it had to be a very *distant* presence. She had seen the entirety of him, and she hadn't run: her decision to stay, to put her desires before her morals, disgusted him. She had once been his Madonna: he had not expected her to be so selfish.

El put the car in park and jumped out, leaving her bags. The house was calling on her to explore, and she hastened to obey. She ran across the gravel, her Valentino sandals slapping against her heels. The portico was a crisp linen white, as were the double front doors. She turned one of the brass knobs and pushed . . .

The hallway was wide, bright and inviting. An entry table and the antique bench opposite were bare and smelled of polish. She moved to the living room, pulled open a sliding door and looked out on the ocean. Gulls squawked, and the water, cerulean and winking in the sun, sloshed toward her and away.

She had no idea what arrangements Bryce had made for his mother, only that he had made them quickly. El couldn't feel his troubled mother's presence at all: maybe it was just the sea, but she thought the house had a refreshed, expectant feeling.

Then a red something caught her eye. She turned and saw a braided rope leash hanging off the back of a chair. The gray dog, had she run off before her master's exile? El supposed it didn't really matter. The veil had fallen from around man's best friend: every owner knew the truth now. A dog might stay loyal or she might abandon you. Either way, she would do what served her best.

El surveyed the room. The plush beige furniture, the Taschen books, the silk rug . . . She walked through the rest of the house, inspecting it with pleasure. There was the broad kitchen fashioned in snowy marble . . . The study overlooking the garden with its tall fireplace . . . Beyond that, the sunroom, from which a path of inlaid stones led to an elegant pool that appeared navy in the shade. El took the path, slipped off one of her sandals and swooped her toes through the water: it was warm.

She strolled to the open-air pool house by the deep end and stripped, laying her clothes on the teak coffee table. A breeze, the first whisper of autumn, raised the hairs on her arms and thighs. Several yards away a sugar maple rustled—a few leaves had already begun to turn. Their crimson faces waved to her in greeting.

She walked to the rippling deep end. She had never quite mastered the dive. That had been the last skill her father had tried to teach her before he'd left. She remembered how it had felt to curl her toes around the rough diving board at the YMCA, to glance down at her father, whose hands had been cupped around his mouth: *Tuck your head! Head down!* But she had always come apart at the final moment, puerile fear gripping her. Time and again she had landed on her belly.

She brought her hands together, left over right, raised them above her head—

She leapt, and her thought, for some reason, was of the hound, the one who'd chased her into Mr. Batten's mansion. Its mournful wail reverberated in her chest as she fell . . .

Her fingers lanced the water, and she barely felt the impact as she allowed herself to be swallowed head to toe. Submerged, she opened her eyes and kicked until she grazed the concrete bottom with the tips of her fingers.

She swam until the shadows on the pool shifted and her hands grew lousy with wrinkles. She splashed up the steps of the shallow end and hurried, dripping, back to the pool house to cloak herself in one of the terrycloth towels she'd seen folded in a linen basket.

Once semidry, she took in the details of the pool house. A humongous TV equipped for virtual reality viewing hung on the wall. There was another fireplace, a full-size fridge, a minibar. Had it been earlier she might've lingered awhile, but the breeze was picking up again and she felt like going inside.

She walked back to the sunroom, sniffling and shaking the chlorine from her hair. When she closed the glass door behind her, she noticed something she had missed before: on a side table sat a bowl of fresh peaches. A vision of the tiered bowl of fresh fruit on Julia's kitchen countertop sprang to mind, and El felt a deep, native certainty in her gut. She wasn't a guest or a tourist anymore. She belonged.

In the end it hadn't been about earning her place. About being talented and famous, making her own fortune. El had been wrong all along to assume that she just had to be good enough, and then she would break through. No. Even if she had made some money, Anna and Julia, their kind, would never have respected her. She would never really have belonged. She only did now because she had been refined to her purest form, her truest nature: to live here, in such a rarefied place, with the worst things imaginable happening everywhere in the world, not just murder but every possible inequity and inconvenience and disaster, to live out of reach, out of earshot, out of touch, and to believe that you *deserved* it—that was the sort of barbaric entitlement money just couldn't buy.

She lounged in the sunroom, eating one peach after another, until evening resolved around her, the shotgun buzzing of cicadas dulled by the lush crashing of waves.

Finally she brought her bags in and lugged them upstairs. The main bedroom and en suite faced the sea of course, and after El showered she turned off all the lights and threw the windows open. Already she was enamored of the tidal rhythm, not the crash of the waves so much as the swell. You couldn't see it in the dark, but you could feel it. The evolution. The moment of suspension when power solidified, when the wave reached its apex and curled its victor's smile . . .

She crawled under the down comforter, between the silky sheets. Closing her eyes she wondered what she would find in her dreams. Intuitively she knew her nightmares were past. There would be no more Anna dying, begging for help, no more gushing head wounds and fires of blood. Now that she had taken decisive action in her life, that recurring, unconscious experience of powerlessness would disappear. What would take its place? She had a sense that whatever she dreamed would foretell her next move. She had acquired this house and soon she would have access to an immense fortune, but she was far from finished. And it wasn't only material things she wanted: the cowed look on Bryce's face when he'd realized what she was capable of had been priceless. How far was she willing to go, how deep was she willing to descend, to feel the thrill of dominance again? In that moment, confronting him, she'd been prey become predator. As she drifted off, she thought she could taste a salty sting on her lips, a taste a little like metal, like the color red . . .

She was in her father's forest again. It was moonless black, but she could see much better in her new body, her warm new body so low to the ground. There was no red anymore—only gold and cool tones, blue and gray—but there was the idea, the idea of red . . .

Something stirred between a pair of hemlocks at the edge of the clearing. She approached, and a great head of matted fur emerged from behind a trunk. It was a dog her own size, also on its own. It looked at her with hard, familiar eyes.

Together they set off at a run.

Why was it so easy now, to find purpose? She'd only had to peer beneath a lifetime's breeding and grooming, and there were all her instincts, gleaming like teeth.

They were getting closer. The hunger in her belly was a dark pain, and she realized she was snarling as her paws pounded the earth, the frozen grass and mud. She and her companion moved in lockstep. Glance quickly and you might mistake them for the same animal.

He was not far now. The idea of red was building like a pressure in her mind. She felt the crush in her companion, too, the momentum, the appetite. Could anything be more natural or impartial? An appetite was the best judge in the world, the best justice.

He was standing at the edge of a frozen pond. He had a leash, and he was calling a name. Whose? Had it been hers, once?

She and her companion crouched low and separated, creeping through the shadows.

Then, he turned. He saw her. He was furious, brandishing the leash, screaming that name—

She dove, and her companion did too.

Together they brought him to the ground. Dragged him to the center of the ice. He gripped the leash as if he expected to regain control at any moment. He had been spared his whole life, spared the onslaught of days and days and years of helplessness, he didn't know to surrender, he didn't know you take a deep breath before the wave drags you under . . .

The ice was cracking. They brought him to bone with their canine fangs and the satisfaction was an explosion of red in her mind, dark red fireworks showering and dripping like willow branches. When they were finished he was white dust, floating through the hole that had opened in the ice. She watched him sink in splintered pieces.

When it was over, her companion was gone. Her twin, her mirror, vanished. There was no one to imitate now, no one to follow. There was only her own brutish want, her own mighty constitution.

ACKNOWLEDGMENTS

My gratitude for everyone who helped me realize the publication of this book is absolutely profound. Some of you I must now embarrass and thank by name.

Thank you to my editor, Gaby, whose instincts are always spot-on, and thank you to Danielle, who shared my passion from the start. I'm indebted to everyone at Putnam who lent their talents to the production of this novel, from copyedits to cover art to marketing: you are all spectacular.

Thank you to my agent, Stacy, who asked to see more of these characters and their world.

Thank you to Marc, intrepid manager and friend, for your endless encouragement.

Thank you to Nick for championing my foray into novel writing. Your mentorship has meant the world.

Thank you to Allie and Allie, to Erin and Julia and Ben, and thank you to the whole Swingers crew—Diana, Keerthi, Kait and Katie. Your early eyes and sharp insights have been invaluable.

ACKNOWLEDGMENTS

Thank you to my family, especially my mom and stepdad. Your love gives me courage.

And thank you to my husband, Ryan, who knows by now that to be married to a writer is to hear the question "Okay, what do you think about this?" throughout the day, usually while you're busy doing something else. You'll never know how much your listening means. How lucky I am to have you as my partner on this adventure, and all the others.

ABOUT THE AUTHOR

Alana B. Lytle is a screenwriter whose recent credits include Netflix's *Brand New Cherry Flavor* and Peacock's *A Friend of the Family*. Her short fiction has been published in *Guernica*. She lives in Los Angeles with her husband and sausage-shaped dog. *Man's Best Friend* is her debut novel.